APOLONIA

ALSO BY JAMIE MCGUIRE

PROVIDENCE (PROVIDENCE TRILOGY BOOK ONE)

REQUIEM (PROVIDENCE TRILOGY BOOK TWO)

EDEN (PROVIDENCE TRILOGY BOOK THREE)

BEAUTIFUL DISASTER

WALKING DISASTER

A BEAUTIFUL WEDDING (A BEAUTIFUL DISASTER NOVELLA)

BEAUTIFUL OBLIVION

RED HILL

HAPPENSTANCE: A NOVELLA SERIES

HAPPENSTANCE: A NOVELLA SERIES (PART TWO)

ΛPOLONIΛ

JAMIE McGUIRE

Apolonia

Jamie McGuire

Cover designed by Sarah Hansen, Okay Creations, www.okaycreations.com

Edited by Theresa Wegand

Proofread and interior designed by Jovana Shirley, Unforeseen Editing, www.unforeseenediting.com

ISBN-13: 978-1501022081

ISBN-10: 1501022083

*To anyone from my childhood who held me back, tore me down, made me cry
or feel worthless, looked down on me, or ever thought that I would fail,
For the people who told me that, as an adult,
I should stop wasting time chasing impossible dreams,
And to my father, the late Darrell McGuire,
for passing on his stubborn pride and rebellious nature.
Every person placed in our lives has a purpose, teaches us a lesson.
Thank you for the motivation to work that much harder to succeed.*

CONTENTS

"Everything that kills me
Makes me feel alive."

—One Republic, "Counting Stars"

ONE

THEY'D KILLED ME, but I survived. While lying on the hotel floor, my long black hair saturated with blood, I'd thought my life was over, except it wasn't.

I had woken up in a hospital, alone, without my best friend, Sydney, and without my parents. Their sacrifice had begun first, and so their murders had been more thorough. When it was time for mine, our killers had been too drunk and too high to be careful—at least, that was what the police report had said.

But I knew the truth.

Five months after losing Sydney and my parents, I'd left for the quaint college town of Helena, Indiana, four states away. I'd gone from a murder victim to a freshman at Kempton Institute of Technology.

Standing in front of my dorm room mirror, naked, I raked back my too-long black bangs. Most girls gained a freshman fifteen. I'd been steadily losing weight for two years. It was hard to feel or taste or hurt after I'd died. There was nothing to celebrate anymore, so eating seemed more like a chore than anything else.

A ratty white towel lay underneath my feet, ready to catch the dark locks that I began shearing away from above one ear and then the other. I had thick and shiny hair that my father had said could have only come from my mother.

The scissors cut away all but four or five inches on top. I ran my fingers over what was left. It felt so good. The sides and a bit of the back were shaved, and the hair left on top nearly grazed my jawline. It was appalling. It was liberating.

I loved it.

Not that many people at KIT noticed me anyway, but if they had, they definitely wouldn't recognize me now. Seventeen inches of shiny black hair that, minutes ago, had brushed the middle of my back were now lying on the floor. Every strand I'd sheared away had once been wet with my blood. Every time I saw my hair in the mirror or touched it, it was a reminder. No amount of shampoo would be enough to wash that night away.

To make sure I wasn't just being impulsive, I had waited, but I couldn't wait any longer.

After showering to wash the scratchy bits of hair from my skin, I stepped out and looked at my new reflection. It was a bit startling but exponentially less repugnant. I zipped up my favorite black hoodie over a worn Kurt Cobain tee, fought with my gray skinny jeans, and then gave the small diamond piercing in the right side of my nose one full turn before grabbing my backpack. I looked back at the mirror, admiring the absence of my tainted hair, and letting the somber thought soak in that, had she been alive, my mother would have died all over again at the sight.

Class one of week one of my junior year at KIT was Geobiology and Astrobiology with renowned astrobiologist, Dr. A. Byron Zorba. Dr. Zorba was what he was called by students, but because he had been my father's mentor when Dad was a student here and later a family friend, I always called the professor Dr. Z.

For reasons unknown to me, Dad and Dr. Z had kept in touch over the years, and my father had consulted with the professor often. When Dr. Z visited, I'd relished hearing about his expeditions and research stories over dinner. The daughter of two idealistic scientists, I not only didn't fit in with other children, but I also had no interest in conformity. When most children were pretending to be firemen or superheroes, I was working toward the Nobel Prize in my cardboard lab. Barbies and boys bored me, and I was sure I bored them. I could monopolize a conversation about the Keck Telescope before most kids knew how to write their names, and Dr. Byron Zorba was my hero.

After my parents' funeral, Dr. Z told me I *was* going to Kempton whether I wanted to or not, and he practically filled out my college application. He also made sure that my inheritance was funneled properly and swiftly into a college fund.

Just before my first spring semester, Dr. Z offered me a position as his research assistant. Living on scientists' salaries, my parents had struggled to pay the bills, and so a work-study program plus a research assistant scholarship would help subsidize my skimpy trust fund and provide for the day-to-day expenses that a college fund didn't cover.

Freshly back from his most recent summer exploration trip to Antarctica, Dr. Z was still on a high from his find—a twelve-inch-by-fifteen-inch, twenty-seven-pound rock. I would be in charge of recording data. Admittedly, the rock didn't exactly impress me, so Dr. Z's enthusiasm was baffling.

I walked into the classroom, immediately squinting from the morning sunshine pouring in from the numerous long windows that lined the opposite wall. Dr. Z's small and messy desk was at the bottom of a steep incline, center stage to dozens of tiny desks attached to uncomfortable chairs.

I joined the line of students making their way to whatever seat they chose, my feet shuffling slowly forward.

"Hey!" a familiar voice said right into my ear.

I leaned away, recognized the face, and began climbing the stairs that hugged the windowless wall. For reasons completely unknown to me, Benji Reynolds had hunted me like a bluetick coonhound since freshman orientation. I had hoped the new do would scare him away. He was clearly a mama's boy and far too attractive and happy to appeal to me.

"Did you have a good summer?" he asked with a huge grin.

I was sure he did. With his golden tan, I imagined him lying by a pool from May to August or running along the beach next to the multimillion-dollar beach home his parents likely owned.

"No."

"Did you even try?"

"No." I was beginning to get annoyed with the stream of students ahead of me who were taking far too much time to choose a seat.

"Hi, Benji," Stephanie Becker lilted from her seat. She was short but had stunning curves, and she twirled a piece of her long blonde hair while staring at him with the most ridiculous look on her face. Her head was tilted, and her eyes clouded over when Benji looked for the source of his spoken name.

"Hi," he said, giving her only a moment of his time before turning back to me. "I was hoping you'd be in this class." His brown eyes brightened.

Even if he did have a strong jawline and a sweet disposition, I still couldn't see him as anything but…well, Benji.

Finally at the tenth row, I sidestepped halfway down the aisle to the same desk I'd sat in the year before. I'd been in that classroom with a different professor the semester before, and I had a strange attachment to that desk.

Benji sat next to me, and I glared at him.

"It's okay if I sit here, right?" he asked.

"No."

He laughed. His teeth were too straight, and his posture was too perfect. "You're so funny. Your hair is...wow," he said, trying to find the best inoffensive adjective.

I waited for him to admit his disgust, but he offered a small smile.

"It's unique and wild and interesting. Just like you."

"Thanks," I said, resentful that he forced me to be nice to him.

He pulled his arms out of his jacket, revealing his perfectly ironed white oxford. Maybe, if the sleeves had been rolled up, I would have forgiven him, but no, they were buttoned at the wrist.

"You could shave it all off and still be beautiful," he said.

"I thought about it."

Benji chuckled and looked down. Any other girl at Kempton would have jumped at the chance to date him. It wasn't that he was unattractive—quite the opposite. We'd had other classes together, and he was one of Kempton's brightest students. It wasn't even that he was dull because sometimes he made me laugh. I guessed I was just waiting for something...different.

Dr. Z was lost in the mess of papers on his desk, and I was glad. The room had already begun to fill, and I didn't want him to make a scene when he greeted me. He was kind but excited about life in general, and I wasn't in the mood for that. But as I relaxed against the back of my seat, his head popped up.

"Rory! I almost didn't recognize you! I just sent you an email! Did you get it?"

Everyone turned to see whom the professor was addressing.

"No," I said quietly, sinking into my seat.

Dr. Z, small and plump with just a bit of silver hair circling the midsection of his scalp that matched his unkempt beard, watched me expectantly.

I pressed my lips together and then bent over to my bag, pulling out my laptop. He obviously wasn't going to let this go. The computer lit up, and I navigated my way to my inbox.

Nodding to Dr. Z didn't satisfy him. His eyes widened, and he nodded his head, encouraging me to continue.

I ran my fingers over the trackpad and clicked on the message he'd sent with the subject line, OPEN NOW. The email contained line after line of data he'd compiled over the weekend from the unimpressive rock. After scanning the bulk of it, I nodded once.

He seemed sufficiently satisfied. "We'll talk more tonight."

A small twinge of guilt panged in my chest. The disappointment in his eyes was evident, but it was a rock. Granted, its material hadn't been recorded on Earth, ever, so that meant it had come from somewhere in the universe. An alien rock. If we still thought the world was flat or if we weren't aware of the surrounding universe, I could understand Dr. Z's excitement, but as it was, it was…boring.

Dr. Z, however, was very excitable and, at times, dramatic. This particular email ended with, *Secrecy is imperative.*

Secrets I could handle. Gossip wasn't a problem. Typing was easy. Listening to his incessant enthusiasm about markings on a rock until three a.m. and then being alert for an eight a.m. course…not so much.

"Cyrus!" Dr. Z said loud enough to catch my attention. "We can talk about your request to be a research assistant after class."

What the hell? I'm his research assistant.

I looked in the same direction as Dr. Z to a pair of dark topaz eyes surrounded by olive skin. The male gender wasn't something I was preoccupied with, so the twinge I felt in my stomach took me by surprise. It didn't matter. I already hated him.

Cyrus sat in the first row, directly in front of Dr. Z. He was so ordinary. He wore a red-and-navy-blue plaid shirt with sleeves rolled up to the elbows and tan cargo pants. I couldn't see his shoes, but I imagined him wearing a stupid pair of brown hiking sneakers. His clothes gave him a casual look, but it seemed forced. *He* seemed forced—his movements, his expressions—as if he were trying too hard to blend in. I couldn't stop staring at the back of his head, noticing every strand of his dark hair, admiring him and wishing for his sudden death at the same time.

"Welcome!" Dr. Z began. "I am Dr. A. Byron Zorba, and you've arrived at Geobiology and Astrobiology…uh…with lab. That's a separate class. Uh…later," he added. "You should also be enrolled in the lab, separately from lecture. If not, see administration. So! Here, and in the partnering lab, you will study organic matter from microbes, rocks, and environmental samples. In lab, you'll extract and, more importantly, interpret these samples. Beyond that, we will reconstruct ancient environments to understand how life evolved within the samples."

"Yeesh," Benji whispered.

"It's really not that bad. Don't be a baby," I said, keeping my voice low, as the professor went over the rules and syllabus.

"I'm still running in the mornings," Benji said. "You should come with me sometime."

"I don't run."

"It's good for you. You should try it."

"I'm not getting up at the crack of dawn to run until I stop freezing. That's not healthy. It's stupid."

Benji just smiled, clearly amused.

"Excuse me, Professor," Cyrus said, holding his pen in the air. "Whom shall I contact—"

I blocked out the rest of his question. The trace of a British accent in his voice and his perfect grammar would never have piqued my attention before, but on that day, it was annoying and snooty.

Not only was Cyrus tall, dark, and handsome, but as class progressed, he also proved to be Dr. Z's most adept and eager student.

Dr. Z paused after answering Cy's latest question. "May I ask…from where do you hail?"

"Excuse me?" Cyrus responded.

"I was curious to know if you happen to be Egyptian?" the professor asked.

I didn't know what expression was on Cyrus's face, but he must have smiled because Dr. Z clapped his hands once, and a wide grin made his already full cheeks puff out.

Dr. Z patted Cyrus's shoulder and shook his finger a few times. "We'll have much to talk about. See me after class."

"Oh Christ, get a room," I snarled under my breath.

The professor's hobby was trying his hardest to be an Egyptian scholar. I thought maybe Cyrus's origin was the reason for Dr. Z's fascination, but that didn't turn out to be it at all. Cyrus never answered the questions that Dr. Z presented to the class, but he asked at least a dozen of his own. He was curious, and I couldn't deny that his questions were a work of art.

Dr. Z answered a few questions before lecturing for just ten minutes, giving us a reading assignment, and then waving us away, twenty minutes earlier than expected.

Everyone looked around, unsure what to do, until I began packing my things. That started a chain reaction, and noise filled the room as students crammed their laptops into their bags and moved to leave.

After our dismissal, Cyrus stood next to Dr. Z's podium, and they spoke in low voices with a lot of nodding and a few smiles.

Oh, hell no. I stood up, grabbed my bag, and walked down the steps, standing in the space next to Cyrus.

"Cyrus has just returned from a summer in Mali," Dr. Z said, smiling.

"Oh?" I said with cold eyes. "You have family there?"

"No," Cyrus said flatly.

He didn't offer further explanation, so I stared at him until he became uncomfortable and looked away. That was my very favorite thing to do to everyone.

"Cyrus is researching the Dogon tribe. Very interesting," Dr. Z said. "He's the third member of our team."

"What?" I said the word louder than I'd meant and in a tone high enough to be embarrassing.

Cyrus nodded once to us both, and then he was gone.

"Are you replacing me?" I asked, my heart pounding. My assistant job was connected to my scholarship. If Cyrus stole it from me, I could be in real danger of losing that money. It was too late to find a student position that wasn't already taken.

"Of course not. You saw the data I sent. You'll never have time for anything else if I don't add someone to the team."

"I can do it," I said, only feeling a tiny bit relieved. "You know I don't go home for the holidays. I don't mind working weekends."

Dr. Z smiled. "Rory, I know you don't mind working weekends, but you should."

He walked out of the classroom, leaving me among his weird sculptures and artifacts. None of it made sense. Dr. Z had always been careful. I couldn't imagine he would invite someone he didn't trust into his precious laboratory. Something about Cyrus felt off, but he didn't seem dangerous or untrustworthy. If the professor had been considering Cyrus as just a third team member, he would have mentioned it before today. The only explanation for my exclusion from this news was that he was planning to replace me. What was more, hastily inviting a new student into his lab wasn't just uncharacteristic. It was troubling.

My eyes were all over the place, looking at a different inanimate object with every thought. I couldn't lose my position as Dr. Zorba's assistant. Everything was riding on it.

The room grew darker, bringing my attention to the large windows. The clouds outside were gray. At this time of year, the weather was more likely to bring in a cold front than a storm. The wind began to blow the few leaves that had just started to fall from the huge oak trees. I pulled one of several tubes of lip balm from my jacket pocket and ran it over my lips. I loved fall up until the night I died. Now, it just seemed ominous.

Clenching my teeth with determination, I lifted my bag and swung it over my shoulder. I refused to lose my assistant position with Dr. Z. Cyrus could take his thought-provoking, eloquently worded questions and shove them up his ass.

TWO

WATER? CHECK. MUFFIN? CHECK. Even handsomer in his black-rimmed glasses, the spot-stealer sitting at the table to my left, working his ass off?

I sighed. *Check.*

We'd been in the basement of the Fitzgerald Building for two hours and hadn't spoken. The boring rock was in a glass case on the other side of Cyrus, and he was simultaneously looking through a microscope and typing his data into the computer.

I pulled my mouth to the side. I couldn't type and study matter in a microscope at the same time. *That's okay. I'll learn how.*

Just once, I'd caught him glancing at me. His golden eyes returned to the microscope so quickly that I thought it was my imagination. At least he didn't catch the other dozen or so times I'd glanced at him.

My fingernails were clicking against the keyboard. *I'm going to have to cut them tonight. It's not like they're manicured or anything anyway.*

I chewed off another hangnail, spit it onto the cement floor, and then took a bite of my pathetic dinner. Muffin crumbs fell onto the table. Cyrus hadn't eaten or sipped a single drop of coffee since he arrived. I set down the mangled mess of bread barely contained in its paper holder.

Focusing on how to compete with perfection over there instead of entering the numbers correctly was going to lose me my spot. I snapped out of it and began typing data as if a fire were engulfing the room and I had to finish to live.

At midnight, Cyrus packed his things, and without saying a word, he walked out of the room and shut the door behind him.

"Yes!" I yelled to no one and lifted both fists in the air. Day one, and I'd beaten him. I was going to stay at least another hour, making sure to tell Dr. Z the next day that I stayed later than Cargo Pants.

Then, I realized it was super quiet without Cyrus's clicking and shifting, and being in the basement alone was actually kind of creepy. But it didn't matter. I was going to stay an hour after Cyrus. An hour was a respectable amount of time to report.

At one a.m., I yawned, cracked my knuckles, and packed my things. There was an elevator with a set of stairs on each side, which I preferred. I had an aversion to elevators, especially alone and at night. That was where I'd met my killers.

After climbing the stairs and pushing through both sets of glass doors out to the front of the building, I noticed a group of students walking and then another group. Scanning the area, I saw that many students were heading in the same destination, and feeling like a lemming, I joined the line.

The group led me five blocks off campus to an old building, down the stairs, and through a door. The sounds and smells were overwhelming. It was a rave, the fake kind with sorority girls and wannabe think-tank members. In the two years since I'd moved east to Kempton, I'd stayed away from raves, parties, rallies, underground fights, and people in general. Yet, here I was, for no particular reason, breathing in heavy smoke, stepping in sticky god-knows-what, and allowing the Top 40 to violate my eardrums.

I turned on my heels and shoved open the door to leave, slamming it right into Benji Reynolds's nose.

"Cheese and rice!" he yelled, holding his face and bending over at the same time. Blood began to seep between his fingers.

"Damn it, Benji!" I said, grabbing his sleeve and pulling him across the room.

A line was formed on the far side of the room. At this type of party, that meant a restroom or keg was close. So, I took my chances and shoved past everyone.

Relieved to see a door instead of a keg, I exhaled. "Thank Christ."

"For what?" Benji said in a nasally voice. He was pinching his nose, his head tilted back. He followed when I dragged him inside.

"Hey!" a girl whined. "You can't cut!"

"Deal with it," I said before closing the door in her face.

I pulled several paper towels from the box on the wall and handed them to Benji. He wiped his hands while I pinched his nose with several tissues.

"Thanks, Rory," he said, his nasal voice muffled.

I sighed. "Don't thank me. I hit you."

"It's not your fault. I was excited. I was coming here and saw you and—"

"Benji"—I closed my eyes and shook my head—"don't."

He nodded, looking embarrassed.

I dampened another paper towel and cleaned the blood off his hands while he continued to pinch his nose and point his chin to the ceiling. He was a head taller than I was, so I had to stand on the tip of my toes to hold the tissue to his nose when his head was tilted back like that.

Someone pounded on the door.

"Just a minute, assholes!" I yelled.

Benji's sheepish smile was annoyingly charming. His short sandy-brown hair was parted and feathered back just so, and his almond-shaped brown eyes disappeared behind a curtain of long eyelashes that any woman would pay good money for. Teeth an orthodontist would be proud of along with a strong jawline would score him any number of nice young ladies. But I was neither nice nor a lady, and I couldn't imagine why he pursued me so ardently.

I hated to admit it, but I was maybe just a tiny bit attracted to Benji. But he was nice. *Too* nice. And I didn't want nice. I didn't want anyone.

"C'mon," I said when his nose stopped bleeding. His shirt and cheek still had blots and smears of crimson. "I'll walk you home."

"I should be the one walking you home."

"I'm not the one bleeding."

Someone pounded on the door, and I opened it. The girls crowding the restroom took a step back as I glared at them and pulled Benji along.

"It's a nice night," Benji said as we walked into the street that led back to campus.

"Yeah, I guess."

"You should go running with me in the morning."

"You shouldn't be running in the morning. Your nose could be broken. Sleep in for once."

He chuckled, dismissing my advice. "Sorry you missed the party."

"I was on my way out, remember?"

"I thought it was weird that you were going there."

"Why?"

Benji laughed. "Because you never go to parties."

"Oh. Yeah." I peeked over at Benji. He looked ridiculous, smeared with blood and smiling. The corners of my mouth turned up.

"Wow, did you just smile?"

I forced my face to relax.

Benji shoved his hands in his pockets. "I can mark that off my bucket list."

"You do that."

We arrived at the Sherman L. Charleston Men's Dormitory, otherwise known as Charlie's. It was once where all the cool, nerdy engineering students lived, but that was before we were born. Now, it was full of run-of-the-mill engineering nerds, like Benji.

Benji checked the paper towel a few times before wiping his nose once more and tossing the blood-saturated napkin into a garbage can ten feet away. It went straight in. He looked at me with a proud smile.

"Night, Benji. Put some ice on that nose."

"Will do. You…you sure you don't want me to walk you—"

"I'm sure. See you around."

I turned around but stopped when Benji's hand gripped my wrist. Out of pure instinct, I grabbed his wrist with my free hand and pulled him over my shoulder, slamming him to the ground. He grunted as the air got knocked out of him when he hit the cement.

"For fuck's sake! I'm sorry!" I said, half-embarrassed and half-pissed that I was being forced to be nice to him again.

Benji groaned.

"Are you…are you hurt?" I felt so awkward. Part of me wanted to walk away, to not care. It would have been easier than standing there, my hands hovering over Benji, unsure where to grab to help him up.

"Even though I know you're unpredictable, you never cease to surprise me. Where did you learn to do that?"

"None of your business. Can you stand?"

"Will you attack me again if I try?"

I rolled my eyes and helped him to his feet. "I didn't attack you. I was defending myself."

Benji laughed once and pointed at his chest. "From me?"

I didn't like the way he was looking at me. It was nice and amused and flirty, every way he shouldn't be.

"You're an asshole. I almost felt bad for a moment, and you're laughing at me."

I started to walk away, but Benji grabbed my wrist again.

I looked back at him and then at my wrist. "Are you suicidal?"

"Obviously," he said and then let go. "C'mon. Sit down for a minute."

"It's cold. I'm going home."

"Then, I'll walk you."

"Benji," I sighed, frustrated. "No. I can take care of myself."

"Clearly."

"You make me crazy! And before you ask, no, not in a good way."

He sat down on the second step and patted the space next to him. "You broke my nose. You can't give me five minutes of sympathy conversation?"

"Is that an attempt at a guilt trip?"

"Yes."

I sat down next to him, crossing my arms.

He smiled. "Are you really cold?"

"No."

"Are you hungry? We could make a McD's run."

I made a face, leaning away from him. "You *are* suicidal. Every time you eat there, you're one step closer to a heart attack."

"Who cares? It's so good."

"I'm not hungry."

We sat there for several minutes in awkward silence. At least, it was awkward for me. Benji seemed content.

"Well...I guess I'd better get going," I said, standing up.

Benji stood with me. "You never said why you went to that party."

"I just needed to get out," I said. "That happens sometimes to me."

"You should try The Gym. It's a good way to burn off steam. Helps me sleep."

"The Gym," I deadpanned.

He laughed. "Yeah. Just try it with me once. If you don't feel better afterward, then you never have to go again."

I thought for a moment. "Maybe."

He shook his head and held up his bloodstained hands. "I'll take maybe."

I left him alone in front of Charlie's, feeling like he was watching me walk away. I didn't look back to find out. Being nice gave off the incorrect impression that I wanted to be a friend or, in

Benji's case, possibly something more. So, I wasn't nice. At least, I tried not to be. Sometimes, the old me bubbled to the surface.

The walk home was chilly and lonely. It was probably because, for the twenty minutes Benji was around, I'd gotten used to the company. That was exactly what I didn't want. Using my card key to get into my dorm, I walked into the hallway, cussing Benji for bringing out that side of me.

I took the stairs as usual but couldn't avoid passing the elevators on the way. My mother's eyes flashed through my mind. I'd seen the line between her brows and the strange look in her gaze just before she died. My father always said she was tough. She was, even as she took her last breath. Her eyes held so much sadness—for being helpless to save me and for the life she thought I would miss out on. She didn't think about herself in those last moments. She was asking me for forgiveness with her eyes, and through the dirty rag tied around my mouth, I gave it to her. I just couldn't forgive myself.

The lock to my room clicked, and only then did I realize I'd just climbed two flights of stairs. My mind had been so far away that I wasn't even conscious of where I was going. It was unsettling. I pushed through the heavy wooden door and leaned back against it until it slammed shut. Reaching behind me, I switched on and then back off the light, turned the lock, and then walked toward my bed, tossing my messenger bag onto the tattered love seat across the room.

Fully dressed, I let myself fall onto the bed, face down into the pillow. A groan escaped from my throat, loud enough for my neighbor Ellie, the bossy, bitchy beauty of the campus to hear. She loved to tell me that my crappy music was too loud, my clothes were too black, and my social life was too sad. It was okay though because I was proud of the fact that I didn't listen to cheesy pop songs or let everyone see my tits in one of four hundred too-tight V-neck sweaters, and I wasn't a slutty, whorish whore. Okay, that was harsh. But in our four semesters at Kempton, she'd had the dicks of at least three professors in at least one of her orifices—and those were only the ones she'd bragged about.

I turned onto my side, hoping, praying that I would fall asleep before the memories came too fast and hard to block out. Instead of going through that painful nightly ritual, my eyes focused on the light seeping in beneath my door. My head popped up. Two shadows partially blocked the light.

Feet.

Every muscle tensed, froze, and caught on fire at the same time. Regardless of how much fear screamed through every vein in my body, I was drawn to the danger. I needed to face it head-on, just like last time. Before common sense could step in, one hand was on the lock, the other turning the knob. The door opened so fast, the air from the hallway brushed against my face.

"Cyrus," I whispered, too shocked to say his name aloud.

He was equally surprised, nearly jumping out of his own skin. "It's, uh…it's just Cy actually. Thank you."

"What the hell are you doing here?"

"Listening."

"To what?"

"Your door."

"My door," I said flatly. An awkward silence fell between us, but then I shook my head, and a freak-out commenced. "What do you mean you were listening to my door? *My* door? *Why*?"

Cy held out his palms, walking into my room. "No, no, please. It's not as salacious as it appears. I was just making sure you were home. Safe." He shut my door behind him, motioning for me to quiet down.

"Why?" I said, my face screwing in disgust.

Cy seemed frustrated and lost. "I…I don't know. You're alone. You do dangerous things. I worry about you."

My eyes narrowed. "You don't know anything about me."

Cy fidgeted. "Dr. Z might have mentioned—"

"Oh, fuck. What has he told you?"

"That you have a foul mouth, for one."

"What else?"

"That you're alone, and you do dangerous things. I just told you—"

"I don't need anyone checking up on me," I said, twisting the doorknob.

Cy held the door closed with his hands. "I apologize for the intrusion. I couldn't help myself. I told myself many times that I shouldn't."

"So, why did you?"

"I don't know. Good night." With that, he opened the door and walked down the hall.

I shut the door and locked it, my anger and confusion quickly doused with an uncontrollable smile.

THREE

"WHO SPENT THE NIGHT?" Ellie was standing a few feet down the hall, locking her door at the same time I was. Her long brown curls cascaded down her back in perfect spirals.

My hair used to be the same length as hers, but she didn't feel like she had to wash blood out of hers every night.

She smiled and shifted her weight to her other hip, her mile-long legs actually covered with tight jeans. I looked down, perturbed that mine were just as tight. I didn't want to be anything like Ellie.

"I have to say," she said, not waiting for my answer, "I'm surprised, whoever it was. Your new haircut is absolutely appalling."

"Good," I murmured.

"What was that?"

"I said, you're a whore," I replied, slinging my bag over my shoulder. That was definitely worth a smile, so I wore one all the way to class.

My thick cable cardigan wasn't enough to ward off the cold, so I kept my arms wrapped tightly around my chest. Everyone else was wearing heavy coats and knitted hats, but I never thought about things like that. I had formulas and data sparking the synapses in my brain, along with horrible memories and now...the golden eyes of the confusing jerk I didn't want to think about.

But I did think about him—a lot. During class, at night, weekends, and in the lab, I wondered about him. It became a game for me to make up his history and background. I'd wonder if he had a happy childhood or if he was at Kempton to run away from an overbearing father. In every scenario though, he was alone and lonely, and no matter how much I wanted to despise him, I just couldn't even if it meant he was planning to steal my research assistant position. I knew he was definitely up to something.

"What do you think his evil plan is?" Benji whispered in my ear.

It had been two weeks since I smashed his nose, and the bruising had finally begun to fade.

"Who?" I asked.

"Cyrus."

"What makes you ask?"

"He's just got that look in his eye, you know? Like he's up to something."

Get out of my head, Benji. "No, I don't know." It was the truth. I didn't know, and hell if I was going to give Benji Reynolds the chance to say we had something in common.

"Lunch today?" he asked.

"Sure," I said, typing Dr. Z's last point into my laptop.

Eating with Benji was a much better alternative to eating alone in one of the cafeterias. He was the only student at KIT who didn't have to blather on about whatever project he was working on, and he wasn't bad to look at either.

"Now, be quiet. I can't miss any notes."

I trained my ears back onto Dr. Z's lecture. With all the wondering and hypothesizing about Cy, I'd become unfocused in my classes, and it was beginning to show. Typically an A student, I was struggling in some classes to retain a B. Dr. Z noticed Bs, and when he noticed something, he wouldn't leave me alone until I made him un-notice.

Just another reason to hate Cy. He was becoming a huge distraction.

"You're doing it again," Benji said.

"Shh."

"Watching him. I'm hoping it's because you're suspicious of him like me."

"Or maybe I'm counting how many times he draws a dot on his paper, which is two hundred and thirty-nine."

"Really?"

"Really."

"How can you tell from up here?"

"I noticed the dots in his notebook in the lab a week ago. Now, I sort of notice."

"I wonder what they mean."

I looked over at Benji's book where he'd doodled letters of the alphabet in different fonts. They were actually pretty good. "What does that mean?"

"That I'm bored mostly."

"There's your answer. Cy just can't draw as well as you."

Benji smiled, seeming satisfied with that answer. What I wasn't telling him was that Cy's dots were always in intricate patterns, and sometimes he added in what looked like hieroglyphics. But I wasn't interested in investigating Cy and certainly not with Benji, so I kept that tidbit of information to myself.

After class, Benji struggled to keep pace with me as I walked to Gigi's Café, just a few blocks off campus. It was our unofficial, completely platonic date spot that we didn't talk about because if we acknowledged that it had become a thing, I would stop saying yes.

"…so I said, 'Therefore, I was correct. A meteor is a flash of light, not the debris.' It's just ridiculous he wasn't aware of the difference at this level."

"Agreed," I said before taking a sip of my water.

I picked at my grilled panini while Benji updated me on his classes, his annoyance with the nerds at Charlie's, and why—even though he was a legacy—there was no way in hell he was joining Theta Tau. He would never give Bobby Peck—the fraternity president, sufferer of Little Man's Syndrome, and Benji's nemesis—the satisfaction.

"So, I know you said you were a little behind in some of your classes," Benji said. He was fidgeting and clearly leading up to something.

"So?"

"So…you want to carve out some time in the evenings to study?"

"I can't. I have to work every evening."

"Not every evening," Benji said with a smirk. "If your grades continue to fall, Dr. Zorba will suspend your assistant duties anyway."

I glared at Benji. "Who said anything about my grades?"

"I just assumed, when you said you were behind."

I tried to remember if I'd even told Benji that much. Telling him anything even remotely personal meant fifty questions and relentless attempts to make whatever it was better. Our friendship was comprised of his relentless positivity and chatter and my bitter quips.

"I don't need your help."

"Of course not," Benji said, dismissing my comment with a wave of the hand. "I would be lying if I didn't admit that I was hoping to benefit from your genius."

I narrowed my eyes. "Did you just backpedal?"

"And flatter you in anticipation that you'd agree to study with me? Yes."

"Do I look like Ellie Jones to you? Flattery won't help your cause."

"Ellie Jones?" Benji said, his nose wrinkling. "What made you bring her up?"

"She moved into the room next to mine."

"Oh," Benji said. The expression on his face mirrored the way I felt about her new living arrangements. "That's…unfortunate."

Benji knew that Ellie never missed a chance to insult me. I wasn't sure why she'd chosen me to torture. Mom once told me that people like her were miserable inside, and making others even more miserable was the only thing that made them feel better. I disagreed. Ellie Jones was just an evil, cum-burping gutter slut.

"So, flattery doesn't work. Will buying your lunch work?" he asked, serious.

"Yes," I said. What was left of my inheritance was being funneled into Kempton, including a meal plan, but if I didn't avoid the irritating cafeteria at least once a week, I wouldn't be able to handle the pressures of KIT. Gigi's Café was my one break from it all, but ten dollars a week on a tiny budget was adding up.

"What if I buy your lunches as many times as we come to Gigi's as long as you help me pass Dr. Zorba's final?" Benji asked.

His request made sense. Dr. Z's finals were notoriously difficult, and I could use the extra study time myself.

"Deal."

Benji slapped his fingers on the table as if he'd won something. When our food came, I tried to keep my attention on the cars passing by and the pedestrians walking their dogs, anything to keep from making eye contact with Benji. He was too happy anyway, and now that we would be hanging out regularly, his eyes were even brighter, and he couldn't stop smiling. It was disturbing.

After lunch, Benji and I walked back to my dorm. We agreed on studying twice a week and then up to three times a week during the two weeks before finals.

"So, we can start tonight?" Benji asked.

"It will have to be before I start my night at the Fitz."

"Okay, we can study from three to five p.m. and grab dinner."

"The cafeteria isn't conducive to studying, and the extra expenditure of takeout defeats the purpose of our lunch deal."

"I can get dinner. It's not a big deal."

I narrowed my eyes at him. "This is sounding complicated."

"Not at all. We have to eat. I have to study. What's complicated about that?"

"Okay, but if anything starts to get messy..."

"Completely one hundred percent mess-free," Benji assured me. He seemed confident enough.

"Okay. My last class is over at two thirty, so I'll grab my stuff and meet you at Charlie's."

"See you then," he said before walking away with a little more skip to his step.

I rolled my eyes and shook my head. Benji Reynolds was incorrigible.

By 2:42, I was standing at the entrance of Charlie's. Pulling out my cell phone, I texted Benji to let him know. But before I could press Send, he opened the door.

He was wearing a pair of gray sweats, a plain white T-shirt, and green Nike sneakers. His white laces were pristine, as were the white soles. They could have been brand-new, but knowing Benji, he probably took a toothbrush to them every night.

Benji held open the door and pulled my backpack from my shoulder at the same time. His biceps bulged as he moved, and it bugged me that I noticed how his skin rippled over the muscles and veins running through his thick forearms. It was probably just because I'd never seen him in a short-sleeved shirt before. Definitely not because anything about Benji could catch my eye. Or at least, that was what I was telling myself.

"Sorry you had to wait out here. I wasn't expecting you so soon," he said.

"Why? I said I was coming right after class."

I walked into the lobby of Charlie's and glanced around at the drab furnishings, wood paneling, and posters only a dork could appreciate, such as *No, Sterile Neutrinos Haven't Been Castrated* and Val Kilmer wearing bunny slippers and an alien antenna headband. It all created an atmosphere that matched the blank expressions of the handful of students sprawled out on the worn couches and chairs. Some were watching the small television while others were staring off into space.

Benji looked up at me from under his brow. "Truthfully, I didn't think you'd come at all. I figured you'd text me with an excuse."

I kind of liked that he anticipated that from me. "Well, I'm here. Where's your room? I'm going to have to pop some Zoloft if I stay down here much longer."

Benji slung my backpack over his shoulder and nodded toward a flight of stairs. I followed him up the steps and then to the right and down a long hallway that was just as underwhelming and unpretentious as the lobby.

Rounding the corner, Benji paused, turned the knob, and swept his arm across his body, gesturing for me to come in. Unlike the doors in the women's dorms, the guys didn't adorn the outside of theirs with dry erase boards or bedazzled letters.

Benji's room was immaculate and high tech. The bed was on one side of the room under a small window with broken dingy white mini-blinds. His gunmetal gray comforter was perfectly made, complete with military corners. The walls were decorated with rolls of electrical and duct tape and wire mesh.

The desk on the opposite side of the room spanned an entire wall. One side appeared to be a workbench, complete with a small plastic container filled with even smaller plastic drawers full of tiny components that required the lit magnifier hovering from the ceiling. The workbench also contained an oscilloscope, power supplies, and coils of different types of wire. In the center of the desk, in front of a brown leather office chair, were four open laptops and one single perfectly sharpened pencil.

Dozens of books and folders were both alphabetized and organized by color in the bookcase that rested inside the long desk on the other side of the room. The books were backlit with blue LED lights glowing through frosted panels that lined the backs of the bookshelves.

On the other side was a pivotal LCD monitor that, because of the movies stacked beside it, appeared to double as a home theater PC.

"I control that via remote and can check email from my bed," Benji said.

Even the walls were customized with white panels. I glanced at Benji, silently asking for an explanation.

"They're backed with multicolor LED lights."

"For what? Mood lighting? Housing allowed you to do this?"

"I get bored," he said. "And I didn't ask Housing. They would have said no. If they find out, I'm sure they'll take it all down."

"And kick you out of Charlie's and probably every other campus residence."

Benji pulled out one of two chairs parked at his desk. "Would you like to do it here, or do you prefer the bed?"

"Excuse me?" I choked out.

My surprise wasn't because I was a virgin. Quite the opposite. After my parents died, I became a statistic, rebelling and giving myself to anyone—male or female—who didn't mind if I lost myself in him or her for an hour or so. The thought of Benji proposing something like sex so casually was unsettling though. He was predictable, and I needed him to stay that way.

"Do you prefer to study at a desk or the bed?"

"Desk," I said, pulling out my own chair. I sat and took a deep breath, letting the adrenaline soak back into my system.

I cracked open the first book, *Frontiers of Astrobiology*, and pulled my notes from my backpack. After Benji finished comparing our notes from the last two classes, we silently read the chapters we were assigned, only stopping when Benji had a question.

At four thirty, someone knocked on Benji's door. He smiled and hopped up from his chair. It was then that I noticed a two-foot-tall plastic ear hanging from the back of the door. I watched him as he walked across the room and opened the door, greeting the skinny, pimple-faced kid holding two small paper sacks. Benji reached into his pocket and handed him some money, and then he kicked the door shut, tossing me one of the bags.

"What's this?"

"Dinner, remember?" he said, bending down to the small refrigerator nestled under the desk. He pulled out a bottle of water and twisted open the cap before setting it on the desk in front of me.

"Oh," I said, unrolling the top of the sack. I peeked in, and the pungent smell of Chinese food saturated my senses. My mouth began to water. I didn't realize that I was hungry until that moment. "Thanks."

"You like chicken fried rice, right? Extra soy sauce?"

"I do," I said, more than a little surprised he knew that. We'd never gone anywhere together but Gigi's Café.

After finishing the last of my rice, I wiped my mouth with the napkin at the bottom of my sack and threw away my trash.

"I'd better get going," I said. "Thanks again for dinner."

Benji beamed. "Anything in particular you want for next time?"

I shook my head as I packed my things. "Just whatever. Beggars can't be choosers."

"You're not a beggar. It's a barter system."

"I'll eat whatever you're buying."

"What if we went out sometime? For dinner. You can drive."

Benji knew I didn't have a car. What he meant was, he'd let me drive his yearling Ford Mustang that was orange with black racing stripes. The engine roared, and everyone could hear him coming. It was his high school graduation present from his parents, and in my opinion, they were hoping it would score him a girlfriend who had an appreciation for expensive things and a nice, reputable family. Unfortunately for him, he had a thing for invincible, mean weirdos.

"No, Benji. See you tomorrow."

"It won't be a date. It's the same thing as today. It's just geography."

"Not gonna happen."

"Mess-free, remember?" When I didn't answer, he changed his approach. "Lunch then?"

"Sure," I said, trying not to think too much about the hopeful smile on his face as I shut the door.

I leaned back against the wall. He was cute, and I liked spending the afternoon with him far too much. I was getting to know him too well. And he smelled too good. Caring was dangerous, for both of us.

The door swung open, and Benji popped into the hall with my bottle of water in his hand.

"Rory!" he called, realizing too late that I was next to him.

I stood up straight, trying to pretend I wasn't just feeling sorry for myself and struggling with my emotions. His face was so close to mine that I could feel his breath on my lips.

"What?" I snapped.

"You forgot your water," he said, taking a step back and then handing the bottle to me. "You okay?"

"I'm fine. You're just exhausting."

Before he could respond, I walked away. Even pretending not to care felt more empowering than the messy cluster of fucks I was giving two seconds before. With every step, the internal conflict disappeared, and the perpetual state of bitchiness that I was used to took over.

"Sorry," Benji called just as my fingers touched the door handle.

And just like that, with that one word, he pulled me out of my comfort zone and back to feeling guilty with a twinge in my chest. I pushed out the door and walked straight to the Fitz, my breath rising up in front of me in white clouds.

Whatever the reason Benji had for liking me, it was the wrong reason. If I had to tell myself that a thousand times a day, I would. If that wasn't enough, I would remind myself that getting involved with Benji would inevitably hurt him, and if I cared about him enough to even entertain the thought of ruining his life by giving in to his stupid crush, I should care about him enough to push him away. I was messed-up. A sob story. A charity case.

Maybe that was why he liked me? He felt sorry for me. That thought, true or not, erased any mushy bullshit going on in my head.

Whatever works.

The lab door crashed behind me as I made my way to my stool.

"Shouldn't you be wearing a coat?" Cy said from behind his computer.

I didn't answer him.

"What is that saying? You'll catch cold?"

"Germs cause colds," I said, picking up my first sheet of data. "It's an old wives' tale, like having wet hair outside in winter can make you sick. That's not true either."

"Old wives' tales have a touch of truth."

"Did you record these isotopic signatures?" I asked, standing and holding up the page in my hand.

Cy looked up and narrowed his eyes. "Not yet."

"They're important, you know."

"I know."

"Then, why are you dicking around with transcriptions?"

Cy took off his glasses and placed them carefully on his desk. He didn't speak. He just watched me.

"I'm angry!" I yelled.

"I sense that."

"Then, why are you staring at me? Shouldn't you be asking me what's wrong?"

"You wouldn't tell me."

"So?" I yelled again, breathing hard. I collapsed onto my stool. A full minute of silence filled the room before I spoke again, "I'm calm now. Thank you."

"You're welcome," Cy said, returning to clicking on his computer.

FOUR

Two weeks into our study agreement, Benji was staring at me, waiting for a different answer.

"Still no," I snapped, a little perturbed he wasn't accepting my answer and letting it go.

He grinned. "You just said you needed a change of venue."

"We can't study at The Gym."

"We can do whatever we want."

I rolled my eyes.

"Is that a yes?" he asked.

"No. It's *still* a no."

"Just once. Come with me once, and I'll never ask you to go again. I'll throw in a freebie dinner, one you don't have to study with me for."

"What am I? A food whore? I said, *no.*"

Thirty minutes later, we were at The Gym. I was in a loose-fitting Rolling Stones tee, black leggings, and high-top Converse, poking buttons on a treadmill and fantasizing about where I would eat my freebie dinner. Benji was next to me, jogging along, spouting information from that day's notes. He wasn't even out of breath, and he was wearing the T-shirt I liked best on him. It was maroon with yellow lettering that said, *Come to the dork side. We have π.*

I clicked a green button, and the treadmill began to move. I held on to the rails as if I were being led to the fiery pits of hell.

Benji burst into laughter. "It's okay, Rory. It's not going to eat you."

"You don't know that," I said.

Benji leaned over and pushed a button a few times.

"What are you doing? Push your own buttons!" The treadmill began to move faster, and so did my feet.

I jogged next to Benji at half the pace, but I was already breathing hard. In high school, I was in volleyball. I could run laps all day and barely break a sweat. I even had friends, and they would beg the heavens for my thick, shiny brown hair and perfectly peach skin. Boys had just begun to notice me. Then, I died and came back an angry shaven and pierced pale hermit who gasped for air after slowly jogging for two minutes.

"How do I turn this off?"

"You don't," Benji said. "You just go with it."

"I don't want to go with it. I want to walk."

"Cardio is good. You never know when you'll have to run for your life."

I raised an eyebrow. "That's a weird fucking thing to say."

"Weird but true," he said, facing forward and pushing his own run-faster button.

I hopped off the treadmill, letting it roll on without me. The water fountain was just a few feet away, so I walked over as slowly as I could without looking crazy to take a drink.

"You must be lost," Ellie said behind me.

I stood up, tense, and then turned around, forcing my shoulders to relax.

"Decided to get a gym membership, did you?"

"No. Just visiting."

Ellie made a face. "What on earth for?"

"I'm here with a friend."

Ellie laughed once. "Now I know you're lying. You don't have any friends." She patted her neck with a towel. Her perky D-cup breasts perfectly filled out a purple racerback top, as did her ass in the matching capri yoga pants. It was almost as if the gods had made a point to sculpt the perfect body and then were too tired to provide a decent personality.

Benji passed Ellie and stood next to me. "Want to try the weight machines?"

Ellie was incensed and crossed her arms.

Benji noticed her then and nodded. "Hey, Ellie."

"You brought her here?"

I looked at Benji, completely confused.

"So?" he said. He wasn't being rude, but that didn't stop Ellie's cheeks from turning red with anger.

"Seriously? You're trying to make me jealous? With...*that*?" Ellie said, laughing once without humor.

I instantly felt sick, and I craned my neck at Benji, who looked genuinely bewildered.

"No," Benji said, shaking his head at me. "No way." He held up his hands.

"Did you..." I couldn't finish. Couldn't even say the words.

Benji shook his head again. "I have no idea what she's talking about."

From the corner of my eye, I could see the beginnings of a grin on Ellie's face. Was she really so horrible that she would pretend to have dated Benji to ruin one of the only friendships I had?

I grabbed Benji's cheeks and planted my lips on his. Benji's entire body tensed, and then he relaxed, pulling my body against his. His mouth parted, and what was supposed to be a quick, hard peck turned into a long, deep kiss with a lot of tongue and a lot of pressure from Benji's fingertips into my skin.

I pulled away and we looked at each other. "I bet she's jealous now," I said, stealing a side-glance at Ellie.

"Who cares?" Benji said, unable to look away from me. Although he hadn't been breathing hard on the treadmill, he was certainly breathing hard now.

Ellie's mouth fell open, and then she walked away, tossing her hair as she turned.

Once she was gone, I nodded to the weight machine. "That one?"

Benji nodded and led me to the contraption, looking a bit bewildered.

I sat on the seat, pulled the metal pin out of the bottom hole, and put it into the top hole. It was my first time in almost three years lifting weights or even exercising. Thirty-five pounds seemed like a good starting point.

I pulled on the bar above my head until it touched the back of my neck and then slowly let it pull away. One rep after another, Benji watched me without saying a word.

"Am I even doing this right?" I said, peering up at the bar as I pulled on it.

"You do everything right," Benji said without hesitation.

I let the bar slip out of my hands, and the weights crashed down.

After a short pause, I sighed. "I was just being a bitch to Ellie. That's all."

"It didn't feel that way," Benji said with a glimmer of hope in his sweet brown eyes.

"You're right," I said, trying to change the subject. "This working out thing does help blow off steam. Maybe I could come here on Saturday mornings. We didn't get that much studying done."

Benji watched me for a moment, and then he looked down and laughed. "Yeah, I can do Saturdays." When his eyes met mine, the disappointment in them stung.

"I'd better get to the lab," I said, pointing behind me with my thumb.

Just then, I felt a searing pain in my backside accompanied by a loud slapping noise that echoed throughout The Gym.

A guy almost a head taller than Benji passed me, smirking. "It's about time you brought a piece of ass," he said.

Benji immediately grabbed him and slammed him to the floor. Benji's elbow stretched back, high into the air, and his hand was balled into a shaking tight fist. Before he threw the punch, Benji pushed away from the guy and stood up.

"I was just kidding, man! Damn!" he said.

"Don't ever touch her like that again," Benji said, a dozen emotions moving across his face. He reached out and helped the guy up. Then, he grabbed my hand, leading me from The Gym to his car.

We didn't speak during the fifteen-minute ride to the Fitz. I picked at the chipped black polish on my nails and stared out the window. The Mustang slowed to a stop at the curb, and my door unlocked with a click.

"I'm sorry, Rory," he said, sighing. "I don't know what happened." He didn't look at me when he spoke. He just stared straight ahead.

"It's fine," I said, shaking my head.

I'd seen a completely different side of him. Before, I was struggling with returning the affections of a semi-annoying nerd. Suddenly, he was a badass. I'd wanted to kiss him again the second we stopped. Now, I was building up the nerve to do it again. He looked at me, and he knew exactly what I was thinking. Benji's line of sight fell to my lips, and his hand reached across the front of the center console and rested on my knee. We leaned toward each other. *Holy shit, I'm actually going to do this.*

His phone buzzed, and the display lit up. Both of our bodies relaxed, and I looked down. The name above the number made my stomach turn. In bold white letters, it read, *ELLIE*. My eyes snapped back up to Benji's. His expression immediately turned desperate.

"I can explain—"

"Liar," I hissed, grabbing my backpack and slamming the door behind me.

I ran up the stairs, through the glass double doors of the Fitz, and turned to the right before running down another set of stairs to the basement.

Cy was standing there with the door held open.

I stopped at the bottom of the stairs and then mentally gathered myself as I walked across the hall and into the lab. My movements felt forced and unnatural as I walked to my stool.

"Are you okay?" Cy asked.

"Fine," I said, staring at the keyboard in front of me.

"Did someone hurt you?"

I shook my head.

"You seem...disappointed."

I could tell that Cy was uncomfortable having this conversation with me, and it meant a lot that he was trying, which only made me feel more emotional.

I took a deep breath. "Only in myself."

"It's okay that you're late. Life is about more than just work."

I looked over at the clock in the bottom right corner of my screen. He was right. I was ten minutes late.

The corners of my mouth turned up, and I peered over at him. "Thanks."

He cleared his throat and began clicking on his keyboard. "You're welcome," he said.

"Can I ask you for a huge favor?"

"Uh...yes, of course."

"Would you..." Ugh, I felt so stupid even uttering the words. "Would you sit next to me tomorrow in class?"

Cy stared at me for the longest time, and then his eyes danced all over the room. He blinked a lot and then simply nodded.

"I know that's a stupid thing to ask. But there's a good reason for it, I promise."

He nodded again and then went back to his data. If I could have at that moment shrunk into a puddle and slipped away under the door, I would have, but instead, I focused on entering every page of data Dr. Z had given us for the week.

The next morning, I waited at my desk for Cy to walk in, praying he would beat Benji to class for once. I was so early that I had to wait outside for the previous class to dismiss.

Once Cy walked through the door and looked up at me, I let out the breath I'd been holding. He climbed the steps, walked halfway down the row, and then sat in Benji's seat.

"I owe you one. Seriously."

Cy was clearly unsure about my request. He probably wasn't aware of whose seat he was commandeering, and I wasn't going to tell him, just in case he changed his mind.

Benji walked in a few moments later with a somber face. He glanced up at me and immediately noticed Cy. I was hoping he would sit in one of the lower rows, but he climbed the steps and turned down our aisle. My heart began to thump against my rib cage so hard that my face was throbbing.

Benji passed Cy and then me before taking the seat on my left side.

I sat rigidly, completely unprepared and hoping Benji would just keep his mouth shut. But of course, he didn't.

His head turned toward me, hesitant and nervous, and then one side of his mouth turned up. "I tried to call you."

I didn't respond.

"I came by your dorm. I guess you weren't home from the lab yet."

I stayed silent, looking straight ahead. From the corner of my eye, I saw Cy glance in our direction.

Benji leaned toward me, keeping his voice low. "Can we talk about this? Please let me explain. Rory, c'mon. *Please?* We just started to get things figured out. I—"

Dr. Z walked in, and I opened my laptop to a blank and ready screen. I typed in the date and tried to stare a hole into Dr. Z's forehead.

Cy leaned forward. "I don't believe she's ready to discuss your issue just yet. Maybe another time outside of class."

Benji sighed and leaned back.

Cy spoke again, "Since there appears to be something upsetting going on between the two of you, it would be polite to find another seat so that Rory can concentrate on her notes."

Benji sank into his seat and nodded, and then he picked up his backpack. He passed in front of Cy and me, and then he climbed the steps, sitting somewhere above us.

"Thank you," I whispered, still looking ahead.

"I would say that you're welcome, but I seem to say that a lot."

I offered a small smile and silently thanked Dr. Z for beginning his lecture earlier than normal.

"We have a lot to cover today," Dr. Z said, "so let's go ahead and get started. Oxygenic photosynthesis…"

FIVE

STUDYING NOW CONSISTED OF ME, my notes, my laptop, and my dorm room. For two weeks, Benji asked me to give him the opportunity to explain—before class, after class, in texts—but every time my anger began to retreat, I would cross paths with Ellie in the hall and hate Benji all over again.

On the first day of October, I was prepared to see Benji outside of Dr. Z's class with that same pathetic, miserable expression, but he wasn't there. I didn't give it much thought until Dr. Z began his lecture, and Benji never showed up. Cy had only taken Benji's seat the one time. After that, Benji got the hint and stayed away. Now that I knew Benji wasn't even sitting above me, I felt very lonely.

I went to lunch and then to lab. Benji wasn't there either. My mind began to wander. I started feeling curious if he was sick, out of town, or something much worse. He'd been so miserable the past weeks, and I just ignored him.

Twenty minutes into lab, I pulled my cell phone from my pocket. Benji hadn't texted or tried to call in two days. I tapped his name and then keyed in a message.

You okay?

He didn't respond. I tried again.

Are you sick?

Five minutes later and still nothing.

I know I've been ignoring you, but you could at least let me know you're all right.

He still hadn't texted me back by the time class was over, so I headed to Charlie's. At that time of day, everyone was going in and out of the front entrance, so it wasn't hard to slip inside and make my way to Benji's door. I knocked. Nothing. I knocked again.

A tall, skinny undergrad with thick glasses stood next to me. "Can I help you?"

"Benji didn't show up for class. Have you seen him?"

He shook his head. "No, but he never locks his door unless he's home," he said, turning the knob.

It opened, revealing his dark room.

"Who only locks his door when he's home?" I thought aloud, peeking into Benji's room

The undergrad shrugged his shoulders. "That's how you know he's not in there."

I shut the door. "Thanks," I said before leaving Charlie's for the parking lot.

The orange Mustang was hard to miss...and it wasn't there.

I walked to Gigi's with my arms crossed over my chest. It was windy and getting colder. I was wearing a long-sleeved white T-shirt with a green short-sleeved T-shirt over that with jeans and boots, but it still wasn't enough to keep me warm. My ears were burning from exposure to the chilly wind.

Gigi's was winding down with just a few stragglers having a late lunch. I wasn't surprised that Benji wasn't there. His Mustang wasn't parked outside, but I still had to check.

I walked out, trying to think where else he would be, and I decided to head to The Gym. If he wasn't there, he probably went home to see his parents for a few days. Maybe he was sick and had to go to the doctor. It wasn't as if he had anyone here to take care of him, including me—the jealous bitch, who didn't even give him the chance to explain, much less apologize.

The sun was low in the sky by the time I reached The Gym. My feet hurt, and my stomach was growling, but none of that mattered because Benji's orange Mustang was parallel parked out front.

I ran across the street and up the stairs, pushing through the double doors. There he was, red-faced, drenched in sweat, and squatting about three hundred and fifty pounds. I walked over to him, too relieved to be embarrassed.

"Benji?"

Recognition lit his face, and he stood up, dropping the bar from his shoulders. He was breathing hard and exhausted, but he still looked just as miserable as he had for the past two weeks.

"You weren't in class."

He put his hands on his hips, trying to catch his breath. His eyes were bloodshot, exhausted, and sad.

"Can we...can we talk outside?" I asked.

He nodded, grabbed his coat, and followed me into the lobby and out the glass door. Then, we descended the steps. I sat on the curb next to his Mustang.

Benji draped his coat around my shoulders and then sat next to me. "I'm sorry I didn't answer your text," he said quietly, looking at the asphalt. "I just couldn't go to class another day and see the anger in your eyes when you look at me, knowing you were just a few feet away and I couldn't talk to you."

"I'm sorry. That was cruel and unusual punishment."

He shook his head. "No, I deserved it. I wasn't honest with you."

"I should have let you explain."

"Not until you were ready. I just had to take a break from being patient."

"You've been here all day?" I asked.

"Pretty much."

My stomach growled, and I covered it with both hands as if that would stop the noise.

"Have you eaten?" he asked.

"I've been looking for you since lab."

"Since lab?" He looked around and sighed. "You went to Gigi's, too, didn't you?"

"And your dorm."

"You walked all over town?"

"Well…yes…I don't have a car."

Benji sighed and hung his head. "I'm such a jerk. C'mon, let's get food."

"I…" I began, hesitating. "I don't care what happened with you and Ellie. It's none of my damn business. I just want to be friends again."

Benji thought about that for a moment. It clearly wasn't everything he was hoping to hear. He pressed his lips together. "I can do that."

"Yeah? I know it will be awkward for a while."

"I promised you mess-free, remember? I'm not saying I'm going to stop pursuing you. I'm just saying I'll take whatever you give me."

I couldn't help but smile. And then I couldn't help myself from elbowing him in the ribs.

He laughed once. "See? Already back to normal."

We stood, and Benji drove me to Gigi's where we had dinner for the first time. Ironically, we both ordered breakfast.

"Full order of biscuits and gravy," the waitress said, placing a plate in front of Benji.

"Breakfrito," she said, smiling as she set my plate down in front of me.

Benji cut up his biscuits with a fork and then shoveled the first bite into his mouth.

"I have today's notes, if you want them."

"I do," Benji said after he swallowed. "But what about the other classes you missed?"

"I'm sure we can make them up."

"I'm not worried about me. Skipping class was my decision."

"Looking for you was mine."

Benji smiled. "I feel like a jerk for making you worry, but I can't deny that it feels pretty good that you were worried about me."

"I'd be a jerk if I wasn't. I mean, yeah, I don't like that you lied to me about Ellie—"

"It's really not what you think, Rory."

"Then, what is she to you?"

Benji shook his head and spoke with a nervous smile. "I guess she was sort of a coworker, but it was *never* anything more than that."

"Coworker?" I asked.

"She was my lab partner spring semester last year. That's why we have each other's phone number."

I rested my elbows on the table and covered my face with my hands. *A stupid misunderstanding. Figures.* "I'm such an asshole. I should have let you explain."

"If you were mad at me, it means you cared enough to get jealous, right?"

"Do you always look on the bright side?"

"Yes."

I smiled at him. We couldn't be more different, but I was beginning to appreciate it instead of holding that against him.

"I'm surprised you can hold up your fork," I said.

Benji paused, mid-bite. "Why is that?"

"You had a bunch of weights on that bar. Were you lifting that much all morning?"

"Pretty much. I've been blowing off stress like that since middle school."

I shoved a piece of breakfrito into my mouth and chewed, narrowing my eyes at him, while I thought about his comment.

"What stress? You seem like someone who had the perfect childhood."

"My parents were great," he said, nodding, "but they worked a lot, and my dad was gone most of the time. We made sacrifices, just like anyone else."

My muscles tensed. I had to stop myself from informing him that he had no idea about sacrifice, but it was just a knee-jerk reaction. Just because his parents weren't murdered didn't mean he didn't have the right to complain.

"What about your childhood? I'm guessing you went to a lot of concerts," he said, nodding to my Ramones tee.

I laughed once. "No, not until the summer after my senior year."

"So, you spent the summer concert-bouncing? That's kind of amazing."

"Pretty much," I said with a small smile. He was right. Not many people could say that.

"Your parents were okay with that? Mine would have freaked."

"They..." I trailed off, trying to think of the best answer that wouldn't lead to more questions. "They didn't really have a say."

He smiled. "That doesn't surprise me at all. I'm sure they know that you would have found a way to do what you want. Makes me wonder what they're like. Raising such a free spirit."

I thought about his comment. I'd never felt like a free spirit. More like someone who was weighed down by her horrific past. But Benji made me see something about myself that I hadn't seen before—the bright side. It was nice to think that maybe my parents were looking down on me, satisfied with my fortitude.

"You're kind of awesome sometimes," I said, smiling at him.

"Yeah?" he said, a hopeful look in his eyes.

An hour after we'd sat down, Benji waved down the waitress and insisted on paying.

"When do you have to go to the Fitz?" he asked.

I looked at my phone to check the time and noticed that both Cy and Dr. Z had called. "Oh, shit. I'm an hour late."

"I'll take you there. I can come in and help you with whatever."

I shook my head, putting my phone in my pocket as I stood. "I just need to get there fast before I lose my position. Shit!"

Benji smiled. "Oh, I can get you there fast."

The Mustang's brakes squealed as we pulled away from Gigi's and then again when we skidded to a stop in front of the Fitz.

I climbed out, holding open the door and laughing. "Thanks for not killing me."

"We still on for studying tomorrow?"

I looked at Benji for a moment, wondering if that was a good idea, and then nodded. *What the hell?* "Sure," I said.

I pushed the door shut and turned to climb the steps, but Benji called my name. The passenger-side window was rolled down nearly all the way by the time I flipped around to face him.

"Can I sit with you in class again?"

It felt strange to keep saying yes to Benji after telling him no for so long, but I wasn't enough of a badass to endure seeing that sad look on Benji's face again. He was a good person. He deserved way better than I could ever give him, but that didn't mean I had to punish him for trying to be my friend.

"Yeah," I said.

Leaving him behind, I jogged up the stairs and into the lobby. My pace slowed as I descended the north stairs to the basement, trying to process the day.

Once I opened the lab door and walked in though, the moment of peace had returned to chaos.

Both Cy and Dr. Z were rushing me, asking where I was, why I was late, whom I was with, and a dozen other questions.

I held up my hands. "I'm sorry! I've been working every night for six weeks! I needed a break!"

"You couldn't call?" Cy snapped.

"I should have called Dr. Z. I'm sorry."

The professor patted his chest. "I'm glad you're okay. Of course, you work very hard and should take breaks, Rory. But please, for god's sake, let me know when you decide to disappear."

Disappear. For the love of all things holy. "Dr. Z, I'm so sorry. I wasn't thinking."

He waved me away, walking toward the door. "Please. We're ahead of schedule, and all thanks to the two of you."

Dr. Z left, locking the door behind him.

"Selfish!" Cy growled behind me.

I flipped around, preparing to let him know that I didn't report to him, but the second I faced him, he crashed into me, wrapping his arms around me, his fingers digging into my skin.

"I thought..." he said, his voice thick with worry.

I just stood there, not knowing what else to do. No one had touched me like that in a long time, yet it felt natural, as if he'd held me a hundred times before. I slowly hugged him back and rested my chin on his shoulder. The longer he held me, the better it felt.

After a full minute, Cy finally relaxed his grip and took a step back.

"My apologies," he said quietly. He looked down and then pushed his glasses up to sit higher on the ridge of his nose.

"You thought what?" I asked.

He shook his head and turned around, retreating to his desk.

"I'm not depressed, if that's what you think."

"I didn't think you killed yourself, Rory."

"Then, what is it?"

"I just...I don't want anything to happen to you."

I grinned, dropping my backpack beside my desk. "Something has already happened to me. You should stop worrying."

Cy opened his mouth to say something, but he decided against it.

S I X

FOR FOUR WEEKS, Benji and I had inevitably eaten two meals a day together, nearly every day, and I'd found I was beginning to look forward to it. My grades had returned to normal, and Ellie had even seemed to be around less. For the first time since I'd moved to Helena, I was smiling more often than not.

Spending time with Benji seemed to take up my days, and being ignored by Cy took up my nights. We would sit across from each other, barely speaking, barely making eye contact. I'd tried asking questions I didn't need the answers to. I'd even tried bringing up the fact that he'd shown up at my door weeks before in the early morning hours to check up on me, figuring that would get him talking. But every time, he would find some way to answer in one or two words or say he was too busy to talk.

I pretended not to notice, but I wanted to punch him for pulling me into that amazing hug as if he gave a shit and then spending nearly a month making me feel as if I were invisible. I wanted to punch myself for caring, for allowing someone to make me feel that way in the first place.

Halloween night, while everyone was dressing up and attending parties, Cy and I were in the basement, punching numbers. The Fitz was one of the oldest buildings on campus, and it struggled to keep itself comfortably heated in the winter and cooled in the summer. The basement was particularly miserable and felt like an icebox on very cold nights.

I sipped my water and then put it down before pulling the sleeves of my sweater further over my hands.

Cy cleared his throat, and for the first time in weeks, he spoke to me first, "I can talk to Dr. Zorba about a space heater."

"He'll never go for it," I said, wiping my lips with the cuff of my sweater. "He wouldn't risk a fire or a significant temperature change affecting the specimen."

"It won't affect the specimen. It came from space."

"Exactly. Where it's cold."

"Who says the planet it originated from wasn't able to retain higher temperatures?"

"Like Venus?"

"Exactly like Venus. I mean…I'm sure that it's possible. I'll look into a space heater."

I watched him expectantly.

"What?"

"No Uranus jokes? I'm disappointed."

"What do you mean?"

I chuckled. "Never mind." My fingers began clicking against the keyboard again, and from the corner of my eye, I was sure that I caught Cy staring at me. I glanced over at him. "What?"

"You're much more attractive when you smile, and your laugh is lovely."

"Uh…thank you."

"You're—"

"I'm welcome. It's okay. I say thank you to you a lot, apparently."

"I just want you to…I don't know what I want."

He stared at me for a few moments more and then continued with his work. My face caught fire as the blood pooled under my cheeks. My fingers wouldn't work after that, and I couldn't concentrate on the numbers.

Cy stood up and left the room without a word. Right about the time I decided to get up and look for him, he returned, setting a Butterfinger on my desk.

"Trick or treat, right?" he said.

"Is that a Halloween joke? I mean, that's cool. I just didn't know you had a sense of humor."

"I'm surprised you're here. There are costume parties all over campus."

I shook my head. "I don't really do parties. Just once in a while when I'm bored out of my mind, but I avoid Halloween parties at all costs."

"Why is that?"

"Fake blood. Dead people. Slutty costumes. None of it screams *fun* to me."

Cy grinned. "I suppose not. We still have an hour or so of work to do. Would you mind if I walk you home when we're finished?"

"Why?"

My response took Cy off guard.

He blinked a few times and then cleared his throat. "I think that maybe my insistence not to form attachments here was incorrect. We spend a lot of time together in this lab, and I'd like to get to know you better. As much as one can in the time I have left."

"You're going back home?"

He nodded.

"When?"

"Soon."

"So, that's why you've been ignoring me? Because you know you're leaving?"

He hesitated. "In part, yes."

"What's the other part?"

He squirmed in his chair. "You...intrigue me."

I wanted to high-five myself. The few times we'd interacted before I thought he was being nice in spite of feeling an extreme loathing toward me. Instead, it was the opposite. To Cy, I was *intriguing*.

I shrugged, trying to pretend I wasn't irrationally pleased. "If you want."

He smiled and then continued with his work. Despite the difficulty I had focusing, I forced myself to get through the pages of data on my desk. My mind kept wandering off, questioning why I felt so drawn to him. Cy wasn't my type. He was leaving. His lack of concert tees told me that we likely had nothing in common. But even then, I had a strong feeling that there was a reason life had thrown us together.

An hour later, I put the last sheet in the bin and turned to Cy. "Need any help?" I asked.

"No, I was just working on a few things for tomorrow while you finished up."

"Show-off," I said, grabbing my bag.

Cy and I walked out of the building, toward my dormitory.

"Would you like my coat?" Cy asked.

I shook my head.

"So," Cy said, shoving his hands into his pockets, "what is your major, Rory?"

"I'm considering Bio Med. I have a thing for Astrobiology though, and Dr. Z and my father..." I began, but got lost in the thought.

"Were astrobiologists? Nothing wrong with having similar interests as a parent. It's quite honorable where I'm from."

"It just feels as though I'm repeating something that shouldn't be repeated." I shook my head. "It's hard to explain."

"No, I get it."

"No, you don't," I said. It wasn't the right thing to say or even remotely polite, but I became weirdly defensive when it came to my pain and memories. No one got anything about me, not even Dr. Z, and they didn't get to say they did. If they understood or related to me, it meant I had to share something that belonged only to me.

When Dr. Z, my counselors, or my social worker tried to offer understanding, I let them know they weren't within a thousand light-years of my truth. Pretending was a waste of everyone's time, and I had endured hell to keep mine. It felt wrong to waste it.

"You're right. That was inconsiderate of me. I'm sorry."

"What's your major?" I asked, trying to pretend I didn't just make our little nature walk completely awkward.

"Interplanetary Culture."

I laughed once. "I'm pretty sure Kempton doesn't offer that."

"I chose Kempton for my semester abroad. It's part of my curriculum at home."

A group of students dressed like various characters of *The Wizard of Oz* jogged by. Dorothy, of course, had hairy legs and a goatee.

Cy smiled, and we continued. "Your culture is definitely one of my favorites."

"You don't celebrate Halloween?"

"No, but if you mean dressing up and begging for candy, then technically, neither do you."

"Touché."

"Did that really just happen? I won an argument?" he asked, grinning.

I narrowed my eyes at him. "Did you just gloat?"

"I guess I did."

"Feel better?"

"Yes. Yes, I do."

"Good. I would say that's out of character for you, but you seem like the gloating type. You're kind of a show-off in general."

Cy seemed offended. "I most certainly do not show off. I am quite focused on remaining in the background."

"No. You're definitely a show-off. All those off-the-wall questions you ask in Dr. Z's class? Show-off."

"I suppose gaining information is not what university is about then?"

"You ask questions a certain way, as if you already know the answers."

"That doesn't even make sense, Rory, and it's actually quite rude."

"I'm not insulting you. I'm describing you."

Cy frowned. "That isn't a very nice way of describing someone."

"I also think you're a little bit…somewhat attractive, and your eyes are incredible. There, that should heal the bruise on your ego."

"No, it doesn't."

I shrugged.

"You think I'm attractive?" he asked.

"Now, you're fishing for compliments. Showing off and now this? Now I know you're a narcissist."

"What?" Cy said, his voice rising an octave.

I burst into laughter, bending over and clutching my stomach. When I finally stood, I lilted a sigh. "Wow. I needed that."

"To insult me?"

"No, to laugh. I was fucking with you, Cy."

His eyes widened.

"I was joking, messing with you, just kidding?"

He nodded, seeming nervous. "Oh."

I shook my head and patted him on the arm, looking up at the four floors of windows on my dormitory. Most of them were dark. "This is me. Thanks for walking me home and for asking this time."

He ignored my mention of him showing up at my door.

"You're never going to explain that, are you?" I asked.

"I don't think I need to."

"So, my hypothesis that you followed me after I left the lab is correct?"

Cy didn't answer.

"Why?"

"I've already told you. I wanted to make sure you were okay."

"That's all?"

"That's all, and for some reason, I needed to see you."

"Why?"

"Why must you ask so many questions, Rory?"

"Weren't you just defending the right to learn while in college?"

Cy lowered his eyes and took a breath. "And just like college, some things we must wait to learn."

"But we learn them."

He managed a small smile and then fidgeted for a bit before reaching for me. He pulled me against him, and my entire body stiffened.

He held his warm cheek against mine and whispered in my ear, "No one knows everything."

He let me go and walked away quickly, his hands in his pockets.

The next day in class, Benji sat next to me and immediately began filling me in on everything that had happened since I saw him last. I opened my laptop, ignoring him for the most part and thinking about the night before. It was nice to walk with Cy and to talk about classes and my major instead of the rock. I thought about how soft and warm his skin was against my cheek and how good he smelled.

Benji prattled on, oblivious to the fact that I was clearly preoccupied, and then Cy walked in. He did something he'd never done before. He looked up at me. Before I did anything stupid, like wave, Cy's eyes drifted to Benji, and Cy's entire face tightened. Benji noticed, too, and they traded strained glances.

Benji leaned into my ear. "Is it just me, or did he give me a look?"

"It's just you."

Cy continued to his desk, and Benji continued with his story about the value of good study habits and his clear superiority over integers.

"Hey…" Benji said, stopping mid-sentence.

"Huh?"

"I can't help but wonder if that was a glint of jealousy in Cy's eyes or just curiosity."

"Neither. You're imagining things."

Dr. Z greeted the class and began his lecture.

Before I could even type the date, Benji leaned in again, his brown eyes lit with mischief. "You don't think I could make Cy jealous? That hurts."

"What is your deal today?"

His playful expression faded. "I saw him walking you home this morning. Are you guys…"

"That was at two o'clock. Why were you hanging around my dorm at two in the morning?"

Benji puffed out a laugh. "I wasn't hanging around your dorm. I was running."

"At two?"

He shrugged. "I couldn't sleep. Are you avoiding the question?"

"No. We're not doing whatever it is you think we're doing. And shh…I'm trying to learn."

"It's okay, you know, if you like him. You don't have to worry about me."

My eyes met Benji's. He looked wounded. "I never asked you to like me."

He shook his head. "No, I know. I just…I will always be your friend. It doesn't matter if you reciprocate those feelings or not. I don't need you to love me to love you."

I pulled my mouth to one side in an awkward half-smile and then faced forward. *He loves me? Since when?*

Our relationship had been strictly platonic since freshman orientation. At least, that was what I thought. I didn't know how to feel about that, much less respond.

"Really?" I hissed. "*This* is how you tell me? Are you serious right now?"

"Sorry, Rory, I didn't mean to—"

"It's okay," I whispered, waving him away. "We don't have to talk about it now."

"Fair enough," he said, his shoulders sagging.

The rest of class, I felt nauseous and panicky, flattered and sympathetic.

"Are we café-ing it today?" he asked.

I just shook my head a few quick times and intentionally didn't look over to see his reaction. Benji feeling hurt was beginning to affect me in ways I didn't like or appreciate. I wanted us to go back to being friends, as we were before, but it was becoming clear that we couldn't. I never asked him to be my friend in the first place or to like me or love me or however he felt about me. *Why should I have to take on this guilt when I tried to keep a respectable distance from the beginning?* It wasn't my fault. He was the one who was dishonest. It ruined everything, and now, Cy was finally coming around.

I could feel Benji's disappointment radiating from his perfectly ironed peach oxford. *What self-respecting guy wears peach—even if the color does look amazing with his skin and eyes—or feathers his hair since 1991, for that matter?* I fought the guilt with anger, and for the time being, it was working.

Class dismissed, and I took my things and darted past Benji, not even saying good-bye. I wasn't sure if he tried. I refused to look.

Since eating lunch at the café was out and the college cafeterias were always too full of obnoxious people during that time of day, I opted to head down to the Fitz and get a few samples lined up and ready for Cy that evening. I was hoping that thought would lead my mind to think more about Cy, but I couldn't get Benji's defeated expression out of my head.

My mind was made up: interaction with Benji would have to be limited. We'd gotten too close, even after the Ellie ridiculousness. He was sneaky, and I was stupid. I should never have kissed him. I knew how he felt about me.

I could feel my entire face compressing into a tight, troubled frown, but both my emotions and my face unraveled when I saw Cy at his desk, already lining up samples.

"Hello, Rory. Surprised to see you here during the day."

"I was going to say that exact same thing to you." I walked over to his desk where he had petri dishes and small square stickers marked with consecutive numbers.

"I guess you don't need me at all," I teased.

"Oh, I need you. Make no mistake about that."

I was standing a bit behind him, so I watched, hoping he would turn around and wink or smile or somehow indicate that what he said meant more.

Nothing. *Fine, I'll help.* "What do you mean?"

Cy raised an eyebrow. "What do you mean, what do I mean?"

"You need me to help you with this?" I said, nodding to the desk.

"Of course."

I nodded. "Good to know. Just wanted to be clear that you didn't mean something else."

Cy fidgeted a bit and then pulled off his black-rimmed glasses, placing them carefully on his desk. "I'm finished for now. I can walk you to your next class."

"What is your fascination with walking me places?"

"It's customary, isn't it?"

"Not since 1920."

Cy grinned. "Just let me walk you. You don't have to be a…hard-ass all the time."

"Oh! Listen to you swearing like a real college student!"

His grin broke into a broad smile. "Really?"

"No. C'mon. *I'll* walk *you*."

We kept a slow pace. Even though the thick cloud cover brought in another brutal cold front, neither of us seemed to notice. We talked about my classes and how out of control Dr. Zorba's beard had become. We laughed a lot, and it was nice to just talk about nothing. We stopped at a food cart, and Cy watched in awe as I ordered a falafel.

"What?" I asked, eating and walking at the same time.

"It's just an odd dish."

"The falafel?"

"Yes, the croquettes in pita bread. Very strange."

"You've never heard of a falafel?"

He shook his head.

"It's a Middle Eastern dish," I said, confused by his confusion.

"Just because it's Middle Eastern doesn't mean I must have heard of it. Are you familiar with all Canadian dishes because Canada is also located in North America?"

"Okay, okay, you win."

"I what? Can you say that a bit louder?"

When we stopped in front of my class, I smirked at his teasing. "Very funny."

"I'm finished with classes for the day," he said, smiling. "I'll see you tonight."

"You're not coming to lab?" I asked.

"I have an appointment."

"Are you sure you don't want to walk me to my next class? And then back to my dorm after that? I'm giving myself a haircut. You can help me with that, too," I teased.

"I can if you wish," he said, his voice steady.

I wasn't expecting him to say yes. "It's kind of ritualistic. I should probably just be alone."

"You don't have to be. I can be there with you."

"I'll see you tonight," I said with an appreciative smile.

Cy walked backward a few steps and then turned to walk away. I stepped into lab to see Benji sitting next to my empty seat with a forced grin and sad eyes.

"You missed out. It was potato soup day at the café."

"I had to set up some samples to save time tonight."

He leaned down to help me plug in my laptop and then pulled out his own. "I can help you in the lab, you know."

"No, you really can't."

"I just feel as if it's taking up all of my Rory time. Kind of sucks."

Rory time? "You kind of suck."

Benji chuckled and shook his head, booting up his computer. "I only take that from you, just so you know."

"And I appreciate it."

Is what I am feeling a…good mood? Do I even remember what that feels like? Whatever it was, it was completely fine with me if it stuck around a while. But then it occurred to me that I hadn't thought about my family all morning, and my good mood immediately dissipated. It felt like a betrayal, disrespectful to go a day without thinking about them. They deserved better from me.

For the remainder of class, I studied microbes, recorded their molecular signals, and felt sorry. Sorry that I didn't save my parents or my best friend. Sorry that I lived and they didn't. And I promised myself that I would never forget about them again.

Benji tried to smile at me a few times, but I ignored him. He got the hint fairly quickly, and I thought it made him feel better that I was behaving like my usual self.

After class, I packed up my things and trudged outside. The sky had been gray for two days, but now huge snowflakes were falling. I pulled at my sweater sleeves, covering my fists with the wool to try to ward off the cold.

I looked down at the bottom of the steps, and there stood Cy. An involuntary smile touched my lips.

"What are you doing here?" I said, descending the ten or so steps down to him.

"I decided to take you up on your invitation to walk you to your next class."

Without thinking, I threw my arms around him. Cy wasn't fazed. He pulled me more tightly against him, crossing his arms across my back and pressing his chin gently into my shoulder. I buried my face into his neck. He smelled so good. I couldn't get enough of it. It wasn't even cologne. It was just him. His skin was as warm and soft as it looked. He let me get as close to him as I needed, and then he let me let go of him when I needed to.

He didn't ask me what was wrong or if I was okay. He just walked with me in silence to my next class.

When I stopped in the doorway, he finally spoke, "I'll wait for you."

Cy had made it a point to remain aloof since we met, and now he was walking me to my classes. A part of me wanted to ask him more questions about why he had gone from one extreme to the other, but I was afraid if I did, it would make things awkward, and he would stop.

There was no use in pretending that I didn't want or need him around more, so I nodded and went inside, relieved to know Cy would be there when class was over.

SEVEN

JUST A FEW DAYS BEFORE THANKSGIVING BREAK, the sidewalks were clustered with red-faced but otherwise chipper students and faculty, almost all of them holding a Styrofoam cup of steaming hot liquid. I didn't drink coffee, tea, soda, or hot chocolate. If I drank anything but water, my throat would feel dry and raw. My father said that Mom must have passed that down to me because she was the same way until she turned forty, and then she tried her first glass of wine, and *that* became her new favorite beverage.

Christ, she was beautiful. Even her last day on this earth with mascara running down her face and a rag tied tightly across her mouth, she was the embodiment of beauty. When my father was happy, he would call her *honey* or *dearest*, and when he was angry, he would say *Charlotte*, but even then, her name sounded lovely. The night we all died, my father said her name in a tone I didn't recognize. A warning. She remained calm until they began tying my wrists, but then she fought them in utter despair.

"Charlotte," my father had said, "sit still, love. It will all be over soon. Just let them get what they came for, and we can go home." He looked at me with calm eyes. "It's okay, sweetheart. It's going to be okay."

That was when she looked at me for forgiveness. She was a ferocious mother bear, unleashing her wrath on anyone who dared mistreat me or disrespect me or made me feel anything less than the amazing being she thought I was. Watching the knots being tied around my wrists and then behind my head, the begging in my eyes, and the torture on my face when I had to watch them hurt my best friend, who I'd known and loved since I was three, killed her hours before she died.

"Rory?"

I was standing outside of Microphysics class, frozen.

"You look lost," Benji said.

"Isn't everyone?" I said, leaving him alone in the hallway.

Benji chuckled as I passed. "That's deep, Rory. We feeling a little emo today? Hey…I'm just kidding…Rory?"

My boots stomped up the stairs to a desk, and my bag fell off my shoulder to the floor. Ice-cold fingers found their way to my chest to touch the stained hair that was no longer there. When I needed to remember her, I would reach for my hair, but I'd shaved it off so that I could forget.

Forget my mother. *Who does that? Was it too much for me to keep the one tangible thing I had left of her?* It wasn't only my blood that had saturated my hair but hers, too. And I'd thrown it in the trash.

For the last three years, Thanksgiving had been difficult for me, and I could feel myself breaking down. It was going to be a rough day.

As the professor instructed straight from the physics textbook, I took unnecessary notes in the margins with shaky hands, not having a clue about what I was writing down on the pages. By the time class was dismissed, my anxiety was nearly intolerable.

Dr. Zorba's office was in the building, so I pushed my way past the other students, focusing on the relief I might feel once I was sitting in his ugly and itchy orange chair. It was there when he'd been hired at Kempton thirty years before.

Without knocking, I pushed my way inside and sat in the chair, focusing on my breathing. In. Out. In. Out. In…out. In…out.

"Difficult morning?" Dr. Z said, not looking up from the paper he was scribbling on.

"I need her today."

"I told you not to cut the hair."

"Too late."

Once I got a handle on my breathing, I noticed someone sitting in the swivel chair on the other side of Dr. Z's desk. It startled and embarrassed me, and then that embarrassment flashed to anger.

"What are you doing in here?"

Cy didn't answer. He just watched as my eyes darted between him and the professor.

"We had a meeting," Dr. Z said.

"About the research?" I said. "Why wasn't I called to this meeting?"

Dr. Z wasn't fazed. "You're worked up, Rory. Calm down, and then we'll talk."

"You didn't know I was having a bad morning. That has nothing to do with my exclusion from a research meeting."

"You're assuming it was a research meeting," the doctor said, his voice low and calm as always. "Remember, Cyrus is also my student. We do have other things to talk about."

"It's not Cyrus. It's just Cy," I said.

Both of them gave me a funny look.

"He's the one who said it," I said, motioning to Cy. I was surprised he hadn't let the professor know that he preferred the shorter name.

Dr. Z just watched me, waiting for me to come to some sort of a conclusion.

"Okay," I said, getting angrier by the minute. "Well, I guess I'd better excuse myself, so you can finish your meeting."

"Sit," Dr. Z said. "We were finished. We can talk about the research since you're both here."

I settled into my seat, satisfied with that suggestion.

Dr. Z continued, "I've determined that this project should be kept between us. All the data should be recorded and put into an encrypted file, and then all the paperwork should be shredded and taken to the incinerator."

I lowered my chin, watching the professor speak. He had a stern look, one I hadn't seen before. He wasn't kidding.

"And we shouldn't speak of it," Cy added, "to anyone."

"What am I missing?" I asked.

Dr. Z intertwined his fingers and rested his hands on his desk. "I've been receiving emails from a Dr. Fenton Tennison. He's from a special division at the CIA, one of the heads of a committee of scientists, military leaders, and government officials. In some circles, this committee is known as Majestic Twelve. He's…interested in the specimen."

I sat up. "So, the rumors are true then?"

Dr. Z sighed. "It appears so, but that's not good news for us."

I'd heard Dr. Z talk about Dr. Tennison before, and my father before that. Tennison was labeled unethical before I was born, and he'd been all but dismissed in most scientific circles. Regardless, he was brilliant, and some research institutions brought him on board until they couldn't deal with his kind of crazy anymore. After Tennison disappeared from the science world, it was rumored more than once that he'd been commissioned by a super think tank within the CIA.

"So, he's interested in the rock—as in, he wants it," I clarified.

"Demanding it. He is stating that it is government property."

"We're going to keep it from him? Can't he just take it?"

"Hopefully not without a court order. Theoretically, that gives us some time to finish recording the data before we move the specimen to a safer location. It's more important than I could have dreamed, Rory. We need to keep it out of hands that might exploit the knowledge there is to learn from it."

"Those special departments don't usually wait on court orders, Dr. Z."

"Which is why we'll do this quickly."

"The CIA wants the rock, and when they come to get it, you won't have it because you're going to hide it from them. Isn't that illegal?"

"Yes," the professor answered matter-of-factly.

Both men looked to me, awaiting my response. Thanksgiving break began in two days, and the campus would be desolate. It was the perfect time to hide out in the Fitz and dedicate all our time to recording Dr. Z's data. It was also perfect timing for me. I wouldn't have to spend Thanksgiving alone, and the project might even help to keep my mind off my orphan status.

"I'm in," I said.

Cy and Dr. Z traded small knowing smiles.

Two. Two glances from Cy since we sat down on our stools twenty minutes before. I'd brought a medium brick oven pizza with me and ate a few slices. I was hoping he'd ask for some, but he never did. Maybe he wasn't glancing at me at all. Maybe he was starving and thought it was rude to ask.

"Want some?" I asked, holding up a slice.

Cy shook his head. "No, thank you."

I put the pizza back into its cardboard box and closed the lid.

After every class, Cy was waiting for me with a smile on his face. He would offer his arm and ask me every question he could think of about everything but my family or my past in general, which I appreciated. We talked about fun things like concerts and food, and we talked about things people weren't supposed to talk about, like politics and religion. Cy wanted to know my opinion about everything but not because he wanted to argue. He just wanted to know.

Benji had asked me to lunch earlier, but I decided to line up specimens with Cy at the lab instead.

It felt as if I was spending twice as much time with Cy as before, and he was talking to me twice as much. But he never talked about himself, and he answered my questions about him with questions about me.

I flipped open the lid. The smell of the greasy cheesy goodness filled the room even more. For the third time, Cy glanced up at me, but he quickly looked back down at his stack of papers.

"Are you *sure* you don't want a slice?" I asked, pulling up a triangle from the rest. The melted cheese made a string from the slice to the pie, and I used my other finger to pull it off and stuff it in my mouth. "It's so good. Best in town."

"It smells delicious," he said, still looking at his paper.

"Then, have some."

"I'm not sure if I should."

My nose wrinkled. "Why?"

"Because I...I've never had pizza before."

"You've never had pizza," I deadpanned. "You're lying."

He looked up at me and blinked, clearly surprised at my accusation. "I don't lie."

I put another slice on a paper plate and held it out to him. "Noted. Now try some pizza. Get the full college experience."

After some hesitation, Cy took the plate from my hands and studied the slice of pizza. The grease had already saturated the plate around the cheesy borders. The pepperoni and sausage glistened.

A corner of my mouth went up. "Unless you're lactose intolerant, take a bite or forever be a pussy in my eyes."

"A-a," he stuttered. "I presume you're referring to one of two definitions for that word. The less vulgar possibility doesn't make sense. The second is preposterous. How could one become a vagina when not taking a bite of pizza? I'm clearly a male—"

"Christ on a bicycle, dude, just eat the fucking thing!"

Cy clumsily picked up the limp triangle and bit off the end corner, chewing with his eyes closed.

"And?"

He took another bite. "It's wonderful. Now, I really must return to my duties." He set the plate down and picked up a pencil, scribbling something in his elegant small handwriting.

I sat, deflated, and then resumed the clacking on my keyboard. *So much for the saying that the way to a man's heart is through his stomach.*

I barely finished a third entry when Cyrus fell off his stool and reached for the closest wastebasket. His body lurched, and he vomited violently into the can.

"Oh god! Cy!" I said, jumping off my stool and joining him on the floor.

As quickly as his groaning, moaning, and hurling started, it stopped, and he sat, leaning against a file cabinet, breathing hard. A thin sheen of sweat covered his olive skin.

"I'm okay," he said, out of breath.

I leaned up to pull a napkin from my desk and held it out for him. He took it without looking at me and dabbed his mouth.

"I am *so* sorry. Are you on a special diet?"

He wasn't a skinny man. He stood at least six foot and filled out his height fantastically. He yanked off his tan twill jacket, and for the first time, I saw that his arms also filled out his shirtsleeves.

"No," he said before dry-heaving one more time. "Well, technically, I suppose I am."

"Why didn't you say so?"

He stood up, almost a head taller than me. "You're a bit intimidating, Rory Riorden."

"You know my last name," I said, watching him climb back onto his stool. "I know next to nothing about you." I stood.

Cy glanced up from his papers once and then looked back down, pushing his glasses farther up his nose. "There's nothing wrong with that. Being familiar is overrated."

"What's your last name?"

Cy let his pencil fall, and he breathed out a frustrated puff. "You wouldn't be able to pronounce it."

I walked over to my stool and sat down. "Try me."

"This is a horrible waste of time."

My eyebrows shot up. "Letting me get to know you is a waste of time? Gee, thanks."

His expression softened. "No, of course not. That's not what I meant. You're very...I like you."

"Enough to check on me and walk me to class but not enough to trust me. Isn't that what this is about?" My voice sounded ridiculously acerbic, but I felt as if he'd just slapped me in the face.

"I'm sorry, Rory. It was absolutely not my intention to upset you. Sometimes, I just feel it's better not to...we're too...I feel too..." He sighed, clearly frustrated. "It's Kazemde."

I didn't flinch. "It's not that hard to pronounce."

He smiled. "You should try to spell it."

"What's your favorite food?"

"I don't really have a local favorite. The food here is...have you heard the adage, *Eat to live, not live to eat?*"

I shot him a look, and he shrugged.

"What's your favorite food at home?"

"It's hard to explain." When he realized I was waiting for an answer, he continued, "It's called *mahallajharad*. It's similar to what you call seafood."

"So, it's a fish?"

"Similar to a fish."

Good enough. "What do you do for fun?"

"My culture is different from yours, Rory."

I raised an eyebrow in disbelief. "Are you saying Egyptians don't have fun? Bullshit."

"I'm saying our fun is studying, learning, and exploring. It's just different, and I know your culture has a difficult time with different. You practice much...disbelief."

"I disbelieve that you think I'm intimidating. You really have the angel-living-in-the-garden-of-evil thing down."

Cy frowned and then returned to his desk. "I shouldn't have eaten the pizza. Very stupid of me."

"Yes, it was," I said, settling back onto my stool.

He made a face. "You told me to."

"I didn't know you were allergic or whatever. That's on you."

"You're not very nice tonight."

"I never said I was."

"That's a lie. You can be very nice when you wish to be."

"I don't lie," I said, mimicking his earlier statement.

"Yes, you do."

"I liked you better when you didn't talk."

"The feeling is mutual!" he said, taking off his glasses.

Once again, I found myself hating him while lost in his weird and amazing golden eyes.

I grabbed my jacket.

Cy sat up, his body rigid. "Where are you going?"

I slipped my arms through the sleeves while I walked toward the door. "I can't work like this."

"But…we still have this stack and the core samples and—"

"They can wait until tomorrow."

"No, Rory, they really can't. Stay. I apologize."

I stopped, still facing the door.

"I'm really very sorry," he said, an edge of begging in his voice. "I felt weak because I was ill, and I disguised it as anger and directed those feelings toward you. Inexcusable. Please forgive me."

I turned. "What are you?"

"What?" he said, shifting nervously in his chair.

"You're at KIT, but you sound like a Psych major."

The corners of his mouth turned up a bit. "I assure you, I am not. Just very aware of and clearly susceptible to human nature. Please sit. Let's finish our work."

I pulled my mouth to the side.

"It doesn't make you weak to forgive someone, you know," he said.

"No, but it gives people another chance to hurt you."

"Did I? Hurt you?" The thought seemed to wound him.

I swallowed. "No one can hurt me. It's like trying to fill a cup that's already full."

Cy's face fell. "Please, Rory, I'm so sorry. I never meant to upset you."

I turned and left Cy sitting alone in the basement.

Running up the stairs, I didn't stop until I burst through the double glass doors. Once outside, I took a deep breath, as if I'd just come up for air. Still going to The Gym on occasion with Benji, I wasn't as out of shape as I used to be, but I was pissed off. No one confused me, angered me, or made me want to tackle-kiss him like Cy Kazemde. What was it about him that made me feel such conflicting emotions? And what was it about me that I couldn't shake off the feelings I had for him?

A person popped up beside me. "You okay?"

I jumped. "Damn it, Benji! What are you doing here?"

"Waiting on you to get off work. I was going to walk you home."

"You're approaching stalker status."

"I thought about that. I didn't really mean to. I just wanted to make sure you got home okay and thought maybe it was my turn."

I knew he was alluding to Cy walking me around, but I didn't want to get into it with him. "How many times have I told you—"

"I know. You don't need anyone. Maybe it's me who needs a friend. Have you ever thought about that?"

That took me off guard. Benji stood there, his hands in his coat pockets, waiting for me to answer. Too much honesty for one night.

The crowd of students usually heading to a party now was nowhere in sight, which only meant one thing—the warehouse. I sighed. That meant paying for a taxi.

"Warehouse party?" I asked, staring at the empty campus. People were not my thing, and parties were definitely not my thing, but at the moment, I would take any distraction to get my mind off of Cy.

"Yeah. Want to go?"

Benji's brown eyes were tired, but here he was, waiting on me to finish at the lab. Something had to be said for selflessness like that.

"Only if I can drive."

Benji smiled. "You got it."

I wasn't a complete asshole. I didn't drive someone else's car like I'd stolen it, but it was fun to take the corners a little fast. Benji didn't seem to mind. Actually, he seemed to enjoy witnessing the smile on my face.

We parked in the open field, a little farther away from the other cars so that they wouldn't ding his shiny doors. Benji's Mustang was pristine, and I knew how far away he parked in the parking lot to keep it that way.

We walked in, and I was instantly lost in the loud music, lights, and cigarette smoke. The warehouse was home to two parties a year, hosted by students belonging to a secret society. No one saw it being put together or taken down. No one knew it was going to happen until it did. And by the time it was over, the secret society had a couple of new members—or that was the rumor anyway.

Benji followed me down the metal corridors. I could barely hear the clanging of the iron catwalk under our feet. I wasn't sure what the warehouse had been used for before, but now, it was a maze of debauchery—new couples making out, keg stands at every other corner, dark rooms filled by couples having drunken sex, and people surrounding a few makeshift tables covered by lines of coke.

We wanted to be engineers, not saints. The workload could drive you out or drive you mad. Everyone dealt with the pressure differently, and finals were approaching. We all had to find an outlet or pop, but no one wanted students screaming, vandalizing, wrecking their cars into trees, secluding themselves, or wielding guns.

Benji pulled open a heavy metal door, and then we walked outside into the courtyard. We followed the covered sidewalk until we reached a small group of students huddled around three kegs. Once we made our way to the front, Benji held a cup under a keg nozzle and waited as the beer dribbled out. He looked at me apologetically. We arrived so late that the kegs were nearly dry.

"There has to be another keg somewhere. You wait here. I'll see what I can find."

I nodded and scraped my fingers through the bit of hair left on my head. The short strands didn't even require work to be coaxed back into place, which was freeing.

Ellie was standing in a doorway with a random stranger. His jaw worked as he kissed her so deeply and sloppily that it made my stomach turn. His lips were sealed and working impatiently over hers. I anticipated that the skin around her mouth would be glistening with a ring of his spit when he pulled away, and a shiver ran down my spine. She had one of his legs trapped tightly between her thighs, and she was moving her hips ever so gently against him.

Ew. Ew, ew, ew. I wanted to look away, but I couldn't.

"Rory, right?"

Oh, thank Christ. Whoever you are, thank you.

"I'm Kevin Monroe. We have Physics II together."

Even if he didn't have that sleazy look in his eye, I knew to stay away. I'd heard about Kevin. He was in his third year of KIT and should have been in jail at least three times for sexual assault. And that was only the number of times the women had enough support and courage to press charges. But for various reasons, the charges kept getting dropped.

He looked down at my breasts and then back at me with familiar scrutiny. He had the kind of look that said, *I hope you're as drunk and easy as I am.*

I took the thank-you back.

"Do you recognize me?" he prodded.

"No," I said, looking away. It was the truth. I'd only heard about him.

"I recognize you. You shaved off all your hair."

"Not all of it," I said, running my fingers through what was left. When pulled to one side, the black tresses I didn't shear grazed my cheek.

"It's hot."

I sighed and looked him straight in the eyes. "Is there something you need?"

He took a step toward me, forcing me to back up just a couple of inches from the wall. "Actually, now that you mention it..." Kevin touched his nose to my ear.

I could smell the alcohol on him before, but now it was pungent, saturating my skin—just like the breath of the men who murdered almost everyone who ever cared about me.

I looked around for Benji. There were several people in the small fenced-in area outside with us, but no one was paying attention. They were all either making out, talking, or huddled around a barrel they were using to light a fire.

I glared up at him and put my hand on his chest, holding him at bay. "Kevin, you need to back off. You're making me uncomfortable."

He took another step toward me. The pressure of my hand meant nothing to him. Now, my back was pressed against the wall.

"Is that so? I didn't think girls who looked like you got uncomfortable. So, does that mean uncomfortable in a good way?" He took my hand and forced it down until it settled on his crotch.

"Call me crazy," Benji said, "but the word *uncomfortable* has a universally negative connotation."

Kevin took one look at Benji and the two red Solo cups he held, and he batted them away, spilling the pale amber liquid all over Benji's green Nikes.

"Back. Off," I said again, my voice low and menacing this time.

I tried to jerk my hand away, but Kevin smiled and kept it in place.

Benji put his hand on Kevin's shoulder, and Kevin grabbed at his wrist, freeing mine. Before either of them could make another move, I moved my hand in a downward motion, forcing Kevin's hand off of Benji. I grabbed the thumb on his offending hand and bent it backward, and with my free hand, I grabbed his throat and slammed him against the wall where I once stood.

"I said, *back* the *fuck* off." My voice was strangely calm, just like my nerves.

Kevin, his eyebrows pulled in and his eyes wide, bobbed his head up and down quickly. I released him then, letting him scamper away.

Benji stood quiet like a rabbit, hoping he wasn't next.

"We'd better go," I said.

"You...wow. How'd you learn to do that?"

I glanced around, seeing that now, of course, everyone was paying attention. "I took a class. C'mon. This was a bad idea."

We walked back inside and began heading down the corridor. Once we turned the corner, I stopped dead in my tracks. Kevin was against another wall—this time, being held by Cy. Kevin wasn't just shocked. He was terrified.

"I'm...I'm sorry! I'll never go near her again."

Cy's eyes were fixed on me, looking as if he'd been caught. Kevin was released, and he took off in a full sprint down the hall toward the exit.

"Why are you here?" I asked, taking one step forward. "What are you doing?"

"Did he hurt you?" Cy walked the few feet to me, looking me over and then touching my arm gently.

"I told you, no one can hurt me." The words seemed insufficient, but I was so baffled by what I'd just seen that they were all I could manage.

Cy pulled me into his arms into a tight hug. It was the second time in as many weeks that he held me that way. I melted against him. His body was rock solid yet so soft. He smelled like soap and sun-dried laundry.

His hand settled lightly on the back of my neck, and he rested his cheek against mine. "I'm so sorry," he whispered.

"I'm really okay," I said, trying to reassure him.

It was at that moment when I realized he was trembling. He was shaking from anger.

"It's okay, Cy."

Benji cleared his throat. "She did just fine on her own."

Cy released me and looked to Benji. "You'll see her home?" Benji nodded. "Of course."

Cy cupped my face, kissed my forehead, and then walked away.

Benji and I walked to the car in silence and didn't speak on the way home either. When he parked in the parking lot and turned off the ignition, he opened his mouth to speak but didn't.

I got out, and Benji walked with me to the front entrance of my dorm.

"Good night," I said.

"I…I'm sorry I left you alone."

"It's not your fault. I had no problem taking care of him."

"It just sucks that he touched you, that he even had the opportunity."

"Men like that…they spend their lives waiting for opportunity and not the good kind."

Benji's expression crumbled, and his head fell. "I'm just so sorry. I know you've been through something awful and—"

"Benji, don't."

"No, I know you don't want to talk about that. My point is, I'm sorry that it happened, and I'm sorry that all I can think about right now is the image of you in his arms and how relaxed you looked."

It took me a minute for my brain to catch up. "Cy?"

"Yeah," he said, stuffing his hands in his pockets and still looking at the ground. His eyebrows pulled together.

"You don't have to talk about this. It's really okay," I said, trying to save us both from his awkward admission.

"No, I do. Maybe not just for you. Maybe I need to say it out loud. I know how you feel about Cy."

"That's impossible. I don't even know how I feel about Cy."

He looked up, and his eyes met mine. "If you'd let me, I could make you feel like that. Safe, I mean. I'm here, you know. I'm not going anywhere. But he's…Cyrus is temporary."

I tried really hard to think of another reason to say no besides the truth, but I didn't have a single one other than my own fears. I was afraid about what might happen if I invested in a real relationship with someone again. There were far worse things than giving Benji a chance, and telling him my fears and why they existed was one of them. "Okay."

"Okay?"

I pushed my hands and arms through the space between his arms and his sides and then held my palms flat against his back. After the shock wore off, Benji pulled his hands out of his pockets and pulled me closer to him, resting his cheek on my hair. He moved a fraction of an inch to kiss my temple.

"This isn't so bad, right?" he said.

He was right. I felt just as safe and warm in his arms. It was different but in a good way. He held me tighter. This was the way a man held a woman when he loved her. Salty tears burned my cheeks. I didn't even know why, but I just wanted to stay there—in a pair of arms that belonged to a man who would never let me go if I didn't want him to.

One of the main lobby doors swung open, and Ellie sauntered out. "My, my…you're just making the rounds, aren't you, Rory?"

I pushed away from Benji and wiped my eyes quickly. "Fuck off, Ellie."

Benji glared at her.

"Who's the new man?" Ellie joked, tapping her chin with her index finger. "I just know that I know him from somewhere."

"If we've met, it must not have been a memorable moment for me," Benji said.

I couldn't help but smile.

"Oh no, darlin', you'd remember, I promise," she said, trying to retain her smug grin.

Benji turned his back to her, and she continued out to the parking lot. "Wonder where she's headed at this hour?"

"Probably to a rendezvous in a professor's office."

Benji chuckled. "I've never liked her. You'd better get some sleep, especially after the night you've had." He hesitated to say his next words. "I can stay, you know. I can sleep on the floor if you don't want to be alone."

"Thanks, but I'm really okay."

"You're sure?"

"Yes. After being threatened twice, I don't think he's going to break into my dorm room just to get his ass kicked again."

"Okay. See you tomorrow."

I nodded, and knowing he wouldn't leave until I was safely inside, I turned and left him standing alone on the stairs.

As I walked to my room, I could still feel Benji on my skin. For whatever reason though, I couldn't shake that Cy was supposed to be in my life, and no matter how much Benji wanted to believe it, Cy didn't feel temporary.

EIGHT

BENJI WAS SITTING NEXT TO ME in Dr. Z's class, but all I could do was focus on Cy—every time he raised his hand or spoke, his green plaid flannel shirt, his staple khaki cargo pants, and how fast he wrote down whatever he thought was important.

I wondered why he thought that particular thing was noteworthy or why he shifted in his chair. I wondered if he thought about the night before and if he would mention it at work that night.

Benji reached for my hand, turned it over, and wrote *LUNCH?* in black Sharpie on my palm. After another glance down at Cy, I peered over at Benji and nodded quickly.

Benji seemed uncharacteristically uptight. He was tapping his pen against his desk one second and bouncing his knee the next.

"You okay?" I whispered.

Benji frowned and tucked his chin. "Yeah," he said, waving dismissively and trying far too hard to be his normal happy self. "Why?"

I shrugged. "Just checking. Last night was weird."

His face relaxed. "Are *you* okay? I worried about you from the moment I left your dorm room until I saw you this morning."

I shook my head and looked back at my laptop. "Don't worry about me."

"I know I don't have to. You can take care of yourself. But it wasn't just that. It's that...well, I've known you for almost two years, and I didn't know you had taken a self-defense class. Does that have to do with whatever happened to—"

"Benji?"

"Yeah?"

"Seriously. Don't."

"Oh, okay," he said, slinking back into his seat. Halfway through class, Benji leaned over again. "We're out the rest of the week for Thanksgiving break. You going home?"

I shook my head, trying not to think too much about his question.

When Dr. Z dismissed the class, I realized I hadn't taken a single note. The first half, I'd spent staring at the back of Cy's infuriatingly beautiful head, and the second, I'd tried not to think about the memory Benji unknowingly pulled to the surface.

Cy stood after gathering his things. He traded just a few quiet words with the professor and then quickly found his way to the hallway. Part of me wanted to stop him and ask about the frightened look in Kevin's eyes the night before. I hadn't seen that kind of raw fear since the night my parents and Sydney—the night I refused to think about. I wanted to know what Cy had said to Kevin that was so frightening.

Benji watched me put away my laptop. "Cy seems like an okay guy, but it's weird that, other than last night, I've never seen him outside of this class."

"Why is that weird? Some days, I don't see you outside of this class."

"Yeah, you do." He slipped on his backpack and then helped me with mine. "He disappears after he leaves here. One day, I followed him, but he turned a corner and...*poof*."

A corner of my mouth turned up. "I'm a little jealous that I'm not the only one you stalk."

"I wish you were jealous."

I shook my head.

Benji laughed once. "I wasn't stalking him. I was just curious."

"No worries. I've seen him outside of this class."

"Like a...like a date?"

"No, like he's Dr. Z's research assistant."

"I thought you were?"

"We both are."

"Oh. I thought he was temporary. You're still working together every night?"

"Every night."

He shifted his weight nervously. "Even over break? Is that why you're not going home?"

"Yes, over break. I'm not going home because, at the moment, Kempton is my home, and no, I don't want to talk about it."

"Oh."

I laughed. "C'mon, I'm starved."

Benji managed a smile and followed me out of the building and off campus to Gigi's Café. Benji and I had been eating there fairly regularly since we started studying together. Now, the waitresses were under the impression we were dating even though I'd set them straight plenty of times.

We walked out to the wooden patio and watched the traffic until our server came out to take our drink orders. We were enjoying a rogue fifty-five-degree November day, and I wanted to spend as much of it outside before I was cooped up in the windowless lab.

"I'll have a water."

"Me, too," I said, watching his nonreaction.

He always made fun of how I drank so much water, but now, he seemed preoccupied.

Benji picked at a sugar packet, looking uncomfortable in a plaid button-up oxford. The sleeves were rolled up to just below his elbows. It was his way of dressing down. He clearly wanted to have a conversation, but he was holding off.

Finally, I kicked his leg under the table.

"Ow!"

"What is it?" I said, trying not to giggle at my grade-school antics.

"What is what?" he said, bending down to rub his shin.

My eyes narrowed. "What are you not saying?"

"I'm not, not saying anything. If you sense hesitation, it's because I'm trying to phrase what I want to say in a way you haven't heard before."

"Is this because of Cy?"

"Because of a lot of things, Rory. I...wanted to wait. I wanted to have this conversation on your terms, especially after what happened with Ellie. I didn't want to risk running you off again. But if I wait, with you and Cyrus spending so much time together—"

"Benji, don't."

"Don't tell me don't. You've stopped me from telling you how I feel about you once a week since we've met. I know there are things I don't know about your past. Maybe I don't need to know them. Maybe one day you'll tell me, and I'll wish I didn't know. Either way, my feelings for you won't change. I don't need to know your past to know that I have feelings for the person you are now."

"I don't even know who I am now. I just know I'm not who I was then. You can't have feelings for someone stuck in limbo like that." I looked away from him. *Purgatory* would be more accurate.

"You're you." He shrugged and smiled. "The woman sitting in front of me is who I want to spend time with, who I want to hold the way I did last night as much as I want. As much as she wants. If you'd just give me a chance—"

The server brought our waters and smiled. "Ready to order?"

"Uh"—I looked down at the menu—"I'll just have the shredded chicken southwest quesadilla."

"The same," Benji said.

"Now, you're just being a suck-up," I said, handing the menu to my left.

The server took it and then spoke, "Actually, that's his usual."

How did I not notice that after coming here so often with him? Was I so focused on not letting him have feelings for me that I overlooked him completely? How could he care about someone like that?

"Thank you, Chelsea," Benji said, not taking his eyes away from mine. "See? Something in common." Chelsea walked away, and Benji folded his arms on top of the table. "How do you feel about me? Think I'll ever make it back out of the friend zone alive?"

I stared at the pedestrians and traffic passing by. Benji was obnoxiously happy and irritating, and in the beginning, I didn't think he was my type at all, but I suddenly feared that if I didn't say something in the realm of him having a chance, I might lose him. His friendship was comforting even if I wanted to kick his ass half the time, and as long as I was being truthful, I wasn't one hundred percent sure he was just a friend.

Regardless of his feelings or mine, I was very possibly on my way toward committing a federal crime. Dr. Z and Cy needed me right now, and that didn't leave any time for a burgeoning friendship to try to become a relationship. Benji obviously came from very respectable stock, and I was every mother's nightmare. And then there was the small matter of a traumatic life event and my immortality. That was a lot for something new and iffy to push through.

"I never meant for us to get in this deep," I said.

"Just answer the question, Rory."

"What if I said not right now and maybe not ever?" As soon as I said the words, I felt my heart knocking against my chest in a panic. *He's going to walk away. He's going to leave me, and I need him.*

Benji stared at me, unable to hide his disappointment.

I swallowed. "Would you stop being my friend?"

"Never," he said without hesitation. "Is that your answer?"

"Maybe. Can I think about it?"

"Absolutely. I'm not ready to give up on you yet anyway."

I folded my arms across the table, too. "Let's go to that party at the Theta Tau house later."

"Another party? You're starting to freak me out a little."

He had a point. I didn't know what was up with my sudden urge to socialize either, but what I did know was that I was getting very sick of the endless cycle of class, dorm, and lab, and The Gym wasn't cutting it.

"Kevin got his ass kicked there last year. He hasn't shown his face since."

"You really want to go?" he asked.

I nodded.

"I'll follow you anywhere."

"Spoken like a true stalker," I said with a smile.

I typed in the last line of data, tossed the paper across my desk, and let it float into the bin. Once it landed safely on top of the huge stack, I stood up from my stool and stretched.

"Break time?" Cy asked, taking off his glasses.

"Yes. Benji and I are going to the Theta Tau break party. Want to come?"

Cy's face blanched. "But we have so much work to do. You can't. We don't have time for parties."

"We always have time for parties."

"But you don't go to parties."

"I do tonight. I've been here for seven hours. I'm going to take a couple of hours and relax. I'll be back."

"Rory," Cy called after me.

"You're still invited!" I called back.

Benji's orange Mustang was running in the street in the exact spot where we'd agreed to meet—a block west of the Fitz. The hot fumes from the exhaust pipe met the cold air and instantly turned into a white cloud.

Benji popped out of the driver's side and jogged around to my side, giving me a quick hug before opening the door.

He was his normally bubbly self on the way to the Theta Tau house, chatting about his dad and bratty sister and what a great cook his mom was.

"You would love them."

"I'm sure they would love me," I said, my words dripping with sarcasm.

"They would learn to," he said, pulling over to the curb in front of Theta Tau.

Less than half of the cars that would normally be parked outside a house party lined the streets. Most of the students had already left for break, but this party wasn't for them. It was for the stragglers, the left-behind, and the black sheep. Those were always the best parties anyway because everyone there had one very important thing in common—the need for an alternative family.

I could already hear the base booming before we reached the lawn. We walked in the front door like we owned the place, and no one seemed to mind—not even Bobby Peck, the Theta Tau president and Benji's nemesis. A small group of already drunk students were in the commons area, but a congregation of people were gathered around the four kegs in the kitchen.

"Jackpot," Benji said. He grabbed two red Solo cups and held them to the man in charge of the faucet end of the keg.

"Welcome!" the faucet guy said.

I couldn't stop staring at the strange painting on his naked torso and the underwear on his head. Clearly, he'd been partying much longer than anyone else in the room. He filled up our cups, and then Benji took my free hand and led me to the front room. We sat in a love seat and watched as a couple acted out a fight they'd witnessed another couple having the weekend before. It was obviously very dramatic and amusing because everyone had tears streaming down their cheeks from laughing so hard.

I sipped the beer, wishing I'd just asked for water instead.

"A much more successful beer hunt than the last party we tried," Benji said, tipping his head back. He'd already finished his first cup and hopped up to get another. "Are you ready for another one?"

I shook my head.

"Well, I'm hoping to get drunk so you'll try to take advantage of me later."

"Not going to happen."

"A man can dream, can't he?" he said, smiling and walking backward a few steps before turning for the kitchen.

I laughed once. Benji and I had known each other for a little over two years, and I had known almost the whole time that he had a thing for me, but this—whatever it was—still felt new and maybe a little exciting.

And then, there was Cy. It was definitely possible to have feelings for two people, but I couldn't have more than a friendship with both of them. *Do I want to be with both of them?*

I watched Benji standing at the keg. He was observing the funny couple, smiling at them, and stealing glances at me once in a while. I wanted to touch him, to be near him, to feel his lips on mine like they were in The Gym.

What I felt for him was different from what I felt for Cy. I wasn't even sure if having feelings for Cy was even accurate. What I felt was drawn to him. I needed him, but I wasn't sure why. There was just something in my gut telling me that he'd entered my life for a reason.

"How could you?" the girl said, pretending to cry. "I thought you were different!"

"I thought you'd put out more!" her boyfriend said in a fake gruff voice.

Everyone laughed.

Benji returned, both hands holding full cups.

I raised an eyebrow. "I guess I'm driving."

"Nah. I'll be done after these."

"Good, because I have to go back to work after this."

"What?" Benji said, disappointed.

I nodded.

"Can I go with you?"

"No."

"Oh, c'mon. I'll be your gofer. I'll go for coffee. Go for water. Sharpen your pencil. I'll be at your disposal."

I shook my head, smiling. "Dr. Z won't allow anyone else in the lab."

Benji downed half of his cup. "Well, that sucks."

"Easy, tiger."

"I'm just trying to drink up the nerve to ask to kiss you."

I stifled a smile. "Please don't." *We might not stop.*

"They don't appeal to you?" he said, pointing at his lips.

"I didn't say that. Just…it's a weird time for me."

"If you hadn't met Cyrus, would you still be unsure?"

His question took me off guard, and he watched my hesitation with waning hope.

"Yes."

"What is it about me that gives you pause?" he asked before drinking the rest of his second cup. For a quiet mama's boy, he sure could drink like a frat boy.

I took another sip. "I don't know why you're interested in me, for one. We don't really"—I pointed back and forth between the two of us—"make sense."

"Who says?"

"Me."

"You're wrong. We make perfect sense."

"The White Stripes tee and the yellow oxford. Yeah, makes perfect sense," I said before taking another drink. Somehow, in my nervousness, I'd managed to drink the entire cup of beer.

"Want another, or are you done?" he asked.

"No, I'm definitely not done. We came to party, didn't we?"

"That we did." Benji left and then came back with three more cups filled to the brim. He was already half finished with his third.

"I will not be outdrank by an oxford shirt," I said before taking several gulps.

"Whoa, there. Slow down. I don't want to be blamed if you don't make it back to work."

"Do I seem like the kind of girl who makes everything everyone else's fault?"

"No. No, you do not."

We both drank to that.

"Where were we?" I asked, feeling pretty good. "Oh, yeah. Our shirts don't go together."

"It's not the outside, Rory. I mean, you're obviously beautiful and unorthodox. I wear button-ups and get nosebleeds, but it's the inside where we make sense."

"What inside? I haven't been nice to you, Benji."

"I'm talking about the inside that *is* nice to me. The girl who tells me where freshman orientation is on the first day. The girl who let me sit next to her in class even though she wanted to be left alone. The girl who pushes everyone aside so that she can help me stop a nosebleed. The girl who walks me home after said nosebleed. The girl who let me hold her. The girl who asked me to this party. The girl who is going to at least try to give me a chance. And more importantly, the girl who had something so awful happen to her that it changed her life, but she didn't use it as an excuse to fail."

"I caused that nosebleed," I said, intentionally ignoring his last comment.

"You could have walked right past me. Some people would have."

I stared at him. His brown eyes were sleepy but happy, and he looked so in love with me.

I put my elbow on my knee and let my cheek rest on my fist. "You're kind of cute when you're buzzed."

Benji leaned forward, put the half-empty cup and the full cup on the coffee table, and then rested his elbows on his knees. "May I kiss you?"

"No," I said, "but you can get me another beer."

He looked down, surprised. "Already?"

I took the cup he had on standby. "Let's play a game. We ask the other a question. If you refuse to answer, you drink."

"Sounds dangerous."

I took a drink and winked at him over the cup.

"Okay, I'll start," Benji said. "What's your middle name?"

"Ann. Boring, right? What's yours?" Benji started to drink, but I grabbed his wrist. "No way! That's an easy one! C'mon."

"My middle name is Benjamin."

"So, what's your first name?"

"It's my turn."

I rolled my eyes. "Fine."

"What's your favorite flower?"

I laughed. "I don't know!"

"Drink!"

"No, wait. I like those globe amaranths. They're beautiful and vicious."

"Like you," Benji said with a mischievous grin.

"So, what's your first name?" I asked.

"Aw, man!" Benji groaned. He started to take a drink and then changed his mind. "It's Franklin."

My eyebrows shot up. "Your name is Franklin Benjamin? Your mom is *mean*!"

We both laughed hysterically. Two cups of beer and twenty-seven questions later, we were both asking questions we would normally be too embarrassed to ask.

"Are you a virgin?" I asked.

Benji nearly spit out the beer he'd just drunk. "Seriously?"

"Yes. That's my question. Answer or drink!"

He leaned in. "Do I kiss like a virgin?"

I leaned in, too. "You can't answer a question with a question."

"No," he said simply. "Are you?"

I shook my head but drank anyway. "Did you have a good childhood?"

"I did. My parents are great. Maybe a little overbearing, but they mean well. I'm really close with my dad."

I smiled. "That's great."

"Why aren't you close with yours?" he asked.

I touched the rim of the cup to my lips, seriously thinking about telling Benji everything, but then I tilted my head back and let the amber liquid slide down my throat. "Why do you hate Bobby Peck?"

Benji narrowed his eyes. "Remember when you asked me if I was a virgin?"

I nodded. "Oh no, you lost your virginity to Bobby Peck?"

Benji threw his head back and laughed. "No!" He chuckled again. "No. He caused a fight between her and me. She dumped me, and now she's with—"

"Bobby Peck? No way."

"Way. I guess I shouldn't be mad at him. He clearly did me a favor."

I smiled at him. "Who's going to drive me back to work?"

"That's," Benji said, pointing at me with the same hand his cup was in, "a very good question. Not you and not me and not just because I don't want you to go back with him. I want you to stay here with me. Do you know how maddening it is to know you like him and that you spend hours with him every night?"

I just shook my head.

"It is. Sometimes, I feel like I'm going to go out of my mind and just storm in there and steal you away."

"Very caveman of you," I said. I was teasing him, but it sounded kinda hot. "Why do you like me?"

"I don't," he said.

Even through the five and a half beers I'd drunk, embarrassment began to seep in. "Oh."

He reached over and entwined his fingers with mine. "I'm in love with you, Rory. I have been for a long time."

"Oh," I said again, feeling my cheeks warm in reaction. Outside of the classroom, those words felt more real. The embarrassment was replaced with nearly uncontrollable lust. No man had ever told me he loved me before Benji—well, except for my dad, and that wasn't the same, not even close.

"Well, well, Benji Reynolds."

Benji and I turned to see Bobby Peck standing behind the sofa we were sitting on. I realized that most everyone else had gone.

"President Bobby Peck," Benji said as if he were spitting venom.

"Where are your keys? I'm going to drive you kids home."

"Um…no," Benji said. "Someone else can drive us. Anyone else."

"I'm the house designated driver tonight. There is no one else."

Benji looked at me, and I shrugged.

"I can't drive."

He blew a puff of air from his lips. "Fine, Bobby Peck, you can drive us home."

"Bobby Peck has to drive me to work," I said, rather amused we were using his full name.

Bobby Peck laughed once. "You can't go to work like this. You'll get fired. Text your boss, and let him know you can't make it."

I pulled out my cell phone. "I'll just text Cy."

Drunk. Going home. Will be there early a.m. Night.

"Okay!" I said, shoving my phone in my pocket. "Taken care of."

My phone buzzed, and I pulled it out again. I squinted at the words.

Need a ride home?

No, Cy. DD has it covered.

Is Benji with you?

Yep.

Okay. Good night.

"Okay! Now it's *reeeeeeaaaaaally* taken care of," I said, laughing at my slurred words.

Benji held my hand, leading me out to his car. He held open the door, and I crawled into the backseat. He climbed in next to me.

"Whoa. This is inappropriate," I said.

"Why is that?" Benji asked.

"Being in the backseat with you."

Bobby Peck laughed. "I know you live at Charlie's, Benji. Where does Rihanna live?"

"Who?" I asked.

"I think he's referring to your haircut," Benji said, trying to whisper and failing.

"Just park the 'stang at Charlie's. I'll walk," I said.

Benji shook his head. I nodded. We both giggled incessantly.

Bobby Peck parked the car and tossed the keys to Benji, and then he pulled a condom from his back pocket. "Have a good night, dude."

"You're still you, Bobby Peck," Benji said. He handed the condom to me. "Can you believe that jerk?"

I laughed and walked with Benji to the entrance. His fingers were still tightly laced between mine.

"I'm going to catch so much hell tomorrow," I said.

"No," Benji said. "I won't let you."

I smiled. "You can't save me, Franklin."

He laughed out loud. "I can do whatever I want. And don't *ever* call me that again."

"I think it's cute," I said.

"Oh, yeah?" he asked. I nodded. "Then, call me that anytime you want."

I grinned. "Good night."

"Let me walk you home," Benji said, playfully tugging my hand.

"I got it."

"It's the middle of the night. I'm walking you home."

"No, you're not. It's stupid for you to walk all the way over there and then back."

"It's stupid for you to walk alone."

We stared at each other for a moment.

Benji squeezed my hand. "Stay with me."

"Yeah, right," I said, walking away.

"I'm serious," he said, pulling me to him. "I'll sleep on the floor."

I thought for a minute, chewing on my lip. "You're not going to let me walk home alone, and I'm not going to let you walk me home. We're at an impasse."

"Correct."

"So, my staying here makes sense, right?"

"Right."

"Okay."

"Okay?"

"Yes. I'll stay if you sleep on the floor."

"Deal," he said, shaking his head, as if my request were the easiest thing in the world.

Part of me wished it had been more difficult for him.

Benji fished his card key out of his wallet, and then I followed him quietly down the hall. He turned the knob, and I walked in. He locked the door behind us.

"What's up with that?" I asked. I tossed Bobby Peck's condom into the trash can but missed. "Why do you only lock the door when you're home?"

"Because if someone wants in, they'll get in. If I'm home, locking it gives me some privacy or a few seconds to prepare if they're breaking in."

"Why would someone want to break into your room?"

He smiled, throwing an extra pillow and blanket on the floor. "You never know." He walked over to his dresser and pulled out a T-shirt. *My favorite one.* "Do you want something to sleep in?"

"Yes, please," I said, catching the tee as he tossed it at me.

Benji grabbed a pair of basketball shorts and retreated to the bathroom. I kicked off my boots and then pulled off my shirt and jeans. The maroon shirt slid over my head effortlessly. It was so soft, and it smelled musky and clean, exactly like Benji.

He knocked on the door. "Are you decent?"

"Not really," I answered. Silence. "I'm just kidding. You can come out."

Benji opened the door. He was shirtless and in bare feet, wearing only the pair of navy blue basketball shorts he'd brought into the bathroom with him. It was the best thing I'd seen since...well, it was the best thing I'd seen ever.

"Hi," he said, looking a little stunned himself.

I sat on his bed, letting my toes move around and enjoy the open air.

Benji lay down on his stomach on the floor, bunching up the pillow between his biceps and letting his chin sink into the down feathers.

I pulled back the covers and turned onto my side, facing Benji. He was looking straight ahead, lying perfectly still.

"Okay then," I said, starting to turn my back to him.

"You look really good in my shirt," Benji said, his voice muffled. "I'm just trying to keep my promise."

"You did promise to sleep on the floor," I said.

Benji slammed his face into the pillow. "I did. I promised. And I will never break a promise to you."

I could barely understand him, but it made me giggle.

He looked up. "There is nothing about this that's funny."

"I don't know. You're pretty funny right now."

"You're really tough, talking from up there when you know I can't touch you."

I stopped smiling and tried not to think too much about what I was getting ready to do.

"What?" he said, taken aback by my sudden change in mood.

I crawled down from Benji's bed. He turned onto his side, watching me move toward him.

I lowered myself to the floor next to him and leaned in. "What if I want you to touch me?"

Without skipping a beat, Benji put his hands on both sides of my face and pulled my lips against his. His mouth immediately opened, and I slipped my tongue inside, caressing his tongue with mine. He moaned in my mouth and laced his fingers at the nape of my neck. I lifted my leg and straddled him, and he rolled onto his back, his hands leaving my neck and firmly grasping my hips.

"Rory," he said against my lips.

"Shh, don't talk," I said, covering his mouth with my hand and kissing down the side of his neck in a straight line. Once I got to his collarbone, he pulled his T-shirt over my head, and then I kept going, planting tiny kisses and licking his skin down his tight chest and then his ribs before stopping at his hip bone.

Abs. Jesus H. God, nerdy Benji Reynolds has abs and that sexy V from his hip bone that points to exactly where I want to be.

I took the top hem of his shorts and tugged gently, kissing and tonguing the places that were exposed as I pulled the fabric down.

Benji's breath caught as I pulled his shorts toward me, over his already hard dick, and then down to his ankles. He kicked them off and then looked down at me, touching his thumb gently to my cheek. He shook his head infinitesimally with the smallest trace of a smile.

I took all of him into my mouth, and he closed his eyes and groaned loudly, every muscle in his body tensed. With one hand on his shaft, I tasted him—sucking lightly, using just a tiny bit of my teeth, and licking the tender underside of his head. He lifted his hips, pushing more of himself into my mouth.

Benji's fingers dug into my shoulder, and before I even had a chance to give him a proper experience, he pulled me up and above him until we were facing each other.

He kissed me again. "I want to be inside you. Please," he whispered against my lips.

I reached up to grab the plastic square I had tried tossing into the trash can. While I tore the wrapper open, I took a second to thank Bobby Peck for being a jerk.

I slid the condom over Benji's skin and then stood, sliding my panties down until they dropped and hit the floor. Stepping away from the fabric, I repositioned myself over Benji's lap, and then I let out a sigh as I slid him deep inside me.

Benji cupped my breasts in his hands, slid his fingers down my stomach, and finally gripped my hips. He lifted me up, pushing me away from him slowly, and then pulled me back down. "Holy...is this really happening?" he whispered, lifting his hips as he pulled mine down against him.

Once we both began to break a sweat, Benji rolled over, placing me quickly but gently onto my back. He grabbed my ankles and lifted them up, letting my heels rest on his shoulders. On his knees, he sank himself inside me even deeper.

I gripped the blanket beneath me, my nails sinking through the cotton and into my palms. The tendons behind my thighs burned in a wonderful way as he leaned against them. I spread my legs wider and let them relax, allowing him to lean in, his chest to touching mine.

As Benji kissed the edge of my ear, I let my legs fall, and I locked my ankles at the small of his back.

"You are so beautiful," he whispered, letting his lips graze my cheek before sinking his tongue in my mouth again.

He pumped and rocked against me, faster and stronger each time, rubbing against every part of me that I wanted him to until I could feel the build, until it consumed me, overtaking my entire body, finally making my thighs twitch uncontrollably. I moaned and let my arms fall back with my hands over my head. Benji reached for them, intertwining his fingers in mine. He rocked against me, each time making the smallest, most amazing humming sound until he came. He squeezed my fingers until his hands shook. His moans sounded euphoric as he pressed his cheek hard against mine.

"You feel so good, Rory. *My God*, you feel good," he said between groans.

He collapsed for a few seconds, breathing hard into my ear, and then he leaned up, kissing me tenderly. "I love you," he said, brushing my hair back from my face. I wasn't sure what expression I had, but it made one corner of his mouth turn up. "It's okay. You don't have to say it back."

He rested his chin on my shoulder, his face buried in the blanket beneath us. I closed my eyes, refusing to think too much about what we'd done or what he'd just said, just enjoying having someone so close who loved me that much. I wasn't sure if what I was feeling was love, but I'd never felt this way before.

NINE

I WOKE UP ON THE FLOOR of Benji Reynolds's dorm room, wearing only a sheet, held over me by one of Benji's arms.

I maneuvered out from under him gently, trying not to wake him. In the dark, it was easy to pretend I wasn't covered in scars but not in the daylight. I hurried to get dressed and then retreated into the bathroom. The toilet flushing must have woken Benji up because he was lying on his side with his head propped on his hand when I came out.

"I'm going to go home for a bit. Take a shower and change before I go to the lab."

"I'll walk you."

"That's really not necessary."

"C'mon. I'm not letting you take the walk of shame. This wasn't a one-night stand for me. I just want to walk you to work."

He wasn't being weird at all, which was a huge relief.

"Okay, but you can't come in," I said.

"Deal."

Benji walked me to my dorm and waited on the front steps while I showered and changed, and then we walked the three blocks to the Fitz, mostly in silence. The campus was empty, and it felt as if we were the only two people on earth. He kept his hands in his pockets, but at one point, Benji offered his arm, and I took it. It was warmer that way, but it was also nice to be so close to him.

When we arrived at the steps of the Fitz, he let go of my arm. "May I say something?" he asked.

"Depends."

"I can't stop thinking about last night. I swear, I won't sweat the fact that you're going to be cooped up in a tiny lab with Cyrus for the rest of the day, if we could do that again."

I looked up at him, dubious.

"The laughing, stupid, fun part...mostly."

"It was fun. I had a great time."

"Okay, I lied. I'll still wonder what's going on between you and Cyrus."

"You don't have to wonder," I said. "It's not like that. I wish I could explain to you what it's like, but it's not like *that*."

"No?"

I shook my head. "It's not like us."

He beamed. "Still mess-free, you know. This is on your terms. On your time."

I touched his cheek. "See you later."

Benji smiled and then slowly wrapped his arms around me, tightening them gradually until I was against him, snug and warm. My arms were around him, too, under his coat. He didn't have an ounce of body fat on him. He was solid, all lean muscle. My head fit perfectly under his chin, and he leaned his head down, resting his cheek on my hair.

He made this wonderful involuntary humming breath noise, as if he were the happiest he'd ever been. It made me want to sink into him even further, so I did, and he held me tighter. I didn't want to move, but I had to. I had federal laws to break, and Benji had a family to go home to for Thanksgiving.

Benji's head tilted back, and I looked up at him. We stared at each other for a long time, and then his eyes drifted to my lips. As good as the hug felt, I wasn't completely sure about making a habit of kissing good-bye.

"Don't worry. I'll ask first," he said. "But I would like to kiss your cheek."

All I could do was nod. Every part of me wanted to remember what Benji's mouth felt like on my skin.

Benji looked at my lips once more, and then he leaned down slowly, touching his lips to my cheek just an inch or so away from the corner of my mouth.

"I can't wait to see you again," he said, walking away.

I smiled, waiting for the warmth in my cheeks to go away before I walked up the stairs and found my way back to the lab— and to Cy.

As I walked into the building and descended the stairs, the warmth turned into tingling. When I walked into the lab, Cy looked up, and I felt as if he knew what had happened between Benji and me.

"You okay?" he asked.

"Yeah! Why?"

Cy frowned at my overly excited answer. "Your cheeks are red."

I already knew that. My entire face was burning. I couldn't answer. I just walked over to Dr. Z's desk, pulled out another stack of pages, and brought them to my desk.

"How was the party?"

"It was a party."

"Benji saw you home?"

"Yep."

"You sure you're okay?"

I looked at Cy for a moment. He was still beautiful, still everything I couldn't stop thinking about since the beginning of the semester, and I still felt drawn to him, but for the first time, I wondered why.

Cy and I worked all day and halfway through the night.

When I returned to my dorm, a clean, folded maroon T-shirt with yellow writing had been slipped under my door, the one Benji had given me to wear the night before, and it also happened to be my favorite that he wore. It came with a note.

> On the off chance you need something
> to sleep in while I'm gone.
> Happy Thanksgiving, Rory.
> I wanted to ask you to come home
> with me, but I knew you were busy, and
> I didn't want to freak you out. Yet. ☺
> I would much rather be with you than
> eating leftover turkey all weekend.
>   Love,
>   Benji

My eyes had just barely peeled open when someone knocked on the door. I had worn Benji's shirt to bed. I loved the way it swallowed me, but I wasn't wearing anything underneath. I slipped on some boxer shorts before trudging across the cold floor. The door whined as it opened.

Cy was standing in the hallway, wearing a black fleece pullover and his token khaki cargo pants. He seemed distracted by my lack of attire. "Happy Thanksgiving. I'm afraid we'll have to start early today. Dr. Zorba wants to move the specimen tomorrow."

I walked away from the open door and crashed back onto my bed. "I don't really do early after pulling an all-nighter," I said, lifting the covers over my head.

"I'd like to take you to breakfast first, if that's acceptable to you."

I turned over, letting every muscle in my face capable of frowning compress and tighten. "Why?"

"I…just allow me this. Please." Cy's expression was desperate.

It made me curious and worried and a little sick to my stomach. *Is it about the rock? The CIA? Dr. Z? Does he somehow know about Benji and me?* There was only one way to find out.

"Uh…okay." I stood up and peeled off my clothes as I walked toward the bathroom.

"What are you doing?" Cy said, turning around and shielding his eyes. His voice was raised an octave, sounding similar to what we non-Egyptians call *panic*.

"Taking a shower," I said, slipping my heather gray cotton panties down over my hips and letting them fall to the floor. I twisted the shower knob with one hand and grabbed a towel with the other, and the water sprayed against the tile floor.

The door closed behind me quickly, but not before Cy uttered the words, "You'll not be long?"

"Five minutes," I said. I smiled as the hot water poured over my face. It was about time Cy was the one who felt unsettled.

We sat inside Gigi's Café, watching large flakes fall from the silver sky. It felt weird being there with Cy instead of Benji, but Gigi's was the only restaurant open on Thanksgiving.

Cy was drinking a small black coffee, and I was sipping my hot water as quickly as I could without burning my tongue. I was wearing three layers, including a tank top, my favorite silver sweater, and an orange fleece vest. My clothes were certainly more colorful than my usual attire, but I felt less like only wearing black these days.

Cy insisted that I dress warmly when I came out of the shower. With his back still turned, he'd said, "It's going to be very cold today and even more so tonight. Please, please take better care of yourself, Rory."

Being watched over wasn't something that had appealed to me for the last two and a half years. But lately, it didn't seem all that bad.

The waitress set a plate in front of me with a steaming breakfast burrito, a small plastic cup of pico de gallo, and the stupid garnish that no one cared about and everyone threw away.

"Your breakfrito," she said with a voice that had been poisoned by twenty years or more of cigarette smoke. She put a bowl of raw spinach leaves and a small plastic cup of vinegar in front of Cy. "Your—"

"Grass," I said with a smirk.

Cy wasn't amused at first, but then his expression softened, and he allowed the smallest trace of a smile to form on his lips.

"Our first breakfast. What's the occasion?"

"I wanted us to have a conversation about the other night."

"What about it?" I asked, suddenly feeling nervous.

He had at least narrowed it down, but I still didn't know if he was pissed that I had bailed on him or if he knew about Benji.

"Are you okay?" he asked.

"Obviously," I said, making a downward motion over my torso with both hands. Not a scratch on me, and I was looking mighty fine with my eleven billion mismatched layers.

I picked up my burrito and took a bite.

"This is serious, Rory. I need to know you'll be okay."

I stopped chewing. "Why?" I asked, my voice muffled by the pound of food in my face.

Cy picked at his grass, moving it around on the bottom of the bowl. He poured the entire cup of vinegar over the green leaves, letting them swim around for a while. "Rory...tell me something you've never told anyone."

"Why?"

"Because I asked you to."

"That's weird."

"You're weird."

"So are you."

"Exactly," he said in a flat voice. "Tell me about what you've buried."

"This conversation has taken an awkward turn, like, before it even started."

"There's a point."

"Okay, so you go first."

Cy took a bite, thinking while he chewed, and then put down his fork the moment he swallowed. "Okay. I believe in fate."

"Lame." My response came automatically even though I was a devout disciple of fate. I needed to believe that what had happened to my parents and Sydney happened for a reason. I needed to believe that they were taken, and I was spared to fulfill some purpose, that the universe needed to leave me here, emotionally crippled and alone in my pain. And as crazy as it sounded, I believed Cy played a part somehow.

"I have a reason to believe. I believe you came here, where Dr. Z was, and that we met for a reason."

I liked this weird conversation. Finally, someone sounded as crazy as me. "Why?"

"Your turn."

"I'm really a lizard," I said, sticking out my tongue and pulling it back in quickly.

"Very funny."

I took another bite of burrito and pointed to my mouth, signaling that I couldn't speak.

Cy seemed frustrated. "Okay, we'll try this another way. Why do you always put yourself in danger?"

"I don't."

"Walking alone in the dark. Antagonizing men with a history of violence against women. Driving so fast that you wrecked your car, which is why you've been a pedestrian for the last twenty months. Walking out too far in an angry sea. Frequenting the dangerous side of town—alone, at night—for absolutely no reason. Getting on the back of a motorcycle with a complete stranger, who was clearly drunk. That's not even half of it."

I squirmed in my chair. Some of those things happened before I knew Cy. Even more happened in high school the six months after my parents died. All of them, no one knew about, not even Dr. Z.

Cy put his elbows on the table. "Spending so much time with Benji Reynolds?"

The last sentence nearly caused me to choke on the bite of burrito in my mouth. I swallowed. "Benji? He's harmless."

"What do you know about him?"

"What do I know about Benji? Not as much as you know about me. How in the hell do you know all of that?"

"Just answer the question."

"You first," I snapped.

"I'm thorough. What you should be asking is how I could learn all of that about you but have to ask what you know about Benji. He has no records. There is nothing available on him or his family anywhere, not even a birth certificate. I couldn't even access his school records at KIT."

"Are you hacking into the school's mainframe?"

"That's not important. You have to stay away from him, Rory. Something doesn't add up."

"You've got that right."

Cy lowered his voice. "You can't trust him. Think about it. A wealthy, preppy kid follows the campus recluse like a lovesick puppy? Have you ever asked yourself why?"

"Are you saying I'm not good enough for him?"

"Of course not."

"Because he's lonely, Cy. He doesn't belong, and neither do I. That's all it is."

"He doesn't belong? He's athletic, personable, and approachable. The women at this school fawn all over him. He could literally have his pick. He chose you and only you. He refuses to even acknowledge anyone else. You're far from naive, Rory. Does none of that strike you as odd?"

I began to feel sick in the pit of my stomach, and my breakfast threatened to come up. "Stop."

"You can sense danger, Rory. You couldn't have missed this. Benji wants to gain access to Dr. Zorba's lab. That is his final objective."

I laughed once. "That's ridiculous. I thought *I* was paranoid."

Cy reached his hand across the table. "How many times has he asked to accompany you to the lab?"

I put down my fork. "Stop it, Cy. Right now."

"I'm worried. I can't protect you much longer."

"I don't need protection. You're kind of pissing me off right now."

"I can live with that. I can't live with knowing that I'm leaving you here to fall into a tailspin until you wind up like your parents."

"You're not making any sense, and by the way, fuck you." I took another bite of burrito for show because I definitely wasn't hungry anymore.

Cy sat back, huffing in frustration and looking around the room. After a few moments, he let his shoulders fall, and he leaned in again. "Promise me, Rory. Promise me, you'll stop tempting fate. I can make a promise to you. You have a beating heart. You have blood running through your veins. No matter what you may think, I assure you, you *can* die. And *you will*, if you continue on this course of self-destruction."

I raised my eyebrows. "It sounds so sexy when you say it." Although I was skilled at masking my feelings, everything Cy was saying was freaking me the hell out. *How does he know those things about me? Why is he so suspicious of Benji? Is he a stalker? Is he Majestic?*

The hand Cy had reached across the table was now a fist, and he pounded it on the table. "Why won't you let me get through to you?"

I leaned forward, whispering forceful words, "Because you're not saying anything! As usual, when you're not being vague, you're asking questions!"

"I have no choice," he said, a defeated tone in his voice.

"But you expect me to. Oh, the irony."

He sighed, holding his hand out again. "Please. What if I say *please?* Stay away from precarious situations and people you know nothing about."

"Like you?"

Recognition lit Cyrus's eyes.

"I know more about Benji than I know about you," I said, shooting him an accusatory look.

"The difference is that *I* actually care about you. I'm not your friend to gain an objective. But I can't help you if you won't help yourself. I have no choice and even less time." He turned to the waitress, and with a hand gesture, he asked for the check.

I hoped he was spouting so much nonsense because he was jealous, but deep down, I knew it was something more.

"Do you ever get tired of speaking in riddles?"

Cy watched the waitress make her way to our table. "I admit, it's frustrating trying to help someone when you can't explain your motives. My sincere apologies. This isn't the way I wanted this to go."

"We're leaving?"

"Yes."

"Okay." I realized that whatever this meal was, we'd both just ruined it, and it was time to let my guard down. "You win. I'm sorry. What do you want to know?"

"Everything," Cy said, pulling out a fifty-dollar bill. He threw it on the table and then stood. "Unfortunately, our time has run out. We have a full day and night's work ahead of us, Rory. We must go now."

"Why is this so important to you?"

"What do you mean?"

"The rock belongs to Dr. Z. You act as if it's yours."

Cy laughed once and shook his head. "No. I know it's not mine. That's ridiculous."

"Are you trying to take the assistant spot from me?"

Cy's expression morphed from irritation to surprise to sadness. "No. No, of course not. You deserve the spot, Rory. And Dr. Zorba cares very much for you."

"Then, why do you work so hard?"

Cy sat without offering a response, and I knew exactly why. He didn't lie. He also didn't want to tell me the truth, but I knew what I wanted him to say. Despite every wall I'd formed over the last few years, despite everything I had tried so hard to become, and despite the feelings I was beginning to have for Benji, I wanted Cy to say it was because of me. That him joining a class that he clearly didn't need, the research assistant job, and all this time we were putting into recording the data wasn't because of some fabled government agency or an alien rock, but that it was all for me.

I needed the weird feelings I had for Cy to make sense, and the explanation I kept coming back to was that I was kept on this earth for a purpose, and Cy would somehow connect the dots.

I decided to be brave, and I reached for Cy's fingers, feeling the warmth of them between my own. Cy squirmed, but he didn't pull away.

"Tell me what your connection is to the research," I said. "Why is it so important to you?"

"It's my fault Dr. Zorba carries this burden," he said quietly. "Please, Rory. We really should hurry."

It might be irrational for me to want Cy to give me some answer from the cosmos, but he was keeping something from me, and it was pissing me off.

"What do you mean, it's a burden?"

He shook his head.

"What if I don't want to go back to the lab? What if I decide to stay here until you start giving me real answers?" I crossed my arms across my stomach. Childish, but this was the weirdest, creepiest, most intriguing conversation I'd ever had. After hearing Cy recount things no one else knew about me, I knew most people would have called the police to report a stalker or at the very least run away, but I guessed Cy was right. I was attracted to risk.

"I can't do this without you, Rory. And I wouldn't want to, even if I could."

And I was attracted to him.

Cyrus took my arm and escorted me from the café quickly. It was then that I saw Benji's orange Mustang pull around the corner and park in the back of the café.

"What is he doing here? He's supposed to be with his family."

"Odd, isn't it?" He continued to keep his hand on my arm and pull me away from the café.

"Is that why you were in such a hurry to leave? Did you know he was coming?" I asked as we walked. "How do you know all these things?"

"I just do," he said, taking my backpack and swinging it over his shoulder. "Need anything else? It's going to be a long day."

I felt for my cell phone in my back pocket, wondering if I should text Benji. "Maybe we can order pizza later, and you can actually answer my questions."

Cy made a face.

"Just kidding...about the pizza."

When we arrived back on campus, Benji was already on the front steps of the Fitz, waiting for me.

Cy glared at him as he passed. Benji wasn't fazed.

"Hey," I said, stopping next to him. Cy continued to the door, and held it open, waiting for me. "What are you doing here?"

"I had to see you," he said, glancing quickly at Cy.

"Benji," I said, smiling nervously, "what's going on? Is there something you're not telling me?"

He held out a small white bag—Gigi's takeout.

I smiled. "I thought you'd be on your way home by now."

"Change of plans."

"Your family decided not to get together for Thanksgiving?" I said as my eyebrows pinched together.

"They called before I got halfway home. Dad was called in to work. My sister works for the same company, so she had to go in, too. Mom wanted to go to her parents'. I wanted to see you."

"Oh. Well," I said, looking down at the sack, "I already had breakfast. But I'll be working all day, so I can eat it later. Thank you."

Benji handed over the sack but seemed tense. "I don't suppose I can talk you into spending Thanksgiving with me? Surely, Dr. Zorba will give you today off."

I looked to Cy, who was fuming. Something was definitely up, and it was pissing me off that I seemed to be the only one who didn't know what it was. "I already said I'd work. I can't back out now."

"Oh. Okay. Well…will you call me before dinner tonight? Maybe we can hang out for a little bit while you're on a break."

"No breaks tonight. We have to finish."

"Why?"

"We just do."

He chuckled nervously. "You have to take a dinner break. Call me by seven, okay?" He was smiling, but he couldn't hide the worry in his eyes.

"I'll probably just grab something out of the vending machine. I have to go. I'm sorry."

His welcoming smile quickly faded, and he called after me, "Call me before seven, Rory, okay?"

"I'll try," I called back, following Cy into the Fitz.

"Did he want to come in?" Cy asked, annoyed.

"No, he did not."

This time, Cy and I sat side by side, working furiously, simultaneously recording data and encrypting the files, saving them on two separate flash drives. Our hands brushed more than once, and although Cy seemed not to notice, I certainly did. Every. Damn. Time.

Finally, I broke the silence. "Are you going to explain how you know all those things about me?"

"No," he said quickly, still typing. He didn't skip a beat.

"Anyone else would be freaked out."

"You're not just anyone. You of all people should know that."

He kept typing, but I paused. As much as I wanted to turn around and force the issue, we had a pile of work, so we continued.

Our faces were so close when we took turns viewing the specimen under the microscope. It was getting close to dinnertime, and I thought about Benji. He wanted me to call by seven.

I decided that shooting him a text would be less likely to start another argument with Cy.

Hey.

Hey! :) How's it going? Close to the finish line?

No. Not even close.

I'm going to pick you up at 7 for dinner.

No, you're really not.

C'mon. I'm going to make you a mini Thanksgiving dinner. With a table and everything.

I have to work.

I'll be outside at seven. Won't take no for an answer.

You're being a little weird.

I just want to have Thanksgiving dinner with you. NBD.

Does it have to be 7?

Yes.

That's weird.

Just trust me, ok? It's a surprise.

I'll see what I can do.

:)

At six o'clock, I hopped off my stool and stretched.

"You must be starving. Why don't you pop out for some fresh air and enjoy the Gigi's takeout Benji brought you?" Cy asked.

"Do you want anything?"

"I brought my own."

"Oh, yeah? Let me see."

Cy laughed once and shook his head. "No. I'll never hear the end of it."

"I want to see," I said, picking his messenger bag off the floor. It was oddly shaped, much bigger than usual. "That's a big lunchbox. What do you have in there? Thanksgiving dinner?"

"Rory, please don't," he said, holding out his hand. He was suddenly serious.

I opened it with a teasing smile and pulled out a hexagonal container. It was empty. "What is this?" I said, frowning at Cy.

He sighed. "It's for the specimen."

"The rock? You're taking it to Dr. Z?"

"No, I'm taking it back."

"To Antarctica?" I said in disbelief.

"No."

I waited, but he offered no more. "Then, wh—"

"Don't ask me, Rory. I can't tell you."

I felt my entire body pull inward. The answer was right in front of me, but I still didn't want to believe it. "You're stealing it from him?"

"I...yes," he said, sounding defeated. "Technically, I suppose I am."

"But...do you..." Tears of betrayal swam in my eyes. "Cyrus. Do you...do you work for Majestic?"

He winced at the way I said his name. "Absolutely not. I'm trying to keep it from them, Rory. The only safe place there is."

"But...why did you let him keep it all this time just to take it away?"

Cy let out the breath he'd been holding. "Because I needed to know what he was capable of learning from it," he said quickly, as if he'd been keeping the words in for far too long.

After a long pause, I let out a faltering breath. "Who are you?"

"A friend. Please trust me, Rory. You cannot tell him. He is safer this way. Do you understand?"

"And what about the data?"

"Once he forms a hypothesis, it will be destroyed."

"By you?"

"No."

"By someone else. Someone you work with. So...you're leaving?"

"Yes."

His answer was devastating. I felt like the air had been knocked out of me. "Are you coming back?"

Cy waited for a moment, scanning my face. He stood and touched my arms. "No. And I'll miss you very much."

I needed time to think without Cy sitting across from me. I picked up my bag and pulled out my wallet. Unzipping it slowly, I removed a five-dollar bill. "I'm going to the vending machine."

Cy took a step toward me. "Will you tell him?"

"You're asking me to lie?"

"I'm asking you to trust me."

I thought about so much in that moment—truth and consequences, lies and protection. I'd been trying so hard for so long to keep it together, to keep people away, so I didn't care. I'd made apathy into an art. And one of the only people on earth I wanted to stick around since I'd said good-bye to existing was leaving me. Every time he opened his mouth, he created more questions and no answers, just like in class. But I believed that Cy wanted to keep me safe, and Dr. Z, too.

"I trust you." Instead of waiting for his reply or reaction, I immediately turned on my heels and pushed through the double metal doors into the hallway and climbed the stairs.

I couldn't explain why I felt such a strong connection to Cy since day one, how—even though I'd felt dead inside for over two years—Cy somehow made me feel a dozen strong emotions from the moment he walked into Dr. Z's classroom. I didn't know much about him, but he knew things about me and wouldn't tell me why. But something deep inside of me said to wait. I didn't know everything, but I knew that Cy was the danger I couldn't stay away from. Learning why might lead me to the answers I so desperately needed to be whole again.

I slipped the bill into the machine and pressed the buttons for the Butterfinger. After hearing the coins jingle into the change cup, I bought a bottle of water and then headed back down to the basement. Cy had his small Styrofoam bowl of uncooked spinach leaves and vinegar.

I stood in front of his desk. He looked up.

"Grass again?" I asked.

"Yes. Much better than a quart of grease and curdled cow's milk or the additives and chemicals in that package you're carrying."

"Cheese is the food of the gods. Milk is high in calcium, and Butterfinger is in the Bible."

"I'm certain it's not."

"It is. You must have skipped over the book of Nestlé."

"Milk. I'll never understand it. Humans are the only mammals who drink the newborn nourishment of another mammal. Disgusting."

"Oh, so you're suddenly better than us lowly humans, are you? Because you look like a cow right now."

Cy stopped chewing the spinach leaves. "I didn't say that."

"Egyptians are still human, last I checked."

"You are correct. Rory…thank you for trusting me."

I nodded, quietly opening the wrapping of my candy bar.

Ten minutes later, I had finished my chocolate, Cy had finished his grass, and we continued to work on recording the stack of data Cy and Dr. Z had gathered. As Cy thumbed through the printouts and I typed, a nearly palpable sense of urgency took over the room. We were nearing the end of our research, and then Cy would take the rock and leave. I would never see him again.

The only sounds were the melody of my uneven fingernails on the keyboard, the intermittent scribbling of Cy's pencil, and the shuffling of papers.

After an hour of near silence, knowing these would be my last moments with Cy, the clicking under my fingers ceased. I took a deep breath. "I'm going to miss you."

Cy kept his eyes sealed over the oculars of the microscope. "Me, too. It keeps me awake some nights…how much I'll think about you when I leave here."

I turned to him, incredibly relieved at his answer. "I'm not asking you to stay. I'm asking you to come back."

He looked to me. "I was going to, Rory, but now, I don't think I…" He stared into my eyes. "I don't think I should."

I leaned in. "I thought you were going to miss me?"

We were so close that I could feel the warmth radiating from his skin. His breath smelled sweet even though he'd eaten probably a quarter cup of vinegar that day. He looked down at my mouth, staring at it with such incredible conflict that it made me feel like we were doing something wrong.

"That's exactly why I shouldn't come back."

TEN

A SNAP SOUNDED, and we both looked down. Cy had been pressing his pencil onto the paper so hard that it broke in half.

He stood up and took a few steps away. "I can handle the rest of this on my own. It's getting late."

"Don't do that."

We were strangers in the beginning. It had taken me weeks to get Cy to warm up to me. He was only the third person I'd trusted since that horrible night. I took another step toward him. I wondered how I would handle him being gone. When he was around, the urge to be next to him was overwhelming. If he didn't come back, I wasn't sure what that would mean, but it didn't feel right. And at the same time, being alone with Cy and feeling the way I did, knowing Benji was outside and waiting to take me to dinner, didn't feel right either.

It was all so confusing, and no matter how much I tried to make sense of it in my head, the more confusing it became.

He shoved his hands in his pockets, as if he couldn't trust himself to leave his hands free. "I wish I could explain everything to you, Rory. You deserve to know the truth about the specimen, about me, about everything. But it's safer for you if I don't. I'm only trying to protect you."

"How many times do I have to tell you? I don't need—"

"Oh, I know. You're fully capable of handling things yourself. But not this time, Rory." He pulled his hands out of his pockets and gripped my arms firmly. "Not this time. And not Benji Reynolds. Stay away from him, Rory. He's not who you think he is." Desperation glossed over his eyes.

"Then, who is he?"

Cy looked away. "That is exactly what is so frustrating about this situation. I can't tell you without risking saying too much."

"*You're* frustrated? You're leaving, and you want me to promise to stay away from my only friend."

Cy shook his head. "I'm so sorry. It sounds terrible when you put it that way. I wish it wasn't that way, Rory. I genuinely wish I could change that for you."

"You're not really leaving. Not for good, I mean."

He nodded.

"No." I shook my head and then laughed the horrid feeling in my gut away. "No. I don't believe you."

"I'm sorry." His expression twisted in frustration. "That word seems insufficient for the way I feel right now."

My eyebrows furrowed. Cy wasn't the first person I'd let myself care about since my parents and Sydney died, but he was the first who was going to leave me. I wasn't sure if I was angry or sad or afraid. "You...you can't just let someone care about you and then go away."

"I tried not to."

"So, you have feelings for me?"

"Of course I do. I care about you very much. I always have."

Cy stared at my lips and then let out a faltering breath. "This is wrong," he whispered. "I shouldn't feel this way."

"Feel what way?" I whispered.

Cy reached out to touch my face, and we watched each other for the longest time. I couldn't tell what he was thinking, and that was incredibly frustrating. His hands slid from my jaw to my shoulders and then down my arms, taking my hands into his.

"I love her," he whispered.

His words confused me, and then when my brain finally sorted them out, they didn't make sense. I hadn't seen him with anyone.

"Who?"

"My betrothed."

"Your...*betrothed*. As in, your fiancée? You're engaged?"

"It's similar, yes."

"She's in Egypt?"

"We're to be married when I return."

I shook my head, and he squeezed my hands, concern in his eyes. "She's wonderful, Rory. You would love her as everyone else does. You remind me so much of her."

I felt sick. "I remind you of her?" *Was this why we were drawn to each other?*

After a brief look of confusion, Cy's eyes lit up with recognition. "In some ways, yes. In others, you're so different. You make me feel things that I've never...but none of that matters. I care for you very deeply as a friend, Rory. Sometimes, I feel that's incorrect, that I feel more than that, but that's wrong. I didn't know it was possible to care for someone like this who wasn't my betrothed. I love you, Rory, as a friend, very much. Too much." He reached for me, but I pulled away. "I want all good things for you. I want you to be happy. I want you to heal."

Those words caught in my ears and made me pause. Enough already. If he was really leaving, it was time he told the truth. "You're talking about what happened to my parents, aren't you? How do you know so much about me?"

Cy froze with the same caught look he had when I rounded the corner at the warehouse party and saw him threatening Kevin. "It wouldn't help any of us if I told you."

My eyes narrowed, full of accusation. "Us? Did Dr. Z tell you?"

"No."

"*How? How* do you know these things about me?" I demanded. My voice echoed through the empty building.

Cy reached out for me. "You were spending time with the specimen. I took it upon myself to learn everything about your background. It was important for me to know who you were. If you could be trusted."

"Since when does someone get a background check to be around a rock? What are you not telling me, Cy? Because you know far more about me than you should. I've been patient, but if you're really going to leave here and never come back, you owe me the truth. What do you know about that night?"

"I've told you more than I should. The things I haven't are the things I'm not allowed to share."

"*Who* are you?"

Cy puffed out a breath of frustration.

"You're really not going to tell me, are you? After everything, you're just going to take off and leave me hanging."

He didn't answer.

"I know there is something more to you being here. I can feel it."

He watched me, and although it was clearly difficult, he remained silent.

I nodded. "Congratulations on your upcoming nuptials," I said, walking to my desk. I picked my backpack off the floor.

"Rory...you are the bravest being I know. I'm not sure I could have survived something like that, physically or mentally. I've seen a lot of things. War. Death. But to watch such brutality waged against your loved ones and to suffer in that way is—"

"*Stop* talking."

I walked around the desk, and for the second time that night, I pushed through the double doors. My entire body felt as if it were moving in slow motion as I shuffled down the dark tiled hallway of the basement to the stairs. A chime signaled the elevator's arrival, and its door opened. It was empty and well lit, welcoming me in, but I just stood there, staring at it.

"You're brave, Rory. Just go in. No one is in there," I said aloud. But my body wouldn't move.

The elevator rumbled and jerked as it climbed the shaft without me and then slowed to a halt at the top.

I climbed the stairs two at a time and exited into the main lobby of the Fitz just as the elevator arrived, and then I turned right, making my way to the north entrance. It was a bit out of the way, but Cy would leave with the specimen tonight, and it would be prudent to leave inconspicuously.

As I pressed the door open, I noticed that the familiar jingle of my keys clanging against each other was missing. I arched my neck, glancing back, and when I didn't immediately see them, I straightened my arms, letting my backpack fall from my shoulders. I flipped it around to check the zipper where they normally hung and then patted my jeans in a panic.

"Shit!" I said, checking my front and back pockets one more time before ripping my bag open to search inside. *What did I do with them?*

I yanked my bag from the floor and rushed to the stairs. The elevator dinged as I passed, but I ignored it. After a few seconds, the cables squealed, and the elevator lurched and rumbled as it climbed again. The moment I took the first step down, the few lights that illuminated the lobby went dark, and the elevator went silent, coming to a stop between floors. Something invisible, in my mind, had kept me out of elevators for over two years. If it weren't for my maddening aversion, I could have been stuck in there.

I continued to descend the stairs in the dark, wondering if Cy had found a flashlight.

"Damn," I whispered, checking my pocket. My cell phone had a flashlight built in. I clicked on the button, and it lit my way. Halfway down, I stopped. A faint sound echoed upstairs. My eyes closed, and I waited, searching the darkness with my ears. A door creaked open, and although it was barely audible, I was almost sure it was the side entrance door. Feet, many feet, shuffled quietly down the hall. I couldn't fathom who would be in the building this late at night but myself, Cyrus, and possibly Dr. Z, but something told me I didn't want to be caught by whoever it was.

The group was almost at the stairs. Without my keys, I couldn't get into the lab, and there wasn't time to knock on the door and wait for Cy to let me in. I ran across the hall to the lab next to ours, knowing it would be unlocked.

There was a large Plexiglas window separating the unlocked lab from Dr. Zorba's. Cy was standing at my desk, scrolling the mouse with one hand and making notes with the other. A few lights were on in the lab. He was using backup power.

I tapped on the window, and Cyrus jumped. He offered a sheepish grin, obviously still embarrassed by our good-bye.

I pointed to the door, trying to warn him of the possible company coming down the stairwell. His eyebrows pushed together, and then he cocked his head, listening. His eyes grew large, and then he waved his hands frantically, signaling for me to hide. I shook my head, suddenly nervous. He was serious.

The heavy metal door of Dr. Z's lab blew open, and a dozen or more men dressed in black and armed with semiautomatic rifles flowed into the room. I slid to the floor and pressed my back against the wall. Alone, in the dark, I wasn't sure if I should stay hidden or make a scene. I could hear Cy demanding to know who they were and why they were in the lab. The men were yelling at him, too, insisting Cy step out from behind his desk with his hands in the air.

My heart was ramming against my rib cage, pumping gallons of blood through my body with such force. My fingers, toes, and eyes were throbbing with every beat. My mind fought to stay in the present, but the yelling and the sound of panic in Cy's voice brought me back to the night when they'd murdered the people I loved most—including who I used to be.

I thought about how much fear I had seen in their eyes, and I knew it mirrored my own. I hadn't been afraid like that since. Why would I? I couldn't be killed. I had died with my eyes on my mother until my lids became too heavy to hold open. The men who had been laughing while doodling on my skin with the tip of their knives had faded to the background while my warm blood had spread out on the carpet beneath me. It had pooled, blanketing me and soaking my hair. The warmth had made it easy to let go, so I did.

After a time, I had awoken in a silent hotel room. No maniacal laughter, no sounds of sharp metal penetrating flesh, no crying or begging, no breathing—not even my own. When my eyes had opened, a curvy red pond lay between my mother and me. She hadn't fallen asleep as I did. She'd died as she lived—with her eyes wide open, watching over me.

My breath had returned then. No one could explain it. Not even me. They'd said I must have passed out, that it was impossible that I had come back to life without medical intervention, and I'd just imagined floating over my own body, watching them carve me like a tree trunk. Even when they couldn't explain how I'd lived despite losing a lethal amount of blood or how I had made it across the hall to call for help, they'd still refused to admit that I died. But I *was* dead, and then I wasn't.

I leaned up to see Cyrus take a step back as a dozen or more men approached him slowly, wearing helmets, dark goggles, and bulletproof jackets, carrying guns straight from a war movie.

Cy struggled as they apprehended him, and then they took him away. One of the men stayed behind long enough to locate Dr. Zorba's rock, and then he absconded with that as well. I heard Cyrus yell out in protest for only a moment, and then the lab fell silent.

A few moments later, the lights came back on. I stood up in the empty lab, in shock, afraid, but only for a moment. If someone had seen my family and me get taken away or heard our cries and helped, my parents might be alive today. Sydney might be experiencing KIT with me. She could have found a boyfriend, fallen in love, and gotten married. Because no one had helped us, the man she would have married would be kept waiting. The children she was supposed to have would never exist. An entire line of people was wiped out, descendants of one of the most amazing people I'd ever met.

Then, I wondered if that was ever her purpose. Maybe she was put on this earth to teach me to be strong, to show compassion for those who were victims of the same heartless sons of bitches that killed her, and to compel her brother, Sam—who was active military and a cop—to teach me how to defend myself, things he wanted to teach her but never made the time.

For years, I'd wondered, *Why us? What about our happy, giggling family made those men choose us?* What about us led to their plan to commit horrific violence that night? Another question I'd had for weeks came to mind. *Why am I so drawn to Cy?* I barely knew him. It had never made sense to me until that moment.

Sitting there, on the floor and alone, I finally had my answers. The deaths of my parents and Sydney left me with the guilt and grief that would empower me to get off that floor. I was drawn to Cy because he would need a savior, and I was the perfect person to save Cyrus. I had nothing to be afraid of. Death couldn't touch me.

Suddenly, my feet were climbing the stairs, dashing down the hallway to the side door. Two black vehicles were flying out of the parking lot, heading south.

"Cy," I whispered.

My eyes began to do something they hadn't done in years. They filled with salty tears and spilled over my cheeks. I wiped them away, refusing to get emotional. Whoever had taken Cy possessed power beyond my own or even Dr. Zorba's, and I had no idea how we could get Cy home, but I'd figure it out. I had to.

After a few seconds of feeling paralyzed from shock, I pulled my cell phone from my back pocket and scrolled through my address book for the professor's number. Hesitation crept in before I dialed. *Should I call him? Call the police? What could they do?* Conspiracy theories and scenes from spy movies flipped like channels through my mind. Calling Dr. Z didn't feel right. *What if whoever took Cy is listening in on the professor's calls? Would I just be setting my own trap?* Calling the police didn't feel right. Cy's abductors weren't worried about local law enforcement.

I shoved my phone into my back pocket and pushed open the door, looking for Benji's car. The orange Mustang wasn't anywhere to be seen. My entire body began to tremble as I tried to come up with rational reasons for his absence. I was late. Hopefully, he'd given up and gone home, but that didn't sound like Benji at all. Maybe they had taken him, too.

Not again. I couldn't let someone take away the people I cared about again. I sprinted across campus, passing the dorms and blasting past five blocks of apartment buildings, until I reached the home of Dr. Z. I'd taken that route many times when I felt myself breaking down and the memories became too loud to block out. This time though, I was running toward the nightmare.

ELEVEN

I WATCHED THE HOUSE for several minutes before finally deciding that no one was going to jump out and grab me if I walked up onto the porch. Knocking on Dr. Z's large wooden door was painful with cold knuckles, but I tried four times. I was glad that I'd been going to The Gym with Benji, or I'd have really been hurting. Standing on the porch, shaking from the November night air, my heaving lungs were gasping for a sufficient breath. The cold burned my throat every time I sucked in, but all I could think about was Cy.

After a few moments and no sound, I pounded on the door again. Thunder rolled in the distance, and the sky lit up, signaling an approaching storm. The wind picked up, and the branches scraped above me. The sun wouldn't breach the horizon for a few more hours, and I worried that Dr. Z was so fast asleep that he couldn't hear my knocking.

I ran around the house, trying to decide which window might belong to his bedroom. All the windows were dark, lit only by the intermittent lightning flashes. "Dr. Z!" I hissed, peering into a window. I saw a bed, dresser...but it was too dark to tell if he was inside. I rapped on the window. "Dr. Z? It's Rory! Please get up!"

I pressed my nose against the window screen and cupped my hands around my eyes, trying to get a better look. No movement. He wasn't home.

Headlights and a loud motor approached and then another. The doors of eight identical green Humvees flew open, and men with guns filed out, quickly surrounding the house. I scurried to the bushes for cover, watching them beat on the door as I had just seconds before. When the soldiers couldn't get an answer, they smashed open the door and entered the professor's home. I peeked in through the window, watching as they pointed their flashlights at the bed. The sheets, pillows, and quilt were undisturbed. He wasn't home and hadn't been all night. After a few more minutes of searching, the soldiers retreated to their vehicles, and I sighed.

"Let's go!" one of the soldiers yelled.

I froze when I realized one was lagging behind. With my back scraping against the sharp edges of the brick, I slid to the ground slowly, trying not to draw the straggler's attention. A pair of black boots rounded the corner and stopped just inches from my hand. I closed my eyes.

You won't see me. Just keep walking. My heart pounded, and I struggled to keep the air in my lungs while I verged on experiencing a full-blown panic attack. I didn't fear what they would do to me if I were caught, but I feared what they would do to Cy if I didn't save him.

I'd only been that frightened once before, just before one of my killers pressed the sharp edge of his knife into my arm. My mother was already lying on her side, the light in her eyes nearly snuffed out—her blood spread around her—but she blinked once to let me know she wasn't gone yet, that she would stay with me until it was over. She lowered her chin, asking me to look into her eyes, to watch her so that we could go together. And so I did while they cut into my flesh and laughed about it. I'd always feel satisfaction from knowing that I frustrated them by not crying out like Sydney. I couldn't. My mother was just a few feet away, and I didn't want to torture her even more. Maybe that was why they didn't spend more time with me. I bored them. And then, they left us to die.

My memory seemed to take me away for years, but just moments later, heavy boots quickly moved toward the Humvees. Motors snarled, and tires ripped down the road. Without a plan for what to do next, I scrambled from the ground and into Dr. Z's garage. He didn't own a car. He walked to campus and used the city bus, but when he needed a different mode of transportation, there was Silver, his ancient moped. It might have been the first moped ever made, and he looked ridiculous trolling down the streets in his helmet and suit and bow tie.

I grabbed Silver's keys from beside the garage door and let my heavy backpack fall to the ground.

The kickstand flew back with barely any effort, and it wasn't long before I was zooming down the road, five blocks behind the Humvees, as fast as Silver could run.

The wind whipped around me, pelting my legs with sand. As brutal as it was, I knew it was only the prequel to the storm. Silver struggled to stay between the white lines as I flicked my wrist and pulled the throttle back as far as it would go. Expletives slipped out from my mouth at every other block as the Humvees moved farther and farther away. They turned east, and I leaned forward, hoping that would somehow encourage Silver to surge ahead.

The red lights of the Humvees were still visible once I turned, and I smiled with relief but not for long. It began to rain and not the light, warm kind that made people look up and smile. It was the hard, stinging cold rain that feels as if it was cutting into your skin.

I kept my distance as we left the city lights behind, but when the Humvees turned down Old Copper Road, I didn't follow. I couldn't chance them figuring out that they were being tailed. Instead of Old Copper Road, I drove another mile south. I knew where they were going, and hopefully, it was where they were holding Cyrus.

The rain was coming down in droves and slowing me down. The dirt road was muddy and too much of a challenge for Silver's small tires. I pulled over into the ditch and laid Silver onto its side, squinting through the rain, in the direction of the old warehouse nearly a mile away. That had to be it—the warehouse that had been closed for fifty years or more and where there had just been a party. The entire perimeter was lit up like Christmas. Never in the history of KIT had the secret society had two warehouse parties in one week—at least, not to my knowledge.

Zipping up my vest, I set out across the field, high-stepping across the brush, trying not to leave my boots in the mud. Terrible thoughts of what was happening to Cy behind those walls crept into my mind. He was of Egyptian descent. Maybe they thought he was a terrorist…or worse, maybe he *was* a terrorist.

And I'm about to break into a commandeered military post and do what? Save him? I could be caught, put in prison, or put to death.

"That only happens in the movies. They don't even kill spies anymore," I said aloud, tucking my chin to keep the icy rain from hitting my face.

I was breathing hard, and the mud had turned thick and impossible. My boot got stuck in a hole, and I began to pull away. As I tried to lean back to push my heel back inside, I lost my balance, overcorrected, and fell to the ground.

Facedown, palms down, flat on my belly in mud and cow crap. *What am I doing?*

A helicopter flew overhead, and I squinted, looking up through the pouring rain. It was landing, probably to collect Cy. I pushed myself up from the ground, pulled my boot as I pulled my foot from the mud, and ran as fast as I could manage through the field until I reached the back wall of the warehouse. Soaked, tired, and out of breath, I felt the rain smearing the mud in streaks down my skin and clothes.

I rested my hand against the door and bent down, taking a moment to collect myself before breaking into a military facility. Suddenly, the door vibrated, and the knob turned. I plastered myself against the wall, turning my head, as the door swung open.

A soldier walked out, lit a cigarette, and then blew a puff of smoke into the night air. His back was to me, so I slid around and along the door until I was inside and then snuck down the hall, hiding in a dark corner under a rusted metal worktable. It was chilly, and my wet clothes were drenched and sticking to my skin. My body shook, partly because of the cold, partly because I was absolutely terrified. I didn't know how to get Cy out even if I *did* find him. He was stubborn and loved to argue about everything. *What if we're caught because he won't come with me?*

Deep voices echoed from the end of the hall. My fingers and toes were so cold that they were throbbing. Seeing a lab coat hanging from a hook on the wall, I crawled out from under the worktable and snatched it. My vest and sweater were bulky and weighed down by the rain. They must have weighed five pounds apiece and hit the floor with a thud when I peeled them off.

Goose bumps rose on every inch of my skin. I wrapped the lab coat around me. My wet tank top was already soaking through the coat, but at least it was an improvement.

Walking slowly down the hall and exercising caution, I checked the rooms I passed, all while trying to keep my teeth from chattering and my wet boots from squeaking or squashing with every step. The minutes passed by, and although it was a miracle that I hadn't been caught, Cy was nowhere to be found.

The warehouse was cleaner, whiter, and brighter than it had been just a couple of days ago. If I hadn't seen it myself, I would have never believed the building could be transformed in such a short amount of time.

Footsteps echoed against iron grates along the floor, this time closer, so I ducked into a dark room. One of the men wore black leather combat boots. The other wore crocodile skin boots with gray slacks. *Hideous.*

"Sir, he's not talking," the soldier said. "Tennison wants to put him on the chopper and fly him out to headquarters. We don't have the experts here to question him."

"Ten minutes, Sergeant," Crocodile said. "Give me ten minutes with him, and then Tennison can take him to Disney World for all I care."

"Yes, sir," the soldier said.

With that, the men headed in opposite directions, but I knew exactly which one to follow.

Crocodile Boots led me down four or five corridors. I lost count. I tried to remember my route, but after a while, I couldn't distinguish one hall from another. When Crocodile Boots went into a room, I snuck into the one next to it.

"The CIA is going to put you on a helicopter in ten minutes, son. After that, I can't help you. I need you to tell me what you know about Dr. Zorba's meteorite. Tell me why you're here."

The man paused, waiting for Cy to answer. After several moments of silence, I heard a deep sigh.

"Just tell me your name. Let's just start with that."

Still nothing until I heard a struggle.

"You're going to tell me everything I want to know, or I'm going to pick up that little weirdo friend of yours and finish the game of tic-tac-toe those psychos played on her skin a few years back."

The words he spoke made me feel dizzy, but I forced myself to remain focused, refusing to let my mind wander back to that night.

After more sounds of struggle, Cy growled, "Get away from me!"

"Are you surprised that I know what happened to her? You think it's a coincidence that her dad was working with Dr. Zorba and his partner and met such a tragic end? Majestic watched Dr. Zorba and Dr. Brahmberger for months before they discovered that signal. We intercepted an email from Marty Riorden to Dr. Zorba. He knew the signal was suspicious. He was going to interrupt their research. Marty's discovery would have taken it in a different direction than what we had anticipated, ruining years of planning and work."

Cy's expression metamorphosed from confusion to recognition. "You...you killed them."

"The real coincidence here is that Rory lived, Dr. Zorba took her under his wing, and ironically, you did, too. Now, I can use her again to get the information I need, just as I did when we questioned her father. It only took half an hour with Rory before he told us everything we wanted to know and even things we didn't think to ask."

I sat against the wall with my knees to my chest and my hands trembling from anger and hatred. We didn't die for money or pure violence or even so that I could be strong enough to save Cy. Crocodile Boots had us killed so that Dr. Tennison could get the validation he'd been seeking. He kept my father from telling Dr. Z and Dr. Brahmberger what he knew about that signal so that they could continue their research. They'd probably been monitoring Dr. Z when he learned of the meteorite in Antarctica. Tennison must have been thrilled, knowing Dr. Z would bring back the rock and do half the work before Tennison stole it from him.

So much violence, so many lives changed forever, ruined and taken away, all so Tennison could take the credit and be hailed for research he didn't do. With Majestic behind him, he had no rules.

I looked around for something, anything, to impale the bastard the moment he stepped outside the room, but there was nothing.

"How could you murder an innocent family, an innocent girl? So that two men who Tennison knew were smarter than him could continue the science for him?" Cy asked, his voice pleading for a reason.

Crocodile Boots laughed once. "I'll let Tennison know your concerns."

"You're monsters," Cy said.

"You know what I'm going to do to that poor girl—again—if you don't tell me what Tennison wants to know. That makes you worse than a monster. No?"

Silence.

"Okay, son. Have it your way."

The crocodile boots clanged against the floor as he stomped away, and I scampered around the corner just long enough not to be seen before crawling on hands and knees into Cy's room.

Before the door could slide shut, I slipped off the white lab coat and rolled it up tightly, wedging it between the door and doorjamb.

Cy was strapped to a chair with white cloth restraints on his wrists and ankles. His eyes nearly popped out of his head in disbelief as I scrambled up to hug him.

"What are you doing here?" he hissed. "Go away!"

I turned to check the hallway before shooting him the dirtiest look I could muster. "Are you kidding me? What does it look like?"

Cy's brows pulled together, and his eyes softened. "Did you hear him? He's coming after you. They'll torture you, Rory. They won't believe that you don't know anything. You have to leave!"

"Let him try, but for now, I'm getting you the hell out of here."

"You must leave, Rory. Leave the way you came. You can't help me."

"Shut up," I said, working on the cloth around his wrist. "I'm already here. I'm covered in mud and cow shit, and I'm getting you out of here. The least you could do is thank me."

Once I unbound one of his wrists, he used his free hand to work on the other while I untied his ankles. By the time I finished one, Cy had already freed his wrist and the other ankle. He pulled me up by the elbow and looked me in the eyes, his face just a few inches from mine.

He wiped mud from the corner of my eye and offered a sweet grin. "Thank you. But you shouldn't have done this, Rory. I don't want you to get hurt."

"You're my friend. You would do it for me, right?"

The corners of Cy's mouth turned up slightly, and then he refocused, his golden eyes flitting about the room. "This way," he said, pulling me by the arm out of the room and down the hall.

"No, this way," I said, tugging him to the right.

His hand tightened around my arm, and he pulled me close. "If we're going to get out of here alive, you must listen to me," he said, looking around. "You're attracted to danger. I feel the impulse to avoid it. Do you understand?" When I didn't answer, he frowned. "I don't have time to explain everything to you. You're going to follow me." With that, he pulled me in the opposite direction.

Not a minute later, there was shouting behind us and footsteps pounding against the metal floor.

Cy pulled me down another corridor and then another. Soon a siren blared, forcing me to press my palms against my ears. Lights along the ceiling began to turn, casting red shadows across Cyrus's face. He jerked his head to the side, trying to listen over the piercing alarm, and then he pushed me into the closest room and against the wall, holding his finger against his mouth.

Soldiers ran past, yelling to each other over the noise. Despite the siren, my heart beat so loudly against my chest that I was scared they would hear it. For the first time, I was truly afraid of what the soldiers might do to Cyrus if they caught us. Whatever they wanted, they were determined to get, and now we both knew what they were capable of doing. Judging by the fear in his eyes, I could tell he knew his fate was bleak if he fell back into their hands.

Once the soldiers passed, Cy pulled me from the room. I struggled to keep up with his long strides. He pulled us into yet another room, this one dark and full of rusted equipment from the warehouse. The cobwebs and cool air seemed like a world away from the shiny prison.

Cy pushed a table to the center of the room and climbed on it, jumping once to pull down an air vent cover. With the cover in one hand, he jumped again, pulling himself up and out of sight. His arm shot back down through the square hole and waved for me to follow. I cautiously clambered on top of the table, but the frightening sound of standard-issue military boots plodding down the hallway made me scramble to reach Cy's hand. His fingers trembled as they extended to their limit, and I hesitated, looking back at the door.

"Rory! Take my hand!" he said over the siren.

I jumped once, reaching for him. I wasn't tall enough to reach. I tried again, missing by more than two inches.

Cy lowered himself further into the room, extending both arms toward me. He had no leverage to pull me up, holding on with just his legs. He was frightened and desperate, but he wouldn't leave without me. "I will catch you, Rory. Jump!"

The footsteps were just a few feet from the door when I bent my knees and reached up with both arms. Cy hooked my fingers with his and then pulled, shooting me up through the vent like a rocket. He turned to grab the vent cover and pulled it up against the hole, sealing us in.

I began to crawl down the shaft, but Cy grabbed both of my legs and dragged me until I was next to him, wrapping both his arms around me. A flashlight beamed in and out of the slits of the vent and then around the room. The legs of the table we climbed onto scraped against the floor when a soldier bumped against it.

"Clear!" he said, motioning the other soldiers to follow. They ran from the room to search the others.

Cy nodded. "They're gone," he whispered. "Follow me."

We crawled on our bellies down the shaft. It wasn't long before I was puffing, struggling to keep up with him. When soldiers were below, we would stop, waiting until they were out of earshot. The shaft was stuffy and dank and had me feeling borderline claustrophobic.

"Cy," I whispered, sweat dripping from my face, "I can't."

Cy pushed up, and a small opening formed above him, letting the rain shower his face. "This way," he said, crawling through the hole.

I made my way to the opening, and once again Cy reached back his hand, waiting for me to grab it. In the next moment, I was on the roof of the warehouse, overlooking the lights of our town, not ten miles away. The rain was freezing, and the sweat on my skin was cooling quickly in the cold night air. I cussed myself for leaving my sweater behind.

Cy pulled off his fleece pullover and handed it to me. "Put this on," he said, looking around, planning his next move.

"Who are those people?" I asked, slipping the soft black fleece over my head. It was dry but wouldn't be for long.

"CIA...maybe one or two branches of military," he said, distracted.

I frowned. "I know that."

He turned, confused by my reply. "Then, why did you ask?"

"Why did the CIA kidnap you?"

Cy looked to his watch. "Oh no."

"What?"

"It's broken."

"There are more pressing matters than your broken watch, don't you think?" I said, pointing to the vent.

Cyrus looked around in thought and then nodded. "Come on."

The fire escape was guarded, so Cy led me to the opposite side of the building. An Army truck was parked nearby, but we were too far to jump. Cyrus peered back at me, making a decision, and then he frowned apologetically.

"I'm sorry," he said, covering my mouth. "Don't scream."

I struggled at first, but then he lifted me into his arms and ran full speed to the edge, leaping the incredible distance to the truck. We landed in the center and then rolled off, hitting the ground. With me still tucked in his arms, Cy pinned us under the truck and waited.

"What are we doing?" I said through his hand.

"Waiting for signs that we were seen."

"Ow!" I said.

He began to search my body with his eyes. "What is it?"

"My elbow," I moaned, lifting up my arm. My shirt was quickly becoming a mess of dirt and blood.

Cy uttered something that sounded like a curse as he pulled up my sleeve to get a better look. He used his fingers to feel the bone and then shook his head. "I don't think it's broken," he whispered. "Can you move it?"

I nodded, gently extending and flexing my arm. Cy's pullover was ripped. I pulled the tear apart with my fingers to get a good look at my arm. The flesh had been scraped away, and gravel was embedded in the meaty muscle. "You were right," I said quietly. "Turns out I do have blood."

Cy rolled his eyes and ripped the bottom part of his T-shirt, tying it around my wound. "This should do until I can clean it. Let's go."

He took my hand, and we ran into the tall grass of the field and then across the road, back into even taller grass. I crouched down, imitating Cy. Every part of my body was freezing, except for the hand enfolded in his. He held on tight as we ran awkwardly across the muddy terrain. Once we were approximately two miles away from the warehouse, Cy finally let me stop to catch my breath.

"I'm not sure if you knew this about me," I sputtered. "But I'm not athletic. Like…not at all."

"Me either."

"You're not sucking in air like I am."

"Let's just say I'm not known for being athletic back home."

"Are you going to tell me what the hell is going on?"

Cy looked around. "I'll try to explain everything later, but for now, we have to find Dr. Zorba, and then we have to retrieve the specimen and somehow get me to the old gas station on the south side of town by four a.m."

"What? Why?"

Cy made a face. "I told you. I'll explain later."

"Dr. Z isn't home. I went there first. Soldiers were there. They didn't find him either."

"You don't know where he went?"

Now, it was my turn to make a face. "If I knew where he went, I wouldn't have gone to his house."

He sighed. "Did he leave a note?"

"I don't think he wanted the CIA to know where he was going."

"We need to go back there. See if we can figure out where he went."

"Why? You were stealing the rock from him anyway, right?"

"I uploaded the final data to him and deleted it from the lab's computers before I was taken. Dr. Zorba is the only one who knows where the complete data files are stored. We have to find him, and it has to be tonight."

Cy turned and took a step, and then he turned back around, pulling me into a tight hug. "Thank you for saving me, Rory. You don't know what you've done."

He turned again, walking back toward town, and I followed.

TWELVE

WE TREKKED THROUGH MUD AND BRUSH and jumped across ditches full to the brim with cold rainwater. My toes were almost frozen and ached with every step. Cy's pullover was warmer than my sweater, and keeping up with his pace was keeping my body temperature even. It seemed like right before I'd break a sweat, he would slow down a little bit.

We crouched in tall grass beside the first paved road. A helicopter had been flying over the area with a spotlight since we left the warehouse, but Cy kept us just out of sight.

"You see there?" he said, pointing. "We're going to run as fast as you can to that old garage, wait for the helicopter to pass over, and then run to the next block."

"How do you know the helicopter will pass over that garage?"

"Go!" Cy said, pulling me up and over the ditch, across the road, and to the garage.

"I wish I had Silver," I said, ducking under Cy's arm and breathing hard. "Dr. Z is going to kill me for leaving it behind."

"I don't think he's worried about that now." Cy checked his watch. After remembering it was broken, he looked away, grumbling something sounding like Arabic under his breath.

"Was it a gift? From her?"

"Sort of."

"Can you just give me a straight answer?"

Cy ducked and pulled me down with him as the helicopter flew over the garage hiding us. The blades were so loud that I didn't bother trying to talk. Once the light had touched everything in the area, the noise got farther and farther away.

"Let's go!" Cy pulled on the coat, but I didn't budge. He turned to me, his eyebrows pulled in. "Come, Rory! We must leave!"

"Okay, but when we get to where we're going, you're going to explain a few things. And I want straight answers. Promise me." I knew this probably wasn't the best time to be difficult, but this also wasn't the best time for him to turn me down. I wanted the truth, and I was determined to get it.

After a second of hesitation, he nodded. "Okay, but we *must* go," he said, holding out his hand.

I took it, and we bobbed and weaved in and out of shadows until we were where I'd started—Dr. Zorba's.

A board creaked under Cy's feet, and he froze.

"I told you, he's not here," I said, following Cy into the professor's hallway.

"Maybe he left behind a clue of where he went. C'mon, let's get you cleaned up."

Cy held my elbow under the faucet until he removed all the residual gravel. "First-aid kit?"

"Try under the sink," I said, nodding.

Cy tried under the sink and then proceeded to open every cabinet in the kitchen.

"Found it," he said.

Cy grabbed the clear plastic box from above the stove, and kneeled in front of me as I sat on one of Dr. Z's wooden kitchen chairs.

Cy sprayed my wound with antiseptic, put far too many butterflies on it, and then wrapped it with gauze. "Truthfully, it needs stitches, but I don't think it's safe to take you to the hospital."

"Agreed. Now, how are we going to find this clue you think exists?"

"Try the easiest path first," Cy said, knocking his fist four times on the doorjamb—twice quickly, the next two slower.

The same knock came back.

My breath caught. Then, a trap door in the ceiling fell open, and a ladder spilled out onto the floor. Cy helped Dr. Z climb down, and I grabbed him.

"You're okay!" I said, hugging him. From the corner of my eye, I saw Cy helping someone else from the attic. Before I even saw her face, I knew who it was and recoiled. "What is she doing here?"

"I could ask the same of you," she said, brushing off her tight sweater.

I frowned at Dr. Z.

He held up his hands. "She had questions about finals. She was unfortunate enough to get mixed up in all of this."

"So, you've been up in the attic with her this whole time?"

"No, just when we heard someone coming. I was afraid someone was watching the house and that if she left they would grab her."

I narrowed my eyes at Ellie. I trusted Dr. Z, but with her deep V-neck sweater revealing at least three inches of cleavage, I knew she was after more than just help with finals.

"Stop staring at me, Rory," she snapped in her Southern drawl. "It's weird."

"Whore," I hissed.

"Rory!" Dr. Z said in a loud whisper.

"It's okay." Ellie grinned. "She just wishes she had breasts."

Her comment forced Dr. Z and Cy to glance down at the pitiful barely B cups on my chest and then at each other, both wishing they hadn't. My blood boiled, mostly because it was true.

"Ellie, that's…quite enough," Dr. Z said, looking uncomfortable.

"Dr. Zorba, I need the flash drive," Cy said.

"The—"

"Yes, with the data we've collected and your complete set of notes."

"Cyrus, I regret that I cannot. It's the only complete file I have. It also contains my thesis. With Tennison snooping around, I cleared everything from my computers and—"

"Good," Cyrus said. "That saves me a trip back to campus. What about your personal computers?"

"They're all wiped. I didn't want my hard work getting into the wrong hands."

"Me either. That's why I need it."

Dr. Z stared at Cy for a long time. "I'm sorry, Cyrus. I appreciate all you've done, but—"

"It's important, Argus," Cy said. "Please."

Dr. Z's eyebrows pulled in, forming a deep crease between them. "Argus is my first name, and no one calls me Argus but my mother. How do you know that name?"

I looked to Cy, wondering how he knew half of what he did. Part of me wondered what side he was on. He had helped Dr. Zorba, but then he was going to steal the specimen from him. To anyone else, Cy would seem like the enemy, but something inside of me told me he wasn't.

"Dr. Z," I said quietly, "give it to him."

The professor's eyes bounced back and forth between Cy and me, and then he let out a sigh in surrender. "I don't suppose you're both working for Tennison?"

Ellie crossed her arms. "Wouldn't surprise me."

"You know all of zero about this, Ellie, so shut the hell up," I hissed.

"We've spent all day in this house and in that attic. I know quite a bit actually."

Cy looked at the professor. "What have you told her?"

"Nothing sensitive," Dr. Z said. "Almost nothing. It's been a long day. We ran out of things to talk about."

Cy took Dr. Z's arm and led him into the professor's study. They conversed quietly, leaving Ellie and me alone to glare each other down.

"Is that who spent the night in your room?" she asked, nodding to Cy.

I could tell she was goading me, so I said nothing. I didn't want to give her the satisfaction.

She laughed once. "What am I saying? He is way out of your league."

My eyes targeted her. "At least I don't have to fuck geriatrics for grades."

Ellie smiled, clearly amused she'd gotten under my skin. "Oh, Rory," she lilted and then circled slowly around me, "I could *smile* at them and get the grades. I don't have to fuck anyone. I'm just attracted to intelligence, which is why I find nothing appealing about you at all."

Just when I was about to spit more venom at her, Cy and the professor returned.

"I have it, Rory. I'm afraid it's time for me to go." He glanced at his broken watch. "I must be at the remaining foundation of that old gas station next to the Old River Bridge at a very specific time. If I'm not, I don't know what will happen."

Ellie leaned down. At first, it didn't occur to me to react. Even when she pulled a small pistol from her boot and pointed it at Cy, it took me a second to register what was happening.

Dr. Z's eyes widened. "Ellie, what on earth—"

Ellie kept her gun on Cy. "Before you scoot along, handsome, how about you give me that flash drive?"

Cy was disturbingly calm. "I knew Tennison had to have a contact on campus."

Ellie laughed, and then suddenly her Southern accent disappeared. "You're a goddamn genius, aren't you? Hand it over."

"But...you're a student." My brain couldn't wrap my head around it. I kept thinking that she must have been sleeping with this Tennison and got pulled into this somehow.

"Rory, really. For someone who watched her mother and best friend get raped and murdered right in front of her eyes, you're so naive." My jaw clenched. She looked at Cy again. "Give me the flash drive, or I'm going to put a bullet right through your heart." She shrugged. "Or the general area of what should be your heart anyway."

My nose wrinkled. She didn't make any sense.

I walked up to her.

"Rory, don't," Cy warned.

I stood between Cy and Ellie. "Don't point that at him," I said, my voice low and full of warning.

Ellie smiled. "You really are thick, aren't you? Get out of my way before I shoot you in your fucking face." She looked around me. "I'm going to kill your little girlfriend, Cyrus. How is that going to sit with your council?"

"Rory, move. Ellie, just...let's all calm down. I'll give this to you if you guarantee Majestic will leave Rory alone. Forever," he said, holding out his fist.

She chuckled. "You know I can't make that promise. There's at least one jackass in our department who can't stay away from her."

"Benji," Cy said.

I looked at Cy and then at Ellie. "You've wanted to believe he couldn't be trusted from day one. That doesn't make sense anyway. Benji's not even twenty, and you immediately assume that he is working for the CIA?"

"I'm willing to believe it," Cy said.

"Of course you are! But it's ridiculous!" I said. "Someone else is out there, watching us, and you're so set on Benji being the bad guy that you're going to overlook clues to who it really is!"

"Aw. Are you going to cry now? Does it hurt your feelings to think that you might not be able to trust the only friend you have?"

Dr. Z watched Cy, Ellie, and then me. "Rory..."

"No." I shook my head. "Just think about it for a second. How many hoops does a person have to get through before being accepted into the CIA?"

"How old is Ellie? They could be recruiting out of high school for all you know," Cy said.

"Yes," Ellie sneered. "Because there's no way I could be older and just be posing as a college student. How did any of you make it into KIT without being able to add two and two?"

"It's not Benji," I said. "She's full of shit for once instead of geriatrics."

She knew Benji was my friend, and she was trying to separate us from our allies. I wasn't educated on intelligence tactics, but KIT didn't accept students on personality alone.

"Keep talking, bitch," Ellie said, cocking her gun.

"You might work for Majestic, but they pimped you out. You're a legit whore after all."

"Yep, I'm going to shoot your pet in the face, Cy," Ellie said, aiming.

I raised my hands, one on each side of my shoulder. "Make her more promises, Cy. I'm super scared right now. Really."

"Rory, take steps back, toward me. Right. Now," Cy said again. This time, his voice was tinged with desperation.

"Okay," I said calmly. "I'm going to take a step back now." Before Ellie could mouth off again, I reached for her gun, pulled it out of her hands, and flipped the barrel so that it was facing her. I cupped the grip of the gun in my hand, getting a feel for it. The move felt as if it all happened in slow motion, but in reality, it was about two seconds.

"Last time I checked, they didn't teach that in self-defense class," Ellie said, clearly surprised.

"I took an advanced class."

It wasn't a total lie. Sydney's older brother, Sam, had picked up a lot of useful things during his time in Afghanistan. He took her death hard, and his way of forgiving himself for not teaching his baby sister how to defend herself was to teach me. This turnaround trick was the last thing he'd taught me, and other than Sam, Ellie was the first person to see me use it.

I was just relieved it worked. I hadn't practiced it in over a year.

I held the pistol in front of me, aiming straight for her forehead.

"Rory, don't!" Cy said.

Ellie took that momentary distraction to bolt, pushing through Dr. Z's screen door. I followed her, but she had already disappeared into the darkness.

"I am so confused," Dr. Zorba said, wiping the sweat from his brow with a shaking hand.

"Can I have the flash drive now?" Cy asked.

I turned to him. "I thought you said you had it?"

"I had to provoke her. Something wasn't right."

I smiled. "Congratulations, Cy. You just told your first lie."

He opened his hand, revealing a screw. "I said I had it. I didn't say what *it* was. Still not a lie."

"Close enough."

"The truth," Dr. Z said, exhaustion in his voice. "If you tell me the truth, I'll give you the flash drive. I just need to know."

Cy looked at me and then to Dr. Zorba. "We haven't much time. They know we're here. They'll come for us." He glanced at me. "All of us."

"Then give me the short version," Dr. Z said simply.

Cy thought about this for a moment and then nodded. "Okay. You might want to sit down, Professor."

THIRTEEN

DR. Z SAT NEXT TO ME on his green crushed-velvet couch. It had seen better days, I was sure. I was also sure he'd found it at a garage sale like the rest of the furniture in his home.

Dr. Z was a humble man even though he'd won a Fields Medal, the Hubbard Medal, and the international Balzan Prize. He was the most respected man in his field, even before his tenure. He expected to win the Nobel Prize in Chemistry one day for his thirty years of research on the calcium-sensitive proteins within cells and their biochemical language. But for a little over a year, he'd been obsessed with newly discovered, unusually regular radio signals coming from an unknown object in Galaxy M82. His oldest and most trusted friend, Lucius Brahmberger, a renowned astrophysicist, had discovered the signal, and together, they had begun investigating the anomaly and Erich von Däniken's paleocontact hypothesis.

Seven months after Brahmberger had first heard the radio signals, he'd disappeared. Dr. Z had remained committed to continuing their research, believing that doing so would lead him to his friend. He had been given a tip from a secret government contact about a meteorite landing in Cape Hallett, an Antarctic Specially Protected Area. Knowing this, Dr. Z had packed his bags and left immediately. When he'd come back, he was more consumed by his work than ever. He had been tracking this particular meteorite since not long after Dr. Brahmberger's disappearance, and Dr. Z was convinced that because of its trajectory, radioactive dating, and reflectance spectra, the rock's origin was the same as the signal's.

He lectured to his classes, giving no one any reason to ask questions. Every other moment of the day, Dr. Z was in his lab, studying his specimen and gathering data. He told me about the rock right away, but no one else—as far as I knew. He was convinced that if he learned enough about the rock, somehow that knowledge would lead him to his friend.

Waiting for Cy to offer some epiphany that Dr. Z had been waiting fifteen months for, Dr. Z was wringing his hands and shifting on the couch cushion. I'd never seen him so apprehensive. Even back when he realized that Majestic was after his rock, he had a confident, mischievous look in his eyes, as if he were accepting the challenge. Nothing seemed to intimidate Dr. Z. He knew then that he was truly onto something, and now that he knew the answer was just a few moments away, he was a wreck, waiting anxiously for Cy to tell him what it was.

"The specimen is dangerous, Dr. Zorba. It's the last piece of a long-dead planet, Chorion. The planet had suffered civil unrest for years before wars, planet-wide devastation, and finally, what we had always thought was a plague led to its demise. The planet had been quarantined for decades. All of Chorion's inhabitants are extinct.

"The remnant, your specimen, is something I've been tracking for a very long time. It contains inactive parasites, and given the right environment, those parasites could spawn. Earth was the perfect place for the remnant of Chorion. Fortunately, the mixture of nitrogen and oxygen in Earth's atmosphere keep them inert, so there was no danger of the parasites reactivating. I tracked the specimen here with the intent to bring it back with me so that we could properly…dispose of it, just as we did the rest of the planet."

I sighed. "We don't have time for this."

"Hush, Rory!" Dr. Z said, frowning and waving me away. "So, you're saying you…you destroyed an entire planet?"

"We had no choice. It was overrun."

"I thought you said the inhabitants were extinct," I said. "How does a parasite exist without a host?"

"By returning to an inactive state. An organic presence along with the right environment reanimates the parasite. Once this happens, planet-wide infestation can happen within seventy-two hours. My planet, Yun, is a little more than twice the size of Earth. Chorion was roughly the same size and population as ours. They were overrun in two and a half days."

"*Yoon?*" I asked, trying to form my mouth around the word.

"Yes, Yun. Its meaning is similar to sunshine."

"Boring. Not even any Kryptonite in this story," I said, my chin resting on my palm.

Cy began to pace. "The head of what you might consider the science department of our government picked up a signal from a neighboring world, Chorion. As I said, that planet had long been considered derelict. We were very excited to pick up on that signal. However, all scans revealed our previous belief was correct, and the planet was indeed barren. Curious about where the signal was coming from and how it was tapping into our frequencies, our Amun-Gereb, Hamech, sent out an exploratory vessel. It never came back. What Dr. Brahmberger picked up on his equipment was not the signal from Chorion, but the SOS beacon from that vessel."

"What is a *hammock*?" I asked.

"Hum-OCK," he pronounced precisely with a slight accent. "He is our Amun-Gereb. He is a…like your President, but he leads our entire planet. He is king."

"Amun-Gereb," Dr. Z said. "As in the supreme Egyptian god."

"That's where Egyptians first heard the word, yes, from our exploratory teams, as they did Osiris, my namesake."

"Oh," I said, nodding.

"The ancient astronauts were real. The paleocontact hypothesis is correct! Please, Cyrus, go on," Dr. Z said, engrossed.

"Contained within the beacon's frequency was an image. Similar to what you call a video here. A crew member, but she was on a different vessel. She was very distraught and injured but was able to report that Chorion was not barren. There was life, but it was not indigenous to the planet or any planet that we had charted within our galaxy. She said the original signal we'd picked up was from an alien spacecraft, the one they had located and boarded. We'd homed in on its beacon. The craft had appeared to be overrun by something else. The crew member said that she'd been infected by the same hostile organism—a parasite—and then she began to convulse. The image stream ended before we could see her full transformation, but by her screams, I assumed it was extremely painful."

Cy closed his eyes for a moment. I knew he could still hear her screaming. No matter how many years passed or how hard you tried, some things never faded away.

"I've been studying humans since Heracleion was discovered."

"The underwater city discovered in 2000 near the Nile Delta?" asked Dr. Z.

"It was an area of interest for our people around Earth's three to four BC. Heracleion was a place our people visited often. There were many statues erected in my ancestors' honor and many scripts detailing our assistance to the Egyptian culture. Part of my function is to make sure our civilization is protected, and the discovery of

Heracleion was alarming to our council. Your oceans are vast and largely unexplored, and so for centuries, we weren't concerned about the relics detailing our visits here, but once Heracleion was discovered, I decided to design a mission to extract any concrete evidence of our existence to prevent any unwanted contact."

"Such a shame," Dr. Z said. "Contact and an alliance could lead to so many wonderful things!"

"You have to admit, historically, humans don't make the best neighbors," Cy said. "It would become, *What do you have?* And then, *What do you have that I can take?* And then, the fighting starts."

I rolled my eyes. It'd be fascinating maybe, if it weren't a huge steaming pile of bullshit.

Cy continued, "Once I realized the beacon had been redirected to Earth, it was decided that I would leave immediately. We realized you were being baited, as we had been. You see, we managed to reverse the feed and bring in broken images from the exploration vessel, and we saw that the entire crew was moving in and out of the ship. It was the crew that had redirected the beacon. The parasites were aware that we had been warned and that we wouldn't be sending more ships to them. They had no way of bringing in more hosts."

"So, the signal we localized," Dr. Z said quietly, "was sent to Earth by the crew."

"Correct. It was our crew who sent the signal to Earth. But it wasn't really our crew. They were…altered."

"Altered how?" I asked, realizing I was on the edge of my seat. His story might be bullshit, but it was entertaining.

"They appeared…mutilated. Their faces were mutated, and their eyes…" Cy seemed to be lost in thought. His face screwed into disgust and horror. He shook it away. "We can't let Tennison keep the specimen, Dr. Zorba. If he manufactures a sustainable alien atmosphere, and the parasites are reanimated, none of us will last long."

"Tell us what to do," Dr. Z said.

"Hold on. I have questions."

"Rory," Dr. Z warned, "this could lead me to Brahmberger. He is still alive, and they have him. They're going to use him to reanimate the parasites. He's the only one who could do this."

"No, I let him tell his story. I let you listen. Now, I have questions."

Cy frowned. "I know you don't believe any of it. I expected that. But we can't stay here. They'll be knocking on the front door any minute."

"Then, we'll go out the back. Why didn't you take the rock the first night you were alone in the lab?"

Cy lowered his chin. "I was going to, but then I worried about how much data Dr. Zorba had collected on his own. He was only giving it to us in pieces. A little bit of knowledge is dangerous. What if he eventually learned the origin of the parasites or even the specimen, and NASA sent an exploratory vessel there? What if the parasites, via their new human hosts, directed the vessel back and infected Earth's populace? And what about the next planet? And the next? When would it stop?"

"We wouldn't send humans that far into space. We have robots for that," I deadpanned.

"We do, too, but had conflicting information. Curiosity is a dangerous thing."

"Why would the parasites redirect the beacon here?"

"It's a flourishing host."

"If the Earth isn't a suitable environment, how will the parasites live outside the environment Tennison creates?"

"Once they are properly embedded in a host, they use that host's acclimation to survive. The parasites, once they control their hosts, will control Tennison's lab, and you can be sure that more labs with those same conditions will be recreated all over the world to make the transition more efficient."

"Okay. Very compelling. I'll give you that. You get an A for creativity. Why do you keep looking at your broken watch?"

Cy hesitated. "I am scheduled to leave. If I am not at the rally point at the predetermined time, I fear…" His eyes lost focus as he retreated into his mind.

"You fear what?"

Cy stepped out of the darkness into the only trace of streetlight coming into the room. "Apolonia."

I wasn't sure if Apolonia was the parasite or something worse. Cyrus's stories were outlandish, but he hadn't cracked a smile. More disturbing, Dr. Z clearly believed every word.

"What is Apolonia?" I asked.

"Who," Cy said. "Apolonia is a *who*, and if I'm not at the abandoned gas station by the Old River Bridge, I'm afraid she'll…she's…emotional."

"*She?*"

"Yes. She'll assume the worst. She'll come looking for me, and that is never a good thing."

"Why?"

"If I don't reach the bridge, you'll see." Lights from a passing car lit up the living room, and Cy went to the window to carefully peek outside.

Dr. Z stood up from the couch and brushed off his polyester pants. "Then, we'd better get you there."

"What about the rock? I thought you were going to take it with you."

"It's important that I make contact with my people. Apolonia and her crew can help me retrieve the specimen from Tennison. I don't want to risk involving you and Dr. Zorba any further."

"You've already involved us. You really think if we sit this one out, they'll let us go?"

Cy thought for a moment. "You're right. We should stay together."

I sat up a bit taller, satisfied that Cy had agreed with me for once. Dr. Z seemed to be pleased with that decision, too.

"What do you mean, her crew? When you say *crew*, I envision pirates."

Dr. Z sighed. "We must go now, Rory. You can be a smart-aleck at Cyrus's destination."

"Before I go running around in the dark in winter, I want more answers."

Cy shifted, clearly impatient. "We can't stay any longer, Rory."

"Just answer this, and then I just have one more question, and then we can go."

Cy nodded, impatient. "Crew might not be the right word. They're more like a retrieval team. Apolonia is the daughter of Hamech. She's a highly decorated soldier and leads the Jhagat, Yun's army. She is the captain of her father's best warship, the *Nayara*."

I swallowed. "And she'll be emotional if you don't show up because…Apolonia is your betrothed, isn't she?"

Cy's eyes turned soft. He looked apologetic, but I wasn't sure why.

"Yes."

Fuck. He really *was* going to leave. *If even half of what Cy said about this woman was true, how could Earth compete with a Xena the Warrior Princess?*

"I'm sorry," Cy said.

"Why?" Dr. Z said, taking a step toward Cy. "Why is Cyrus sorry, Rory?" His eyes shifted from Cy to me and back again. His cheeks flushed with anger, and his lips formed a hard line. "Was he dishonest about being involved? You haven't...uh..."

"What? No!" Cy said, clearly shocked at the accusation.

"No," I said, closing my eyes. Dr. Z was the closest thing I had to a father. His even having to ask was embarrassing enough.

"Good," Dr. Z said, taking another step toward Cy. "Or else you would have to worry about more than just Tennison. Let's get you home."

FOURTEEN

WE FLED OUT THE BACK DOOR, conscious of four vehicles coming down Dr. Z's street and following each other closely. The Old River Bridge was on the outskirts of town and at least a half hour drive. Traveling on foot and hiding in the shadows meant it would take us half the night.

I looked at my watch. "What time are you supposed to meet her?"

"By sunrise," Cy said. "Without my *sola*, I can't be sure."

"Do you have a car?" Dr. Z asked.

Cy shook his head. "I only went to your class and the lab. It wasn't practical."

"Uh...Dr. Z? I forgot to tell you. It's about Silver."

Dr. Z's expression compressed. "What about Silver?"

"Can we discuss this later?" Cy asked, clearly irritated.

Dr. Z frowned at me. "We'll talk about it later."

He walked off from me, and Cy raised an eyebrow.

We continued to the Old River Bridge, sticking to the shadows and avoiding the streetlights and any open shops. A helicopter could still be heard in the distance, and I wondered if any of the local news channels had noticed and reported on it yet.

Headlights hovered over the asphalt a mile away, and I dived behind some bushes. Cy gently pushed down Dr. Z's head and helped him to kneel beside me. My socks were marinating in cold rainwater, and my skin felt soggy and raw. Only the knees of my jeans were wet, but the puddle of rainwater was traveling up the backs of the denim, and soon, my pant legs would be completely saturated. Aliens, Xena, fringe departments of the CIA I could handle, but *nothing* was worse than wet clothes.

"Oh, shit," I said, stopping in my tracks.

Cy walked back to me. "What is it?"

"Benji wanted me to meet him outside at seven. What if they took him? What if he's at the warehouse?"

Cy sighed and kept walking. "They didn't take him."

"But what if they did?" I said, chasing after him. "What if they have him, and they're hurting him?"

Cy turned. "How can you be so naive, Rory? He's with them. You heard Ellie."

"She was lying. She does that."

"Why won't you see him for what he is?"

"How did he make Majestic, Cy? Did they recruit him in middle school?"

Cy shook his head. "I'll let him tell you."

"He's not Majestic. I know Benji. He wouldn't hurt me. He wouldn't hurt anybody."

Cy didn't answer, and I began to wonder if I was trying to convince him or myself.

Mud, cold temperature, and brush began to wear on all of us. We'd only been walking for twenty minutes when the professor began to slow his pace. Cy and I tried encouraging him, but the longer we walked, the more he struggled.

"I just…can we rest? Just for a moment," the professor said.

"Just for a moment," Cy said.

Dr. Z leaned against a tree and then slid down to the ground. His breathing was labored.

"Are you all right?" I asked, touching his shoulder.

He chortled. "Not as young as I thought I was." He looked up at Cy. "How old are you?"

Cy smiled. "We have a longer life span. In your years, it would be equivalent to my early twenties."

"What is it in your years?" I asked.

"Our cycle is different. But if I calculated my age in twelve-month cycles, I will turn seventy-five this year."

Dr. Z and I both looked at each other, and Dr. Z smiled. "Well then, I'm not the oldest here."

I made a face. "It's not funny anymore, Cy. What's really going on?"

Cy didn't flinch. "I can understand the skepticism, but you know me. It's all true."

I frowned. "Break's over. Let's go."

We continued through a slice of wooded area next to the highway, hiding when cars passed. It was more grueling than walking along the asphalt, but it was better than getting caught.

"What will happen when we reach the bridge? If she's there?" I asked. My voice sounded small.

Cy didn't answer right away. He cleared his throat. "I'll go with her."

"Will you even say good-bye?"

We walked in silence for a few minutes. It occurred to me to prod him for an answer, but I just couldn't. It seemed trivial with everything else going on. But when Cy stopped, turned, and pulled me into his arms, I was glad I had given him the time he needed. I was melting in his arms while he held me exactly the way he had at the bottom of the steps the day I didn't know I needed him—the first day he walked me to class. Back then, that embrace was letting me know that he was there. Now, it was an apology that he couldn't always be.

"Good-bye," he said quietly. His voice was quiet and sad.

"Even though your story is the craziest load of crap I've ever heard, I'm out here, walking around in the dark, through the mud, with you. I came for you, Cy. We're all probably going to prison. You're just going to get in that ship…and what? Wave and say, 'Thanks for risking your lives for me.'"

"You don't even believe in that ship."

"I believe in you."

"This is not easy for me, if that's what you think."

"Then…let's make it easy." I shrugged, forcing a hopeful smile. "I just don't want to miss anyone else. I know what it's like. It's too hard."

Cy stared into my eyes, every regret and sorrow scrolling across his face. "I will miss you, Rory. I will miss you most of all."

I nodded and then let my arms fall to my thighs. "Okay then."

"If you want to turn around and go home, I would understand," Cy said.

"I don't need you to love me to love you," I said, remembering Benji's words and, for the first time, understanding what they meant. There were so many different kinds of love. I didn't have to love him romantically. I could love him enough to see him home, wherever that was. "You're still my friend. I care about what happens to you, and I'm still going to see this through to the very end."

Before Cy could respond, a familiar engine growled, and I spotted headlights down the road.

A broad smile spanned across my face. "It's Benji!" I said, running toward the road. Relief rushed over me. They hadn't taken him. He was okay.

In the next second, Cy wrapped his arms around mine and lifted me off my feet.

"What are you doing?" I asked, struggling.

"You might trust him, Rory, but I don't."

"But—"

"Shh!" Dr. Z said, ducking behind a bush as Cy pulled me down and covered my mouth.

The Mustang passed slowly. Cy and the professor ducked when they realized Benji had a flashlight and was shining it into the woods.

"Rory!" Benji called in a loud whisper from his orange Mustang.

"He has a car," I said through Cy's hands. "At this rate, we won't make it by Christmas, much less the morning."

Cy shook his head.

I begged Cy with my eyes. "He's worried about me. Please let me let him know I'm okay."

"Rory!" Benji called again. The Mustang passed us, continuing down the road.

Cy let me go, and I sat on the ground, devastated and angry. I wanted to run after Benji, to ask for his help. My gut said that he could be trusted and that he would do anything he could to help.

A tear fell down my cheek, and I wiped it away.

"You should forget him," Cy said. "He'll only hurt you."

"Why are you so threatened by him?" I asked, shaking. "You don't know everything, Cy. You said it yourself. No one knows everything. And I'm telling you, whatever you think you know, you're wrong about him."

"I know that you're attracted to danger. Have you ever thought that maybe that's why you're drawn to Benji? Because he is on the wrong side?"

I stood up, wiping the mud off my hands onto my jeans. Benji was so far from dangerous that I might have laughed if I weren't so offended. "He's on *my* side."

"I'm not arguing with you, Rory. We can't trust him. That's the end of it."

We continued walking, cold and exhausted. My breath puffed out a fleeting white mist with every other step. Dr. Z had been wheezing for the last five or so miles. Cy's encouragements came more often. He stayed at the helm, and the darker the night sky became, the more desperate he became.

When the sky began to show the first signs of daybreak, Cy's encouragements were louder, and he sounded more like a drill sergeant. "We must hurry. No more breaks! It's just over the hill!"

I sighed. The hill was five miles away. "We've got to get on the road, Cy! It will be so much faster."

Cy thought a moment and then nodded. "Agreed. Let's go! Let's go!"

The sky began to turn colors. Cy was a good quarter mile in front of me, and Dr. Z was farther behind me than that.

Cy turned back, and I waved him on. "It's okay! Go! We'll catch up!"

A low, throbbing sound came from the other side of the hill. Cy seemed to recognize it and took off in a sprint, more than a sprint. He seemed to have switched on the nitro and surged ahead. A few moments later, he disappeared over the hill. I picked up the pace, afraid that he would see Apolonia and leave before I could see him one last time. Dr. Z was falling farther behind.

"Hurry!" I called to him, but my voice was drowned out by the pulsating noise.

Just before I reached the peak of the hill, Benji's Mustang appeared from the other direction, stopping abruptly the second he saw me. The roaring thrum was so loud I couldn't hear him coming.

Benji jumped out, ran around the front of his car, and wrapped his arms around me as he crashed into me.

"Christ, Rory!" he yelled over the noise. "You're freezing!" He yanked off his coat and draped it around me. "Are you okay? I've been looking everywhere for you!"

I had two fistfuls of his shirt, burying my face in his chest. "I'm so sorry I didn't call you!"

He held me at arm's length to look me over. "You're covered in mud. What the heck have you been doing?"

"I…" I looked in his eyes. He wasn't waiting for me to give away all my secrets. He was genuinely confused and concerned. I had trusted Cy more than once during this crazy night. It was his turn to trust me. "How did you know to look for me here?" I was yelling close to his face like we were in a dance club. The pulsing noise was so loud that it seemed to drown out everything else, even my thoughts.

Benji glanced at the hill and then back at me. "Because that's where everyone else is."

"What?" I said, pushing away from him to run to the top of the hill.

Military vehicles were surrounding a large craft, every curve of its hull smooth but not shiny. Strange symbols spanned a quarter of its length, and the light coming from its underbelly seemed to glow from its casing. It was hovering just a couple of feet off the ground over the remnant foundation of the old gas station on the far side of the bridge.

"It's the *Nayara*," I breathed.

"The what?" Benji asked.

"Her ship," I said, trying to swallow the lump in my throat. There was no denying it now.

The *Nayara* had come to take Cy away. He would board her, and I'd never see him again.

"Whose ship?" Benji asked.

Dozens of soldiers had encircled the craft, most pointing their automatic rifles. Others were pointing Geiger counters or video cameras.

"It's been there for over an hour, just sitting there. I looked for you all night. When I couldn't find you and you didn't answer your phone, I figured you were...with Cyrus."

I turned to him, a little offended. "Seriously? You thought I'd just hop off your floor and get into Cy's bed?"

Benji looked ashamed. "I couldn't sleep, so I went for a run to blow off some steam. It passed right over me, and then I saw the Humvees heading this way. I ran back to my car and drove this way, thinking there would be a roadblock or checkpoint or something."

"Are there any?"

"A few orange-and-white barricades, but no one is manning them. I just drove around them. It looks as though they called everyone to the site once the movement started."

I glanced down, looking for Cy. I didn't see him, but I did see the man with crocodile boots standing in the middle of it all. No gun. No camera. Just staring at the ship with his hands on his hips.

"I don't know. I just had a feeling you'd be here."

"Benji," I said, looking up at him, "can I trust you? I mean, *really* trust you?"

His eyebrows pulled in. "Of course you can."

I hugged him tightly. "Thank you," I whispered, just as Dr. Z jogged the rest of the way to where we stood.

Another loud sound filled the air as I caught movement out of the corner of my eye. It sounded like a dubstep foghorn. My hands automatically covered my ears to protect them. The noise was deafening.

The ship was lifting slowly into the air, and an LED-like glow lit up the edges of the ship. The *Nayara* was powering up. My ears were ringing. Benji and Dr. Z were tugging at their earlobes and moving their jaws around, too.

The sight was breathtaking. The lights and lithe movement of the ship were unlike anything I'd ever seen. It wasn't hovering clumsily as it lifted away from the ground, like one of our clunky mechanical crafts. No sound of an engine, just the pulsing of an electrical source. No scorch marks on the ground.

"Sweet zombie Jesus, I'm looking right at it and still don't believe it."

"Incredible, isn't it?" Benji said, keeping one arm around my shoulders, rubbing his hand up and down my arm, trying to warm me up.

Another sound, this one familiar, was muffled by the ship. Cy was running toward the huge craft, waving his arms, screaming, "Apolonia! Stop! Apolonia!"

Just as he said her name the second time, the ship pulsed for just a second, like the breath taken before a scream. In the next moment, gun-like barrels fired from the ship at the vehicles and soldiers. The sound and heat penetrated my bones, even a quarter of a mile away. Benji and I were pushed backward. I covered my face. Benji covered me. Bullets weren't coming from the gun-like barrels protruding from the front and sides of the ship. They looked more like fire in gel capsules. The capsules exploded on contact, but they also spread, igniting everything they touched. The fluid didn't splatter though. It jumped.

"Incredible," Dr. Z said, the scientist in him captivated.

The men scattered and then began firing back. The ship gracefully rocked back and forth as the capsules rained down on everything. Cy stood on the edge of the woods, waving his arms, his screams silent.

"C'mon!" I yelled, pushing out of Benji's arms. "Take me across the bridge, Benji!"

"Rory, that's crazy! You'll get yourself killed!"

I opened the passenger door. "Cy is going to die if we don't, and if he dies, we'll *all* die."

"Wait. Seriously?" Benji said as Dr. Z and I crawled into his car.

"Let's go!" I screamed.

Benji scrambled into the driver's seat and turned the Mustang in a perfect doughnut in the road, tires squealing, and then he stomped on the gas, racing toward the chaos.

Apolonia's ship lifted higher into the sky, still targeting the soldiers and vehicles on the ground. The pulses coming from the ship were rattling Benji's car. I clicked my seat belt and steadied myself with both palms on the dashboard.

Cy was far enough away from the mayhem but still waving his arms. She was blowing up everything. The surrounding trees were ablaze, and almost all the military vehicles were incinerated. He was right. Apolonia was emotional. He hadn't shown up at the correct time, so she was going to punish those who had come in his place.

"This is insane!" Benji said.

"Yes, but it's important! Go!"

Benji jerked the wheel left, turning the Mustang off the road and into the grass. We sped over the uneven ground, stopping less than one hundred yards from the burning woods. I reached for the door handle, but Benji grabbed my arm.

"What are you going to do?" he asked, panicked.

"I'm going to get him out of there! He won't leave until he's in that ship or until he gets himself killed!"

Without waiting for a reply or permission, I jumped out of the car and immediately broke into a sprint, running toward Cy. He was still waving both arms toward the sky, hoping Apolonia would see him. Fire blazed all around us. We didn't have much time.

Crocodile Boots had gotten inside the last remaining Jeep, but it was spinning its wheels, centered over bodies and the wreckage of another vehicle. The *Nayara* suddenly turned all her guns on his struggling Jeep.

Cy saw what was about to happen and ran to stand between Crocodile's vehicle and the *Nayara*.

"Apolonia! I'm here! Stop this!" Cy said. He took another deep breath and yelled something long and beautiful in what had to be his native language.

Just as the *Nayara* powered up to fire, silence fell. No pulsing, no foghorn, just the flickering and popping of the burning vehicles and earth around us. The ship lowered to the ground.

A door opened. Cy didn't hesitate. He bolted for the opening and disappeared inside.

The man in the crocodile boots stepped out of the Jeep, took off his belt, and threw it into the *Nayara*. It wasn't until it disappeared that I realized what it was—a grenade belt.

"Cy!" I screamed.

Crocodile Boots wrapped his arms around mine, barely struggling to keep me in his grasp. He watched and waited, and then he smiled when the front of the ship exploded, sending it to the ground on its side.

The earth cratered under the *Nayara's* weight, and the ship pushed a massive mound of dirt in our direction. Crocodile Boots didn't move. He just watched as the huge craft barreled toward us.

The *Nayara* came to a rest, lying lifeless on the other side of the mound of dirt that had stopped just a few yards from the toes of my boots. Her underbelly was no longer glowing, and a gaping hole exposed her insides.

"Easy now," Crocodile Boots said in a raspy voice. A toothpick bounced between his lips as he spoke. His shoulders were broad, and his smile was just as sleazy and cheap as his suit.

The five soldiers in the Jeep jumped to the ground and surrounded us. Their AK-47s were pointed at *Nayara's* wound.

"Should we proceed, Dr. Rendlesham, sir?" one of the soldiers asked. He was speaking to Crocodile Boots.

He has a name after all.

"Inside. We just want Cy. Kill everything else."

"No!" I said, fighting him with every step.

Finally, he threw me to the ground and straddled my hips. He gripped my wrists and held them against the dirt. A piece of steel was lying beneath my left arm, and it dug into my skin.

Unable to move, feeling sharp metal slicing through my skin, I was in our hotel room again. Sydney was crying in the bathroom, and my mother's eyes were staring into mine. They were bloodshot, and the skin around them was wet and smeared with mascara. Blood was dripping from the wounds in her skull from where they'd nearly beaten her to death with the telephone.

You're not alone, her eyes had said.

I'd managed a muffled, "It's not your fault," from behind the dirty rag tied across my mouth.

I wish I had told her then that I would come back. I would come back, so I could stop this idiot piece of shit sitting on top of me from destroying the world.

Rendlesham's disgusting voice brought me back to the present. "You're quite the pain in the ass, Rory. More than one little girl should be."

The more I struggled, the more the twisted steel cut into my forearm, but I ignored it and smiled. "I'm not finished yet."

"Oh, you are. You're finished all right," he said, leaning into my face. When he spoke, spittle dropped from his mouth and landed just under my eye.

Suddenly, Rendlesham was tackled from the side and knocked to the ground. I scrambled to my feet. Benji was holding Rendlesham to the ground, and the soldiers were trying to decide if they should open fire.

"Run, Rory!" he yelled, struggling.

Conflicted, I took a step toward Benji. He was going to get himself killed.

"Get the hell out of here!" he yelled again.

I turned on my heels and climbed the dirt hill. One of the soldiers grabbed for my ankle, but I kicked him in the face and kept climbing.

"Shoot her, idiots!" Rendlesham said.

"No!" Benji screamed.

A few bullets hit the dirt beside me before I rolled over the top of the mound and then scrambled into the hole of the hull. Stripped sharp pieces of charred metal scraped my legs and arms as I crawled along the wreckage, but the soldiers were already over the hill and shooting at me.

Farther inside, I tripped and stumbled through the darkness. I could see the beams of flashlights shining on the walls of the ship several yards behind me. They were inside. It was my first instinct to find someplace safe to hide, but hiding wouldn't help me find Cy. If he was still alive, he was probably critically injured and needed help. I had to keep going until I found him.

"Cy?" I half-whispered, half-yelled. I crawled on my hands and knees, feeling in front of me, hoping to come across the door Cy entered. He couldn't be far from it. "Cyrus!"

Within moments, I was in a narrow corridor. My hand landed in something cold and slimy. Hard bits also rolled around on my fingers. I reached out farther, and I felt a sharp edge and then a nose and a chin.

"Oh Christ. Please, no," I said, my hands trembling.

FIFTEEN

I YANKED MY HAND BACK.

"Cy?" I said, my eyes filling with tears.

I felt over the rest of the body. The clothes were slick and tight-fitting, not at all like Cy's jeans and shirt. What was left of the hair was very short and spiky, different from Cy's soft waves and curls. Exhausted in every way possible, my body collapsed against the wall, and I cried quietly, covering my face with my clean hand. It wasn't him. Cy could still be alive.

After a few minutes, I wiped my hand on my jeans and my nose on my shirt. I hadn't felt that alone in a very long time. Cy was hurt somewhere in a strange ship, and Benji was outside, either captured or dead.

Tears spilled down my cheeks. I'd left him there to die. I should have stayed with him. Instead, I ran away like a coward. *How am I going to save anyone?* I wasn't even brave enough to get into a fucking elevator.

Once my eyes adjusted, a faint red light at the end of the hallway caught my eye. I crawled toward it, over more slick-clothed bodies, through more sticky blood, and what felt like guts and bone. The red light led me to a larger room with connected desks, chairs, and darkened monitors. Maybe a control room or bridge. I wasn't exactly familiar with spaceships.

"Cy?" I called out just loud enough for someone close to hear, hoping I hadn't missed his body in the black corridor. I stood up. My entire body complained. My arm was covered in warm blood—my own. The rest of me was covered in the blood of others.

I leaned against a desk, beyond exhausted. I had wandered too far away from the point of the explosion. It wasn't likely that Cy had gotten this far inside the ship in that amount of time. Rendlesham and the soldiers might have already captured him. Maybe they'd captured Dr. Z, too. I was alone in a dark busted ship, tripping over dead bodies. I couldn't imagine how I would come out of this one on top or how, if Apolonia and Cy were dead, we would be able to stop Tennison and Rendlesham from activating the parasites.

An unfamiliar smooth voice speaking an unfamiliar language whispered something menacing in the dark, and then a familiar voice spoke back in warning.

I turned, seeing Cy and his betrothed. Apolonia was holding a sword to my throat. She was breathtaking. Her skin was a bit lighter than Cy's, and her long black hair fell in soft waves to her elbows. It was propped up somehow from the underside and then left to cascade over like a waterfall. She had two thick braids running across the top of her head and a heavy red stripe running across both of her eyes and nose, from temple to temple, making her pale blue eyes—that were just a few shades away from white— look even brighter. Her curve-hugging crimson uniform didn't leave much to the imagination, showing her toned shoulders, arms, and abs, and she was almost as tall as Cy. She looked both futuristic and savage.

She could be in a workout commercial or a hair commercial or a lipstick commercial, I thought as I noticed her shimmering plump lips. *My day just got much worse.*

"Don't make any sudden movements," Cy said.

"Don't worry. I won't," I said, slowly holding up my hands.

"You don't have to do that," he said and then spoke something to her.

She answered.

"English, please," Cy said to her.

"English feels unpleasant in my mouth," she replied. She spoke my language but awkwardly and with a severe accent. It made her seem less frightening even though she was looking at me like she wanted to take my life.

"Put down your weapon, Apolonia," Cy commanded. He spoke much harsher than he had ever spoken to me.

She obeyed but remained in a defensive stance.

I wanted to hug him, but I was afraid to. She could cut me in half at any moment.

"I'm so glad you're okay," I said. Every muscle in my body seemed to relax at the same time.

Apolonia muttered something in their native tongue. Cy reprimanded her. It was then that Apolonia pulled Cy's arm around her neck, and I saw that his leg was bleeding. No wonder she was unhappy with my comment. He wasn't okay at all.

"What did you come across on your way here?" Cy asked.

"A lot of dead bodies," I said before swallowing.

"We need to get you out of here and cleaned up, and I—" Cy stopped mid-sentence, let Apolonia go, and then limped over to me, pushing me to the floor. "Hide. Under here." He directed me under the desk. "Don't come out, no matter what. Understand?"

"But—"

"Just listen this once, Rory! Don't come out until I say otherwise."

I nodded and then sat still as I heard him grunt and groan as they turned to flee. A dozen pairs of footsteps were trying to be quiet and failing as boots pulled at the sticky blood in the hallway. The sounds grew louder as they approached our location. I sank back into the leg space of the desk as they entered the room just before Cy and Apolonia were able to escape.

"Cyrus," Dr. Rendlesham said, delighted, "who's your friend?"

"Stay back," Cy said.

I leaned up, peeking over the desk. Cy was standing in front of Apolonia, his palms out. Apolonia wasn't cowering. She stood, her feet shoulder width apart and both of her arms at her side. Her chin was down, and she was staring at the soldiers from under her brow. Her ice-blue eyes glistened, even in the dim red light.

Holy shit, she is intimidating.

"Doctor, call off your men. She will kill them. And you."

Dr. Rendlesham wasn't fazed. He chuckled and then called for backup into a small mic on his wrist. "We have five AKs trained on her, son. In about thirty seconds, it will be twenty. You should be telling her to stand down, not the other way around."

Cy warned Apolonia in their language, clearly begging her to be patient. Then, he spoke to Rendlesham again, "I'm asking for the lives of your men, Doctor. Have them lower their weapons. Let them go home to their families."

One of the soldiers laughed once.

Rendlesham shook his head. "I'm giving you one more chance, Cyrus. Have her surrender the sword, or one of my men will blow her head off."

"No. They won't," Cy said. He looked at the soldiers. "Please understand. The only reason any of her crew is dead is because of the explosion or impact. They're highly trained warriors. You're no match for her. I know you have kids waiting on you at home." He took a step. "She is lethal. You don't even have to put down your weapons. Just back away and leave her ship. She's already angry that you—"

"Enough," Rendlesham said. "Take the shot, Smith."

One of the soldiers lifted his gun, but he hesitated.

"No! Don't!" Cy said, simultaneously holding out his hand and taking a step.

Smith aimed at Cy and pulled the trigger. My scream was obscured by the echoing blast of the gun.

Cy looked down, seeing a smoking hole in his right shoulder. He fell to his knees and then onto his side. The entire room fell silent. My hands covered my mouth.

Apolonia watched Cy fall to the ground and then looked at the group of soldiers before her. Her eyes were no longer a pale blue. Her pupils dilated until her irises were onyx, and the blackness bled into the whites until they appeared to have been replaced with two balls of polished granite. She crouched slowly as she pulled her sword before her.

The soldiers backed away a fraction of an inch and positioned their weapons.

"Fire!" Rendlesham commanded.

"No!" I screamed.

The bullets left the chamber, and Apolonia spun, matching their speed. Her sword deflected the bullets, sending them back. Four of the soldiers fell, and she head-butted the fifth, sending him to the ground. Once he was on his back, she shoved her sword into his chest with a quick twist. His screams were instantly cut off.

Rendlesham stumbled back, but more footsteps were rumbling in the hallway. Two dozen soldiers filled the room and surrounded her. The corners of her mouth turned up into a devilish grin, and then she taunted them with words I didn't understand.

"Sir?" one of the soldiers said hesitantly.

Her eyes lacked compassion or fear. Her flawlessness revealed that she wasn't human, but her eyes exposed her inhumanity. I didn't imagine any of these men wanted to spar with her. That much beauty with that much malevolence was unsettling.

"Kill her, goddamn it!" Rendlesham barked.

Deafening blasts filled the room, and I fell to the ground, unwilling to witness Apolonia's death. Bullets bounced off every wall, sometimes ricocheting off the front of the desk I was using as shelter. My hands flew to my ears, and I yelled against the noise. It was the only way I could block out the soldiers' horrific screaming.

The rounds of bullets came less often with every soldier's cry. I leaned up, and Cy's betrothed was a blur of turns, thrusts, flips, and slashes. Within minutes, she was the only one left standing among at least twenty-five bodies.

I ducked back under the desk. I was afraid of no man, but Apolonia wasn't a man. She wasn't even a woman. She was death encapsulated in perfection—a frightening thing to behold.

Benji suddenly came into view. I was so glad that he was okay, and I wanted to hold him so much that my entire body literally pulled an inch or two in his direction. He was on his knees in the mouth of the hallway, desperately waving at me to crawl the fifteen or so feet to him. I waved him back, hoping he'd save himself.

C'mon, he mouthed.

I shook my head, waving him away again.

He stretched his neck to try to see around the desk, and then with his jaw set, he crawled over to me. I shook my head faster. As soon as he was within reaching distance, he lunged at me, pulling me tightly into his arms.

"I thought you were dead!" he whispered, half-laughing, half-puffing.

"You are so stupid!" I hissed. "She's going to kill you!" I shouldn't have asked him to risk his life—again—but I didn't let him go. I couldn't.

Benji cupped my face. "I said I'd follow you anywhere."

I covered his hands with mine and then offered an apologetic small smile, but when I heard the sloshing of Apolonia's feet through the blood of the soldiers, I put my hand on his chest and pushed Benji back against the desk next to me.

Apolonia kneeled beside me, her face just inches from my cheek, but I didn't dare look at her or her freaky-ass black eyes.

She spoke something beautiful but frightening.

"Just don't hurt him," I said. Accepting that she would use her sword to slice through me, I closed my eyes. Just because I would come back didn't mean it wouldn't hurt. I wasn't exactly sure I could come back after being cut in half anyway.

"Stand. Up," she said, clearly annoyed.

I did as she demanded and brought Benji with me, but I stood in front of him.

"What are you doing?" Benji asked, trying to trade places with me.

"Stop moving!" I said, my voice breaking. I was sure at any moment she was going to decapitate him.

Apolonia's eyes were blue again, and she rolled them at us. "I will not hurt you. Cyrus would not like it." She turned, pointing her sword at the dark hall. "Is he with you?" she asked.

Dr. Z sheepishly stepped out of the hallway.

My shoulders fell. "Yes," I said, smiling at my professor.

"You look terrible," Dr. Z said. "Glad to see you're alive."

Apolonia left us, stepping over bodies to reach Cy.

I hurried over to him as fast as I could limp. I'd hurt my leg somehow, and with every step, the pain got worse. "Cy! Are you all right?"

He groaned. "No."

"Oh, for fuck's sake, I thought you were dead!" I said.

Apolonia glared at me as I helped her help Cy to his feet.

"My injuries are the least of our problems. We need to"—he growled as we stood him up—"get the specimen and get Apolonia out of here. If she doesn't make contact with her father soon, he will end the world before the parasites can."

"What does that mean?" Benji asked, frowning.

Cy took one look at Benji and then glared at me. "What is he doing here?"

"He's helping," I said. If Benji didn't have Cy's protection, Apolonia would waste no time relieving him of his head. I got the feeling she didn't care for humans. Any of us.

"How did he know you were here? You know we can't trust him!" Cy said.

"He was looking for me. He saw the *Nayara* this morning while he was running. She's sort of hard to miss."

"He just happened to be running before dawn?" Cy said, snarling at Benji.

"He always runs in the mornings! Would you please trust me for once?"

Cy locked his eyes on Benji. "I know what you're up to. If you do anything to get either of these women hurt, I will kill you myself."

Benji looked at me, confused and hesitant to respond. "I would never do anything to hurt Rory. She's more important to me than she is to you."

"Why is that?" Cy seethed.

"Because I…that's none of your business."

"Rory is my business," Cy said.

"As flattering as this is," I said, "we have shit to do. Let's get Cy stitched up."

Cy and Benji stared each other down until Apolonia tightened her grip on Cy. "Agreed. We should move. Check for survivors," she said.

Apolonia left for a moment, and then the bridge was lit with something other than a red emergency light. She returned and sat Cy down on a chair, directing Dr. Z to stay with him. Then, Benji and I went with her to check the bodies in the hallway. Every time we couldn't find signs of life, Apolonia became more and more angry. After the sixteenth body, I was beginning to feel afraid to be around her. We reached the breach in the hull and saw that Rendlesham's Jeep was gone.

A flicker of silver caught my attention, and I turned to see a woman lying next to the torn hull. She wore the same uniform as Apolonia but in gray, and she was speaking in Cy's language. Her skin was golden brown like Cy's, but her irises were black, contrasting the light paint forming a rectangle across her eyes from one temple to the other. Her pixie-length silver hair was what had caught my attention. I could see that her side was hung up on mangled metal.

"Apolonia! Here! She's alive!"

In the next moment, Apolonia was at the young woman's side, cupping her face, speaking comforting words.

"I hope she makes it," Benji said. "If not, Apolonia might stab one of us just to make herself feel better."

The young woman grinned at me. Her teeth were red, covered in her thick blood. "English. I can speak your English."

"What can I do?" I asked.

Apolonia spoke to her, and the woman nodded. It didn't look like a pleasant conversation. Before I understood what was happening, Apolonia slid her sword into the holster strapped to her back. Then, she took the woman's legs in one arm and her neck in the other, and in one quick move, Apolonia lifted her straight up off the debris that had impaled her. The woman didn't scream or cry out. She just held her breath.

"Holy shit," Benji said, staring at Apolonia with the woman in her arms.

I was thinking the same thing. The young woman wasn't many years away from being a girl, and she had already displayed an intense amount of bravery and self-control that I had only seen once before—in myself.

"Come," Apolonia said. She carried the young woman back to the bridge.

"Where are Cy and Dr. Z?" I asked, panic welling up in my throat when I didn't seem them where we left them.

"They must have made their way to the…" Apolonia looked to the woman in her arms. "*Shehaucht.*"

"*Shehaucht*…erm…in…infirmary," the woman said.

For the first time, I saw Apolonia flash a nonthreatening smile. "Cy has shown Dr. Z the way to the infirmary. It is forward."

We entered an all-white room, every surface made of the same strange cloth-like material. Even the walls, floors, and small surgical tables and beds were composed of this gauze-cheesecloth combination. I assumed it was to keep the room sterile.

It was brightly lit but not so much that I needed to squint. I glanced up at the ceiling but couldn't find the source. There were no bulbs, no lamps. Everything seemed to glow from the soft natural light, giving me a strange dreamlike sensation. It was a bit unsettling—the bright yet forgiving lighting—and even more so when I realized that every item in the room was clear, as if I had on X-ray, high-definition glasses.

Benji smiled at the sight of Dr. Z tending to Cy's wounds.

Apolonia carefully placed her comrade on a bed that looked more like a large rectangular table, two over from where Cy was lying. She wasted no time pulling out trays and equipment.

"Is she a doctor, too?" I asked Cy.

"No," Apolonia answered. "Tsavi is the doctor," she said, nodding to the woman.

Tsavi was bleeding from her ears, too. I wasn't sure about alien anatomy, but they looked human, and I imagined that bleeding from the ears wasn't a good sign for them either.

Cy called out, prompting Apolonia to rush to his side. My stomach tensed, and my cheeks flushed, but it wasn't jealousy.

It was that I couldn't bear losing someone else. It was too much to stomach—that, and so much blood. I hadn't seen that much blood since—

My eyes felt heavy as I placed my hand on the nearest bed to steady myself.

"Rory?" Benji said.

"Is she okay?" Cy asked.

Benji forced me to look at him as he pulled down the skin under my eyes a bit. "I don't know. Rory?" He began checking me over, looking for any signs of injuries.

My mouth wouldn't work. I was too tired to respond, too deep in sadness.

"She's bleeding!" Benji said.

My feet left the ground, and then I was lying flat on the table next to Tsavi.

"Help her," Cy said, his voice sounding as weak as I felt.

I thought he said it again. Although, I wasn't sure since he spoke in his native language.

I turned my head and stared into his beautiful golden eyes. He always had a calming effect on me, even when I hated him. He was dirty, covered in grease, soot, and blood, but he was still beautiful. *Like my mother just before she died.*

"I'll be okay," I said although it was too quiet for anyone but Cy to hear.

He reached out for me, and I mustered up the last of my strength to lift my hand to touch his fingertips.

A ripping noise above drew my attention. Benji was pulling gently on my arm, assessing my wound. The light shining from behind his head nearly blacked out his face, but I could still see his sweet smile.

"I'm not going to let anything happen to you, Rory. I promise."

SIXTEEN

MY EYES OPENED and blinked a few times. It wasn't a surprise. I'd come back from much worse. It wasn't even a shock to find myself in the bright white infirmary of a spaceship. But it was a surprise to see Benji Reynolds leaning over me, resting his head on my bed. He'd stayed with me, sitting on a weird-looking but clearly uncomfortable stool, sleeping hunched over, not wanting to even go as far as the next table over.

His fingers were resting over mine. His breathing was slow, deep, and relaxed. He looked so peaceful.

Tsavi.

Cy.

I lifted my head and looked around. Aside from mine, the tables were clean and empty, as if the other two patients had never been there. I was wearing a light-blue shirt and pants I didn't recognize. The fabric was incredibly soft.

"What the hell are these?" I asked. "Alien pajamas?"

Benji lifted his head and blinked, trying to focus. "Oh, thank God you're okay."

"What happened?" I asked, supporting myself with my elbows.

Benji rubbed his eyes with one hand and rested the other on my arm. "You had a significant laceration in one arm and a bullet hole in your thigh. It was clean. Exit wound."

I looked down. "It doesn't hurt."

"Apolonia did something. She had this little..." He was trying to draw it in the air. "Anyway, you don't even have a scar. Lost a lot of blood though." He frowned. "I should have caught it. I was sitting right next to you and didn't even notice you were wounded."

"Don't be too hard on yourself," I said, grunting as he helped me sit up. "Neither did I."

"I don't know what the hell is going on. I'm just glad you're okay."

He touched my cheek, and I heard Cy clear his throat. He was standing in the doorway with Dr. Z just behind him.

"Glad to see you're still among the living," Cy said, walking into the room.

"You, too," I said, looking past him. "Where's Tsavi?"

"Here," she said, walking around Dr. Z in the same clothes as me. "You humans are not as fragile as I thought you would be."

"You're not as green as I thought you'd be," I said with a tired smile.

Benji helped me off the table, and Cy hurried over to help as well.

"I've got her," Benji said.

"I see that," Cy grumbled, and then he hugged me. "I was worried for a bit."

"You shouldn't have been. I've told you a million times—"

"And I've told you once, you're not invincible, Rory. Lucky but not invincible."

"I don't know," Tsavi said. "Judging from the extent of the scars she has, I would say she has survived many wars."

Instinctively, I crossed my arms, first over my chest and then my stomach. It felt like a violation. My scars revealed my past, and the only way I controlled that night was to keep it hidden. I'd only allowed a few people to witness some of my scars but never all of them.

I looked up at Benji, and he offered an understanding small smile. He'd seen them.

"I would not call it luck," Apolonia said, frowning. "We should get going. *Nayara's* communication systems are not functional. Once Hamech learns of the crash, he will burn everything he crosses until he finds me. We should already be on our way. You let her sleep too long."

"She needed it," Tsavi said. "Can you walk?"

I let go of Benji. "Can you? Last I saw, you had a head injury."

Tsavi smiled. "It would take more than that to slow me down. Apolonia should have been a doctor."

Apolonia offered a small smile. "Then, I would not have been given *Nayara*." She touched a wall and looked up, her expression sad.

"When we make contact with your father, we'll retrieve her, but right now, we need to find a way to reach him," Cy said.

"What?" Benji said. "Like a broadcast system? There's a radio station on campus."

"Too risky," Dr. Z said. "If Rendlesham starts shooting at us again, we don't want an innocent student to get in the way."

"It's still break. There won't be many people left on campus," Benji said.

"Still too risky," Cy said, looking sheepishly at me. "We've already involved one student too many."

"Amen," Benji said.

"You involved yourself," Cy snapped.

"And I'd do it again," Benji snapped back without hesitation.

"And why is that?" Cy asked. No one missed his accusatory tone.

"What are you getting at? Why don't you just ask me whatever it is you think you know?" Benji asked.

"How do you just happen to be everywhere at the right time? The fact that you have attached yourself to Rory is questionable in itself. You're not even remotely her type. You look like the kind that would be chasing Ellie Jones or Laila Dixon."

I frowned at Cy. "Laila Dixon? From administration?"

Cy shrugged. "She's more Benji's type, voluptuous and oblivious."

Benji took a step toward Cy. Apolonia took a step toward Benji.

"How would you even know my type?" Benji asked in a controlled but defensive tone. "I'm sure you don't mean to say *I'm* the suspicious one. You've been lying to Rory since you met her!"

That seemed to infuriate Cy more than I'd ever seen. "And what's your truth?" he said through his teeth.

"I haven't lied to her," Benji said.

"What have you omitted?" Cy said, unyielding.

"Omitted? Let's talk about omission. You don't lie? Please. Not being honest *is* lying, Cyrus. Don't fool yourself."

Cy's jaw worked under his skin. "I haven't lied to you. But he"—he pointed at Benji—"hasn't told you who he really is. Tell her, Benji, or I will."

The line between Benji's eyebrows deepened. He was clearly troubled by Cy's threat. He looked to me, trying to find the words to say next.

His expression made me nervous, even more so than Cy's threat.

"I've tried to tell him that we can trust you," I said. When Benji didn't return my smile, I paused. "You said I could trust you. You meant it…right?"

Benji struggled for a response.

"Benji?" I asked, leaning down until we were eye-to-eye.

"I didn't want to lie to you," he said, reaching for me. I took a step back. "If you'd asked, I would have told you. I swear, I've tried. I kept waiting to find the right time, and then there just wasn't a right time."

No matter how many breaths I took, the air couldn't satisfy my lungs.

Benji looked desperate. "If you remember our conversation at the café, I was working up to it. I wanted you to know, but how could I tell you? You wouldn't have believed me, not until you knew the truth about Cy."

"Who are you?" I asked.

Benji opened his mouth to speak, but nothing came out. He shook his head. "I don't want you to hate me."

Cy spoke, "He's Benji Reynolds, son of Agent Frank Reynolds, chief intelligence officer for Majestic Twelve."

I looked at Benji, my mouth gaping open.

Benji took a step toward me. "Rory, just let me explain."

"Tell me it's not true. That's the only thing I want to hear from you right now."

Benji looked up at me. "It's true."

I stepped back, physically evading the truth. "So, you were a plant, just like Ellie? I was your target?"

Dr. Z was immediately next to me, holding my arm. He always knew what I needed. And right now, I needed not to fall onto my knees in shock.

Benji came to my other side, but I pushed him away. "I knew what Cyrus was. Even before that, I knew Majestic was watching Dr. Zorba. I know this looks bad—really, really bad—but I wasn't using you, Rory, I swear. Dad said he wanted me to watch out for your safety. Heck, *I* wanted to watch out for your safety. And by the time I knew what Majestic really wanted, it was too late. I'd already made a decision by then."

"We do not have time for this," Apolonia said, crossing her arms over her stomach.

"No, we don't," Cy said, reaching out for me. "C'mon, Rory."

"What kind of decision?" I asked, facing Benji.

Benji shrugged, as if it should have been obvious. "That I was in love with you."

Dr. Z watched for my reaction. "If you recall, Rory, Ellie also said that there was one member of Majestic who couldn't stay away from you."

"Well, Ellie was right about that." Benji lowered his chin, staring me straight in the eyes. "Look at me, Rory. You have to know. All I've ever wanted was to keep you safe."

Tsavi grinned. Cy looked as if he wanted to end Benji's life, and Apolonia looked impatient.

"Rory," Cy said, bending his fingers a few times, asking me to come to him.

"What was too late?" I asked.

Benji took a few steps toward me and then cupped my shoulders. Purplish half-moons under his dim brown eyes revealed just how sleep deprived he was from looking for me the night before and from watching over me on the infirmary table. His shirt was wrinkled, and his hair was tousled. "It was too late for them to convince me to help them because whatever side you were on was where I wanted to be."

I fell into his arms, and he pressed his cheek against my hair, squeezing me tightly against him.

"I knew they were coming for the rock. That's why I wanted to get you away from there before dinner. I was going to try to get you both out before they came. But I've had to plan every move carefully, Rory. I couldn't help you if I didn't have inside information. I wanted to tell you everything. It just had to be the right time."

Cy laughed once and then turned around to face me, his fingers laced on top of his head. "He can't go with us, Rory. We *can't* trust him. He's Majestic!"

My mouth formed a hard line. I understood this was important to Cy. Everyone in that room had a lot at stake, but Cy didn't know Benji like I did. "Do you trust me?"

Cy's eyes bounced between me, Benji, Dr. Z, and finally, Apolonia. Her eyebrows moved infinitesimally toward each other. Cy took a breath and looked at me again. "Do *you* trust you?"

I reached for Benji's arm, and he moved toward me. "He wouldn't do anything to hurt me, Cy. I believe that."

"It's settled then," Tsavi said. "They'll return any moment, this time with more men, and we have to make contact with Hamech."

"Be mindful of the fallen crew," Apolonia said. "We will retrieve them and take them home to their families."

With glossy eyes and a small smile, Tsavi spoke, "They died an honorable death. Hamech will give them grand *Kahtpech* funerals." She watched Apolonia for a moment and then went into the other room before quickly returning with short, thin robes for Dr. Z and me.

Dr. Z thanked her and then put his on. There was no zipper, but the front seamlessly joined together as if by magnets.

Dr. Z's eyes widened, and he smiled at Tsavi. "It's very warm, thank you."

"My pleasure."

Cy smiled at Tsavi. He appreciated his people being kind to humans, and Tsavi seemed to like us. The feeling was mutual. She seemed more…human—at least more so than Apolonia. Knowing Cy, I couldn't imagine what made him fall in love with such a dry, emotionless, and angry person. He once called her emotional. I couldn't disagree more. From what I'd witnessed, it was unclear if she even had a soul. Cy was a warm, kind being. He begged the soldiers—men who were out to harm all of us—not to engage his betrothed, so we wouldn't have a massacre on our hands. *How can he love such a monster?*

Apolonia walked to a door and tapped her finger on a rectangle full of strange symbols. They lit when her finger made contact, and when the door slid behind the wall, a closet full of weapons was exposed.

"What are you doing?" Cy asked.

Apolonia threw a small palm-sized weapon to Tsavi. It looked like the rubber grip on a bicycle but solid.

"We need weapons, Cyrus," Apolonia answered.

"We can't continue harming the humans. We have you and your sword. That's all we need."

Apolonia touched Cy's face tenderly, but her expression still seemed emotionless. "I have already lost so many. I can't leave Tsavi defenseless."

Cy nodded and turned to Tsavi. "Try not to kill anyone."

Tsavi smiled. "Of course."

Cy and Apolonia led the way out of the ship, followed closely by Tsavi and Dr. Z. Benji and I straggled behind. He helped me over bodies and wreckage even though my wounds were healed.

Other than fatigue, I felt fine, but I let him worry about me anyway.

Finally, daylight hit my face. The cold air hit me at the same time, and my next breath came out in a cloud of white mist. My eyes squinted, and I lifted my hand, shielding my face from the morning sun. Benji pulled the robe from my other hand and held it up.

"Dr. Zorba called this warm. It's a millimeter thick and has no liner."

"I guess we'll see," I said, slipping my arms into the sleeves. The front melded together, and instantly, the cold dissipated from my body. "The fabric must include some special form of technology. It's better than my goose-down coat."

"And all this time, I thought you didn't own a coat," Benji said with a teasing smile and a wink.

We climbed down from the *Nayara* and over the mound of dirt the ship had excavated during its crash landing. The wreckage and debris from the battle were still smoking.

"Where are the fire trucks?" I asked. "The police?"

"Rendlesham has quarantined this area, I'm sure," Cy said.

I strained to see the top of the hill we came over. "I wonder if those roadblocks are manned."

"Definitely," Dr. Z said. "I've been thinking about Apolonia's need to contact her father. The old KIXR building is ten miles from here. It's been for sale for years, and it is old enough that the signal won't be as efficient."

"So, we cannot use it?" Tsavi asked.

"No," I said. "Efficient broadcast signals make the signals weaker for someone to pick up in space."

"That's right," Dr. Z said. "Old radio programs were broadcast from massive ground stations that transmitted signals at thousands of watts. In theory, those signals could be picked up relatively easily across the depths of space. This is exactly what we need—an inefficient old station. Kempton's communication head went out to take a look five weeks or so ago—you know, for spare parts for the radio science department. They weren't willing to sell it without the buyer taking the entire building, but he said all the equipment and the towers were still there and intact. I can't be certain that the equipment and towers are still functional, but I'm sure three KIT students, a KIT professor, and three beings of assumed superior intelligence could get it up and running."

"That's assuming a lot," Benji said.

Tsavi, Cy, and Apolonia turned to look at Benji.

"What?" he said. "I'm sure they've built on past inventions and ideas just as we have. They're a much older race. But that doesn't necessarily equal higher intelligence."

Cy narrowed his eyes. "I learned to speak nearly every language on your planet, including how to write them, colloquialisms, and your ridiculous contractions in the two months it took me to travel to Earth after I tracked the meteor here."

"Can you compose a symphony?" Benji asked.

"Can I...what?" Cy said, clearly perturbed.

"My point is, we're all good at something. Languages appear to be your strength."

I elbowed Benji. "They already don't trust you. You're not helping yourself."

He pulled out keys. "I have the only car, and it's fast. Does that help?"

SEVENTEEN

WE ALL STOOD, hidden by the woods, staring at Benji's orange Mustang. The paint was obnoxiously conspicuous, the engine was offensively loud, and the backseats were two captain's chairs instead of a bench.

"What?" Benji asked.

"We should just put a sign on it that says, *CAPTURE US*," Cy said. "And there are six of us."

"I can make two trips," Benji replied.

Cy shook his head. "We need to stay together."

Benji frowned. "Why?"

"You're right," Cy said, holding out his hand. "Your car is necessary, but you're not. Hand over the keys."

Dr. Z sighed. "Whatever we do, we must do it now. I'm sure there will be more soldiers coming at any moment."

"Cy—" I began, but Benji took a step in front of me.

"I realize we haven't much time, but you're not taking my car and leaving me in the woods to walk home. I want to help, but I'm not an idiot."

"Okay," Dr. Z said, holding up his hands. "I'll stay behind."

"No one is staying behind. We can all fit," I said. I took Benji's keys from his hands and pushed a button on the keyless entry remote. The trunk popped open, and everyone stared at the empty space. I climbed in, lay on my side, bent my knees, and propped my head with my elbow.

"This is ridiculous," Cy said.

Benji smiled at me. He broke something off his keychain and then tossed his keys to Cy. "You wanted to drive, right?" He climbed in, too, and made a show of getting comfortable next to me.

"What are you doing?" Cy growled. His patience with Benji was waning.

"It's cold, and there are two too many bodies versus seats in the Mustang. I'm volunteering to keep Rory warm." With that, he reached up and pulled down the trunk lid.

It was pitch-black, and for a moment, I wasn't sure if this was a great idea. I could hear Dr. Z and Cy discussing the directions to the radio station and then Cy and Apolonia speaking quickly in their language. It didn't sound like a pleasant conversation.

The trunk lit up, and Benji's face was just a few inches from mine. A tiny flashlight was in one hand, and he was propping his head with the other. "My dad said to always keep one of these on my keychain. He said I would thank him one day. Thanks, Dad."

I laughed. I couldn't help myself. It was slightly enjoyable watching jealousy on Cy's face, and I sort of liked the badass side of Benji.

The motor snarled, and we began moving. As Cy went over bumps, Benji and I giggled. I wasn't sure where the radio station was, but I assumed Cy would have to take back roads to get there. I didn't realize until the ride began to get really bumpy that Cy would have to stay off-road until we cleared the roadblocks.

"I hope your car isn't too damaged after this."

"I hope we don't get stuck or that Cy doesn't drive us off a bridge. I don't think we thought this through."

"He wouldn't. He doesn't like you, but he has a weird compassion for humans."

"Is that—ow!" he yelled. Cy had taken a bump too fast, and Benji banged his head on the trunk lid. He rubbed his head and then pounded the side of his fist against the interior wall of the trunk. "Take it easy! He probably wants to make sure we're too rattled to cuddle."

I smiled. "He's got his hands full with the warrior princess."

"Oh. I wondered if they were…if so, he's doing a poor job of hiding it."

"Hiding what?"

"How he feels about you."

"I think you just get under his skin."

"Very likely. I'm the competition."

"He's in love with her, Benji."

Benji grinned. "Thanks."

"For what?"

"Not denying that I'm competition."

I grinned. "I'm glad you're okay. I shouldn't have asked you to drive me to the ship."

"Me?" he said, his eyebrows shooting up. "They're not after me. If I hadn't seen you over that hill when I did—well, I was about five minutes away from a full-blown freak-out. For a second,

I thought you were in that ship with Cy. Either the ship would leave and I'd never see you again, or the soldiers would shoot it down and you'd get hurt. I wasn't prepared for either outcome."

"So, it wasn't all an act then? You didn't want the rock?"

Benji's face compressed, and he leaned toward me. "I don't care about the rock. You're the only thing I've wanted since the day I met you."

"But you wanted to get into the lab."

"The only reasons I wanted in the lab were because you were there and to make sure Cy wasn't hitting on you."

I laughed and leaned in, touching my lips to Benji's for just a moment, before Cy hit another bump, and we both banged our heads on the ceiling.

After half an hour, the Mustang finally came to a stop, and the engine turned off. I was relieved, but Benji looked a bit disappointed. The trunk popped open to reveal Cy standing over us. He held out his hand to help me out.

"Are you okay?" he asked. "Sorry about the sharp turns. Helena is crawling with Humvees. We had several close calls. It's not easy sneaking around in an orange sports car."

"It was a little rough but not bad," I said, stealing a glance at Benji.

We followed Dr. Z to the front door of the radio station. None of us were surprised that it was locked, but Benji successfully picking the lock with some wire from his trunk surprised us all.

"What?" he said.

"Where did you learn to do that?" Cy asked. "That's a fairly expert move for a conservative engineering student."

"My dad taught me. He also taught me how to shoot a gun, start a fire, hotwire a car, and filter water effectively. He's seen a lot during his time in the Majestic Twelve program. He wanted to be sure we survived if something happened."

"He didn't show you how to stop a bloody nose?" I asked.

Benji shrugged and grinned. "Dad didn't have to teach me how to play dumb if a beautiful girl was willing to take care of me."

I narrowed my eyes at him, but his mischievous grin was contagious.

"Do you always carry a lockpick in your trunk?" Cy asked.

"It's two paperclips, one bent like so," Benji said, holding out his hand. "They were in my backpack in the trunk."

"Amazing coincidence, that's all," Cy seethed.

A raggedy, skinny gray cat meowed and rubbed itself against the wall of the station and then against Benji's leg.

"Aw, poor guy," Benji said. He tried to pet him, but the cat maneuvered out from under Benji's hand and kept rubbing his side against Benji's other leg.

"Looks like you've found a friend," I said.

"Animals and kids love me," he said before smooching at the overgrown kitten.

We all started following Dr. Z into the radio station, but Cy motioned for Apolonia and Tsavi to guard the front door. The building was sectioned into two different-sized rooms with a wall and a single narrow door. The front section contained the DJ booth, speakers, a desk, neon signs, chairs, and a bathroom. The back, from what I could see, looked like storage. Both halves were dark and full of equipment and cobwebs.

The professor hobbled to the DJ booth and sat down, looking over the knobs and buttons. "Someone find a power source. I'll try to figure this out in the meantime."

The cables behind the DJ booth led down into a hole in the floor, so Cy, Benji, and I fanned out, searching for an electrical box.

Several minutes later, Cy and I met in the center of the back wall without finding anything.

"I'll check outside," Benji called to us.

"You do that," Cy muttered under his breath.

"Why are you so hell-bent on hating him?" I asked.

"I'm just waiting for him to betray you."

"You mean, us."

"No, I mean, *you*. One can't be betrayed by someone one doesn't trust." He sighed, frustrated. When he spoke again, his voice was calmer, "This is a bad idea, Rory. His father is Majestic. Benji has been raised with that allegiance, and you think *one girl* is going to make him switch loyalties?"

"Why didn't you make him leave then?"

"Because you wanted him to stay."

"Since when do you listen to me?"

Cy checked over his shoulder, and then his eyes met mine. "I do care for you. When Tsavi, Apolonia, and I leave this planet, I don't want you to be alone. If Benji is what he says he is, then you're going to need him even if it makes me physically ill to put any thought into that scenario."

"So, you're allowing Benji to stick around because you want us to be friends just in case he's not a lying Majestic minion?"

"Precisely, but not friends, an asset."

"We're already friends."

"Yes. This concerns me."

"Why?"

"I've already told you, Rory."

"You care about me."

He nodded.

"Lame." I walked away, but he gripped my wrist.

Cy kept his voice low. "Do you have any idea how difficult this situation is for me? I didn't mean to…I didn't come here meaning to get close with anyone."

"Let's be honest. You don't get to deny me Benji because you're jealous. If you choose Apolonia, then you can't claim me, too."

He released my wrist, clearly disgusted. "You're wrong. I wouldn't do that to you or to her."

"I guess *one girl* can make someone completely contradict everything he thought was right."

"Now you're comparing me to him?" Cy said, his face twisting to anger.

"Are you saying you're not jealous?"

"Jealousy is a human emotion, one I do not possess."

"I thought you didn't lie."

Cy began to say more, but the lights came on, and Benji careened through the door with a huge smile on his face and that ugly cat in one arm. "Found it!"

In that moment, I realized how close Cy and I were. He noticed it, too. In unison, we stepped back, putting distance between us, fidgeting and failing miserably at appearing casual.

Benji picked up on it, and his smile disappeared. "Everything okay in here?" The cat wriggled out of Benji's grip and ran into the back of the building.

"Everything is great," I said, leaving them both for the front area of the radio station.

"What did you say to her?" Benji growled. When Cy didn't answer, Benji caught up to me. "Rory...Rory!" he said, grabbing my arm gently.

"I'm trusting you, Benji. If you make me look like an ass for it, I'll never forgive you."

"I'll do everything I can to get them home," he said, nodding in Apolonia and Tsavi's direction, "and keep you safe. I swear on my life."

"What about your dad?"

"I respect him. Doesn't mean I believe in everything he does."

"And what is that exactly?"

"That Cy and his people pose a threat. That they want the rock Dr. Zorba found because it could protect our planet...from them."

"Why would they think that? If that were true, Cy would have just taken the damn thing and gone home."

"Is that what he told you?"

"Yes. Because it's the truth, not to mention common sense."

"What else did he tell you about it?"

Having eased into the back and forth rhythm of our conversation, I almost answered. But something stopped me. "You're asking a lot of questions about the rock for someone who doesn't care about it."

"Sorry," Benji said and then let go of my arm.

Apolonia and Tsavi took turns keeping watch while Dr. Z, Benji, Cy, and I tended to the wiring inside and outside the radio station. I was stripping copper wire with a box knife and needle-nose pliers, and the boys were wrapping the copper around the antennae and linking it to the various wires of the station. Every once in a while, Benji would take a break and try to coax the cat over to him. It looked as if it had already been electrocuted once, so I wasn't surprised that it wanted nothing to do with Benji while he was wrapping copper wire.

"Your father would have to pass into the atmosphere within fifty miles vertically in order for this frequency to reach him. You could record a message on a loop," Dr. Z said to Apolonia.

Benji clipped his wire. "There are several radio antennae on the north hills. This radio station must redirect to them. It's possible we could divert the beam, redirect by linking the ground signal to the antennae. Hamech's ship could intercept the signal. If we knew the ship's trajectory, we could even point one of the dishes here in that direction and bypass the antennae all together."

"I do not know," Apolonia said.

Dr. Z shook his head. "He would have to be monitoring those antennae in order for him to pick up the signal. If we only had a way to know for sure that they were receiving the signal..."

"Is it possible, Apolonia? That his ship could be monitoring those antennae?" Benji asked.

"It is possible," Apolonia said, her voice monotone. She was emotional all right with the one emotion she had—anger.

Benji shrugged. "It's better than nothing."

The more time that passed, the more nervous Cy seemed. Even Apolonia's stoicism began to weaken. None of us were sure how much time we had before Hamech found his daughter's busted ship, and that made every passing moment even more frightening.

My throat felt dry and scratchy, and from the way Dr. Z was clearing his throat, I knew he felt the same way. We hadn't eaten or drunk anything since the night before. No one had taken a bathroom break since early afternoon. When the boys started working with the wires, we had to turn off the power. We were all dehydrated, cold, and hungry, and that made it hard to focus.

"Rory, you're looking pale. You should rest," Dr. Z said.

"I'll rest when this is over," I said.

Apolonia spoke in their language to Tsavi. Tsavi nodded and then looked to Cyrus.

He nodded. "They're right. You should rest. Your wounds are still healing at a cellular level. Humans require REM sleep. Your body likely needs to return to that sleep cycle to complete the restorative process."

"Don't you need to rest, too, then?" I asked.

Cy glanced at Apolonia and Tsavi and then offered a half smile. "We're not human."

I twisted the last copper wire and tossed the pliers to the ground. "Okay, I'll rest." In truth, I was fighting exhaustion but gauging the rest of the tired eyes in the room, not more than anyone else.

The temperature outside had fallen dramatically in the last hour, and the old building was turning into a meat locker. I chose the space under the desk. It was surrounded by other taller equipment, and I hoped the parts of me not covered by the alien jacket wouldn't feel the draft.

I curled up on my side, bending my arm and using it as a pillow. The cement floor was ice cold. I looked around, seeing a tarp draped over a speaker.

"I'll get it," Benji said, grabbing it as he walked toward me.

I moved, waiting, as he folded the tarp and then placed it where I was lying.

"Thank you," I said, moving into the same position I was in before.

Benji stood up without a word, but within a minute, he was back, draping a woven blanket over me. "My dad insisted I keep a blanket in the car during the winter just in case. Turns out he was right about that, too."

"But not everything," I said, shivering under the blanket.

Benji rubbed his hand up and down my arm, trying to help me ward off the cold. "True."

"You're not on the same side anymore."

"Nope."

"How does that make you feel?"

Benji thought for a minute and then grinned. "Pretty good. He also taught me to think for myself."

"Do you think he'll forgive you?"

"I don't know. Guess we'll find out when I end up in a federal prison…or not."

I returned his smile and felt my stomach flutter when I realized he was shifting to lie down behind me. The radio station was fucking freezing, but that wasn't the only reason I wanted him next to me. Benji had been pursuing me a long time. It wasn't until Cy came into the picture that I was able to feel anything. Ironically enough, it was for Benji. Now that that door had been opened, I couldn't seem to get enough of him.

The second Benji's body was next to mine, the shivering slowed, and I sank back to get even closer.

"That makes twice in six hours," I said.

Benji put his arm over the top of me and pulled me against him. "Must be my lucky day."

I grinned and reached up to touch my fingers to his. He took my hand, lifted it to his mouth, and then touched his lips to the back of it.

"I've missed you," he whispered.

I turned my head, touching my forehead to his chin. "Nothing will ever be the same again, will it?"

"I don't know," he said, sighing. "I guess it depends on what you're referring to. If you mean our lives before we got mixed up with aliens...probably not. If you mean our friendship before you spent the night...probably not."

"At least you're honest."

He touched his lips to my temple. "I don't want to go back to the way it was. You would have never let me hold you like this before."

"I don't know. You were growing on me."

"Yeah?" he said, looking down at me.

I rested my head back onto my folded arm. A few months before, being alone didn't faze me. Having a boyfriend never crossed my mind.

"Cy will be leaving soon," I said.

"Good riddance."

I rolled my eyes.

Benji chuckled. "I'm only half serious." I could feel his breath blowing my hair as he spoke. "Does that mean something? For us?"

"What do you mean?"

"When he leaves"—he hesitated—"am I just the one who's left?"

I frowned. "No. It doesn't mean anything, except that he's leaving."

Benji fidgeted. He clearly wanted to say something but didn't.

I nestled against him. "I don't know if you and I would ever work out, Benji. But what I do know is that, right now, I'm lying here in your arms, and it feels like we're all where we should be."

"So, why are you still here? We could leave, you know. You don't have to put yourself in danger for him."

I looked over at Cy and Apolonia, smiling at each other and stealing small touches every once in a while.

"He's my friend, and I love him."

"So, you're saying you love him...as a friend?"

"I just love him. I thought it was something else, but I think helping him is just something I need to do."

"Lucky guy," he said. A combination of jealousy, hurt, and disappointment darkened his face.

I turned onto my back, looking up at him. "It's different with you." He tried to soften the tension around his eyes, but it was still there. I touched his cheek. "In a few hours, I'm going to tell Cy good-bye. But if I had to do that with you, I couldn't do it, Benji. I couldn't survive it if you left me."

Benji leaned down, touching his lips to mine. It didn't matter who else was in the room or what they thought. The right pair of arms was around me, and that was all that mattered.

Benji pulled away and began to make smooching noises with his lips. I looked up at him like he was crazy until I realized that he was trying to coax the cat into coming closer.

"What is your obsession with that cat?"

"I like a challenge," he said.

"If you want him to snuggle with us, you should at least name him."

"Okay. What do you suggest?"

"Oh no, I've never had a pet. This is your deal. You name him. Are we even sure it's a *him*?"

"Good point. It should be something unisex. Snuggles?"

I frowned. "That is the lamest name ever."

"Yes, but it fits the moment. Just go with it. C'mere, Snuggles. Here, boy…or girl."

The cat was actually falling for it, and it came closer until Benji could pet it a few times.

"See? He doesn't think it's a lame name."

"She does, too. And when she finds out you don't have any food, she's going to patiently wait to catch you in a weak moment, so she can scratch your eyes out."

Snuggles found a cushy spot on the blanket at my feet and padded a few times with her front paws until she finally settled in. I wasn't going to complain. She was warm.

"Yes. She looks vicious," Benji said, his mouth just in front of my ear.

Before long, my body melted against Benji's, and I felt myself drift off. But I didn't dream. It was just a warm, sweet darkness, the kind I had sunk into when I died. All I wanted was to lie still, heavy and relaxed against Benji. In that moment, it felt okay to just slip away even if it was forever. Staying there was easy. It was the waking-up part that was hard. This time though was even harder.

My body lurched, and voices around me grew louder.

"Jesus! She was convulsing!" Benji cried, his hands hovering over me. "What...what do I do?"

"She needs water," Cy said from somewhere close.

"I'll go," Benji said. "There's a gas station a few miles away."

"And what do we do if you're caught?" Cy asked.

"We don't have time to argue! I'm going!" Benji said. "Stay with her!"

The whole world seemed compressed into a tunnel. The only thing I could feel was nausea and pain. Every nerve screamed. Every muscle tightened. I knew that if I tried to walk, I would fall.

"Try to relax, Rory," Dr. Z said.

Cy's hands touched my arm. "It will be over soon."

My body lurched again. For someone who was so dehydrated, I seemed to be vomiting buckets. My palms were flat on the concrete, covered in whatever my stomach was rejecting. Maybe my whole body was rejecting what Apolonia had done to me. Maybe she had done it on purpose. Maybe she had been trying to kill me. I found the strength to look up at her through the sweat pouring into my eyes. She was standing over me, next to Tsavi. Her expression was as empty as always.

"What did you..." I said, but I couldn't finish.

Once Apolonia recognized what I was accusing her of, her face finally flashed an expression—anger.

"You think I did this to you?" She took a step, but Tsavi held her back. "I saved your life," she spit out. She looked to Cy. "This is who you are so fond of? How could you care about someone so weak? Look at her! Sweat dripping from her like an *epocshta*."

Tsavi pushed her back, out of sight. I could hear them arguing in their native language.

Cy put a gentle hand on my back. "She's just upset. I told you she's emotional."

"I don't know what an *epocshta* is, but I think I'm offended," I said before gagging back another wave of nausea and vomiting.

Cy brushed back the strands of my hair that fell into my face. "Don't worry about that now."

"What is that? That language?" I said, my voice sounding like tires over gravel.

Cy looked at me, his eyebrows pulled together. He was scared. "Ahnktesh."

"Ahnktesh," I said. "It's beautiful."

"Don't talk, Rory. Save your strength."

I vomited again.

"She didn't mean to," Cy said, a begging tone in his voice. "None of us could know it would have this effect. Please be okay," he said before kissing the crown of my head.

If I felt better, I might have appreciated Cy caring for me, even in Apolonia's presence. Being near death was probably the only time she would allow it.

At some point, Benji came back with water, wet paper towels, and gas station food—Cheetos, spicy pork rinds, soda, candy bars, and Slim Jims. If it all didn't make me want to puke again, I would have thanked him. The only thing that could have made that lineup any better was ramen noodles.

Benji sat beside me and pulled my head onto his lap, pouring the water into my mouth. The water came right back up for the first ten minutes, but after that, I felt better with each swallow. Two bottles of water later, I felt nearly back to normal.

Cy and the professor helped me move my things to the other side of the room. The mess I'd made on my bed left us looking for more things to keep us warm. Apolonia rinsed off my clothes by pouring a bottle of water over my head. The alien clothes dried within seconds. My hair didn't. At least it wasn't as long as it used to be, or it would have never dried.

The cat ran away when Apolonia gave me the improvised shower, but it returned when it realized Benji had food. Apparently, cats liked pork rinds and Slim Jims.

With a new tarp beneath us and four extra-large C-Mart sweatshirts that Benji had bought from the gas station to use as a blanket, Benji, Snuggles, and I were huddled together again.

"Be sure the lights are off, Cyrus, and then let's try the power," Dr. Z said from the DJ booth.

Cy did as he was told, and Tsavi went outside to switch on the power.

"Testing," Dr. Z said into the microphone. He pushed the earphone closer to his right ear. "Agh," he growled, pulling off the earphones and letting them fall to the control panel. "We're not there yet."

"Not yet," Cy said. "But we will be."

A spotlight shone through the front window, and everyone who was standing ducked down. Apolonia, crouched and silent, walked across the room to look out.

Her body relaxed. "They are gone, but they might be back. We should stay hidden."

"Should we find something to drape over the windows?"

Cy shook his head. "We can't take the chance of them noticing. They'll stop to take a closer look." He looked around the room. "Maybe we should all get some rest and try again in a few hours."

Apolonia took a step toward him. She'd taken down her hair, and the black waves cascaded down past her shoulders, settling at her elbows. "I am not sure we have a few hours. I have been out of contact with Hamech for most of the day. If he tracks the *Nayara* to her last communication and sees that she is down...if he does not find me inside the ship...the bodies..."

"Agreed. But we have to rest. Just a few hours. We can't continue like this."

Apolonia nodded, still unsure. She and Tsavi made a pallet on the other side of the room. Cy made his a few feet away from the DJ booth and Dr. Z.

The room soon grew nearly silent. The only sounds that could be heard were the professor's snoring and Benji's deep breaths.

"I'm glad you're feeling better. I can admit now that I was afraid," Cy whispered.

"That I was going to die or that Apolonia had tried to kill me?" I whispered back.

"The former. She wouldn't hurt you. I know she's—"

"Cold? Unfriendly? Hostile?"

He chuckled quietly. "I was going to say intimidating."

"Are you in a lovers' quarrel?"

"What's that?"

"Why is she sleeping across the room from you?"

He glanced over to where Tsavi and Apolonia were sleeping. "We have very old, very different traditions. It is out of respect that we don't lie together before the wedding night."

"Oh. So, you haven't, uh..." I trailed off, watching as his eyes lit up, and then his face displayed utter disbelief at my conclusion.

"No, I mean, yes. Not that it's appropriate at all to be discussing. We just don't feel it's suitable to lie together amid strangers."

"Strangers?" I said, raising an eyebrow.

"Anyone. I wouldn't lie with her unless we were alone. Even after marriage, upon visiting family, a couple doesn't sleep in the same bed."

I let my chin rest on my fist. "How long have you been together?"

"Seven years, your time. Betrothed for one. I always knew of her, of course. She is Hamech's daughter. It never occurred to me to try to win her affection. She seemed so out of reach. One day, her unit was assigned as security to an exploratory mission, my first as a senior science officer. She saved my life. We were friends first, and then she—by some miracle—fell in love with me. I know she seems cold, but she was raised without any margin for error. She doesn't tolerate weakness"—he laughed once—"well…except for me. We are to be married when I return. Hopefully, after this debacle, Hamech will still allow it. Hopefully, *she'll* still allow it."

"Why wouldn't she?"

"My friendship with you…unsettles her."

"Should it?"

Cy looked down to the floor. "No."

I smiled. "It's okay. I can see that you love her."

"If I've…if I've seemed confused about the nature of our friendship, please accept my apologies. Being here, so far from home, and spending so much time with you…you make it very easy to forget."

"I'll take that as a compliment."

"You should."

I settled back onto my side, listening to the awkward silence we'd left in the air, until I heard a ruffle coming from Cy's direction.

"It's so strange to feel so strongly about two women who are so different. Sometimes, I wish the situation were different. But it's not, and it's wrong of me to think that."

"So, stop."

"You don't know how much I wish I could."

"You said it yourself, Cy. You love me… as a friend. I had a friend once that I loved that much. She was like a sister to me. And then I had Benji. And now I have you...for a few more hours at least."

"You're an incredible human. I shouldn't be surprised that the way I feel about you is so confusing."

"*Love* is the most overused word in the English language. It's confusing to everyone. Some people live their whole lives and never get it right."

"Thank you. I don't think I would have truly understood if I hadn't met you."

"Well, how about that? I finally get to be the one to say, you're welcome."

EIGHTEEN

I'D FOUND MYSELF IN WONDERLAND, a place where the impossible wasn't pretend anymore. A time when death was temporary and believing that humans were the only intelligent beings was nothing less than arrogant. Secret government organizations and spaceships. The end of the world.

When I peeled my eyes open, it was the first time that my dreams were more realistic than real life. It was also the first time I felt Benji Reynolds draped over me like a blanket and wished I could stay there forever.

The humans were still on the floor, and the aliens were awake, testing the equipment. It at least appeared to be working. Now, they were trying to calibrate it so Hamech's ship could pick up the frequency.

I wriggled out from under Benji and joined the others in the booth. "How's it going?"

"Almost there," Apolonia said, a trace of a smile on her face.

"Would you care? If we all were blown to smithereens?" I asked and immediately regretted it. "Wow. I don't even know why I said that."

Cy looked to Apolonia, but he wasn't annoyed. "Didn't I tell you? She loves danger."

"Clearly," Apolonia said, still smiling slightly.

"Did someone somehow procure coffee this morning? You're both questionably chipper."

Tsavi laughed once and then covered her mouth. "No. We just enjoyed watching your snuggle time with Benji."

My cheeks instantly set fire. "Glad we could entertain you." Embarrassing, yes, but it was good to see Apolonia and Cy in a better place.

Dr. Z hobbled from his pallet, stretching, yawning, farting, and groaning. "I've had worse nights, but that was brutal for this old man."

He sat on the worn red fabric of the rolling DJ's chair and took the headphones from Apolonia. A look of disgust replaced her smile.

Dr. Z scratched his whiskers, and his eyes squinted at the control panel. "We need to redirect the signal, yes?"

"Correct," Cy said. "We've tried diverting the beam with unsuccessful results."

"What about transfiguring it to a microwave frequency?" Benji asked, pulling his coat tighter around him.

"Transfiguration…" Dr. Z pondered Benji's idea for a bit and then looked up at Cy. "It's worth a try."

While Cy and Dr. Z began working with renewed enthusiasm, Benji and I stood back. I had been sick and cold since we arrived at the radio station and hadn't eaten any real food in almost twenty-four hours. I was happy to let them figure it out.

"Their moods seem strangely upbeat," Benji said quietly.

"Last night's spooning likely satisfied the warrior princess that I wasn't after her fiancé."

"Oh. So, they're engaged?"

"Allegedly."

"And how do you feel about this alleged engagement?"

I turned to Benji. "I feel fine. Do we have any water left?"

"We do," he said, pulling a bottle from behind him and holding it out to me. "See? You do need people."

"It's not a good thing." I glanced at Cy. "As you can see, they just leave."

"I won't," Benji said without hesitation. "I'll be here for as long as you'll let me."

I pulled up one side of my mouth, trying to form some sort of a smile. Snuggles was rubbing up against Benji's leg. "Must be time for breakfast."

Benji made me take the water. "Try drinking this first."

I took a sip.

"Does this earn me a first date?"

"I fuck on the first date, so nope," I said, walking to the back of the building.

"You do not," Benji called after me.

Any moment, Cy and the professor would make the magic connection to allow Apolonia to make contact with her father. They would save the world without anyone knowing. Hamech would float down in his king-sized space module and pick them up. They would locate the rock and then dispose of it at the Bad Rock Disposal. Cy and Apolonia would be married quickly after that—however long it took them to get home—and they would have two-point-five beautiful and hostile alien babies.

Dr. Z would go back to campus and find something else to obsess about. Benji would go back to living alone at Charlie's—unless he kept the cat—and I would keep being Dr. Z's research assistant…and maybe even grow out my hair. Maybe.

How could we experience something so life-changing, only to return to our mundane existence? Although, maybe it was more likely that the professor, Benji, and I would be arrested and sent to federal prison, but not before Apolonia's daddy blows us all to hell.

For some strange reason, I was more okay with the latter. I glanced over at Benji. No, it wouldn't be okay. Maybe it just made more sense for something bad to happen to me.

I looked over my shoulder at Cy and Apolonia standing very close but not touching. Tsavi stood over Dr. Z, watching him work. Benji was across the room, fiddling with the ugly cat. We were all connected, and this group made sense in a weird, hodgepodge way. We were six people who had no business being in each other's lives, much less caring about one another, but decisions were made years ago that shaped us like puzzle pieces, and now, we fit together.

"I, uh…I think I have something. I think I have something! Quiet!" Dr. Z said, holding his hand in the air.

Cy leaned over Dr. Z, speaking Ahnktesh quickly but beautifully into the microphone.

I walked toward the front area, but before I made it to the doorway, a loud boom threw me in the opposite direction. I landed on my back. A terrible high-pitched ringing in my ears drowned out all other noise. A few seconds later, Benji was above me, his face covered in dust and dirt, and small pieces of debris littered his hair. He was speaking, but I couldn't hear him above the ringing.

Benji shook his head and then pulled me up and across the back room to the back door. Tsavi was already outside, using her strange weapon to take out the knees and shoulders of the soldiers shooting at us. She grabbed my arm and pulled me across the alleyway to the next building. It was still dark in the early hours of the morning.

Benji stayed behind, trading punches with a soldier and finally getting him on the ground. I glanced back, pulling away from Tsavi, to see Benji grab the soldier's weapon and then run to catch up. By the time he joined us, the ringing in my ears was beginning

to subside. Tsavi was barking orders at Benji, who was holding an
AK-47 as if he'd held one since birth.

"Rory? You okay?"

I nodded and then pulled my arm from Tsavi's grasp. "Feeling
a little manhandled at the moment."

"You were stunned," Tsavi said. "We didn't have time to
wait."

"Where are Dr. Z and the others?" I asked.

"Last I saw, Apolonia was engaged in some serious hand-to-
hand combat while Cy was helping Dr. Zorba out," Benji said.

"So, they're coming?" I asked.

Benji shook his head and then looked to Tsavi. A soldier came
around the corner, and Benji gunned him down.

"Shit! Benji! You just killed him!" I said, covering my mouth.

"We can't stay here," Benji said. "We're vulnerable. We've got
to keep moving."

Tsavi nodded once. "Agreed. We can circle back and get
the car."

"In theory," Benji said. "Let's move." Benji took my arm and
kept me with him, pointing the AK-47 in every direction he
looked, which was a lot of directions. He looked less like the Benji
I knew and more like the soldiers I saw in the *Nayara*.

We weaved in and out of the shadows. The farther we trekked
from the radio station, the more I worried that we would lose the
others.

"Your dad taught you to shoot one of those?" I asked.

"He taught me to shoot a lot of things," Benji said so quietly
that it was barely audible. He didn't look at me when he spoke.
Instead, he glanced around corners, up, down, and behind us.

"You didn't bring us out here to kill us, did you?"

Benji stopped and looked down at me. "What?"

"We're separated from the others. You could kill Tsavi and me,
and you could tell them any story you wanted."

Benji glanced at Tsavi, who was several feet ahead and
checking the street we were about to cross. He stared into my eyes
and gripped his weapon. "I'm sorry," he said, frowning, "but
what's it going to take for me to dig up that seed that Cyrus
planted? Do you honestly think I could ever hurt you? Kill you,
Rory? Seriously? That hurts."

I looked down at his rifle. "You're carrying a huge, crazy-looking gun. You took out a highly trained soldier to get it. I don't know what to think, except that there's a whole side of you that I don't really know at all."

Benji searched my eyes for a moment and then touched my face gently. I opened my mouth to speak, but he put his mouth on mine, slow and tender. His mouth was warm and soft, exactly the way I remembered. He pulled away, touching his forehead to mine. "You know me. I'm the guy who's been following you around, gladly taking your crap for two years. I'm not any different, except maybe not as pathetic as you thought."

I shook my head, but the rest of my body was frozen. "I never thought you were pathetic. Too happy, yes."

"Too happy?" he said, raising one eyebrow.

"Annoyingly so."

He grinned. "Maybe it was just being around you."

Tsavi sighed, clearly uncomfortable witnessing our exchange. "Okay, you two. It's time to circle back. I haven't heard gunfire in a while, and I just saw a fleet of military Humvees driving east."

Benji took my hand, and we followed Tsavi, but we didn't circle back. We *ovaled* back, taking the route that was parallel to the way we escaped.

More people were in the street, looking stunned and confused, pointing at the hole in the KIXR building.

Tsavi stopped and climbed into the backyard of a house sitting across from the radio station. There was no car in the drive, and the lights were dark.

"The police will show up here soon," I said.

Benji shook his head. "They're not in charge anymore."

I began to get nervous. The entire northwest corner of the building was gone, bricks and concrete reduced to rubble. If Cy, Apolonia, or Dr. Z were still inside, I was afraid they weren't coming out.

With each passing minute, panic began to set in. Benji's Mustang was still parked in the same place, covered by large pieces of metal siding and smaller pieces of concrete. Hopefully, the front windshield was still intact.

"Stay here," Benji whispered. "I'm going to check for tracers and things."

"Tracers and things?" I said, feeling anxious about him going over there alone. "What are tracers? And what *things?*"

"A tracer is basically an expensive GPS. *Things* could be something more...invasive...like explosives."

My eyebrows shot up. "Oh, so are you saying your dad also taught you how to defuse a bomb?"

"That he did not," Benji said, cradling his rifle under his arm and running across the street. He immediately slid under his Mustang like he was Chuck Norris.

"I think he's enjoying this," I said.

"That's a defensible notion," Tsavi said, nodding a few times before grinning down at me.

The people in the street seemed to be too afraid to get to close to the building, but some of them were on their cell phones, pointing at Benji.

"We should go look for them," I said. "What if they're hurt?"

"Patience," Tsavi said, her voice low and calm.

"I don't believe it," I said, seeing the ugly, smelly cat. It was rubbing against Benji's green sneakers, which were poking out from under the Mustang as he searched the underbelly of his car.

"Wasn't the cat inside when they blew up the front half?" Tsavi asked, bewildered.

I wasn't even going to make a nine-lives reference. It was too easy.

Benji scooted out from under his car and petted Snuggles.

"Really? Is he really going to do this now?" I said.

Benji jogged back to our side of the street, huffing as if he'd just finished his daily run.

"What was that all about?" I asked.

"You want the good news or the good news?"

"Uh, the good news."

"No explosives. I did find a tracer though. That could explain how they found us."

"How is that good news?" I asked.

"I also found a piece of string, and Snuggles now has a pretty new collar with a shiny tracer for a tag."

Tsavi nodded. "Well done."

"Thanks," Benji said with a wide smile.

Tsavi tensed and motioned for us not to move. She made a noise that sounded kind of like a bird. The noise echoed back, and she nodded. "It's them. Let's go."

We ran back across the street, meeting Cy and Apolonia at the Mustang. Dr. Z hobbled around the corner, clearly in pain.

"Christ, are you okay?" I asked, helping Cy help Dr. Z to the car.

"How many times have I told you *not* to call me Christ?" Dr. Z said, winking at me.

I rolled my eyes. "He's fine."

Dr. Z and Tsavi sat in the back. Apolonia sat on Tsavi's lap, and I sat on Cy's lap while Benji drove. Benji didn't seem happy about the new seating arrangement at all, but Cy and Apolonia weren't comfortable with the lap situation. Tsavi paled when we suggested she sit on Cy's lap, and there was no way I was going to plant my ass on Apolonia's thighs.

"What now?" Benji asked, backing away from the radio station. "The only other station in town is on campus."

Cy thought for a moment. "We are running out of time and options. We still don't know where the specimen is, and Hamech could be heading toward the *Nayara* at any moment."

"The warehouse," I said. "That's where they took Cy. They set up shop, and it didn't look temporary. The rock could be there, and hopefully, they'll have equipment we can use to contact Hamech."

"What if you're wrong?" Cy asked. "What if we get there, and they've gone? That's not exactly a plan."

Benji pressed on the gas. "It's the only plan we have."

NINETEEN

BENJI PULLED THE MUSTANG into a field half a mile east of the warehouse. The engine was loud, and none of us felt announcing our arrival was a good idea. I climbed out of the passenger-side door, and Cy followed, quickly leaning the seat forward for Apolonia and Tsavi to climb out. Benji struggled to help the professor.

"Maybe Dr. Zorba should sit in the front next time?" Benji said.

"I'm fine," Dr. Z said. "Stop fussing. You're making me feel older than I already do."

We walked quietly through the field, staying off the road. The warehouse and surrounding grounds were brightly lit. They were still there and didn't want surprises.

"So, what's the plan when we get there?" Benji asked in a soft voice. "How are we going to get in with the perimeter lit up like they're interrogating the grass?"

"The humans are going to stay outside," Cy whispered. "We're going to have to make a pretty far leap onto the roof."

"The way we got out?" I asked.

"Rory!" Dr. Z said, almost too loudly. He bent over and put one hand on his forehead. Silver was lying over on her side, wet and muddy. The professor sat her upright and pushed the kickstand down with his boot. "This is...unacceptable!"

"Shh!" Cy said, holding out his hands. "I understand you're upset, but we can't get caught over a moped."

"Silver is not just a moped! I saved for months for her. She is garage kept. She's nearly fifteen and look at her! Perfect condition. That doesn't just happen, you know."

Apolonia and Tsavi stood together, their faces displaying the confusion and astonishment at the professor's behavior. Dr. Z used the sleeves of his alien jacket to try to rub off some of the mud but gave up.

He turned to me, clearly angry. "If you treat my prized possessions this way, then don't borrow them!" he seethed.

"Yes, sir," I said, cowering. As my eyes focused on the muddy ground beneath my feet, I tried to stifle a smile. No one had gotten angry at me like that since I had parents. It felt pretty fantastic.

We continued on without Silver, creeping low and quietly through the tall grass of the field. Some parts of the ground had finally dried. Some were still muddy. No one knew which areas until one of us stepped ankle-deep into the muck.

Where the spotlights of the warehouse met with the darkness, we waited.

"Do you have a plan yet?" I asked.

Cy gestured for me to walk over to him. I joined him just out of earshot of the others.

He fidgeted. "I need to tell you something."

"If it's about Benji—"

"It's not," he said, cutting me off. "It's about you. Thank you. Thank you for everything you've done since the day I met you up until this moment. Despite the...circumstances...you've been a true friend to me, Rory."

"Is there another way to be a friend?"

"I've seen a lot of things during my time here. You would be surprised."

"No. I wouldn't."

Cy laughed once and looked down. "I guess not."

"If we could go back to the beginning, I'd do it all again. I just...I know you can't stay. I just know what it feels like to miss someone, and I'm not looking forward to it."

Cy wiped a speck of mud from my cheek with his thumb and flicked it to the ground. "Part of me wishes I *could* stay."

I glanced over to Benji, who was failing at pretending not to be watching us. "I'll be okay," I said with a smile. I turned back to Cy. "So...the plan..."

"We're going to make our way inside the warehouse, track down the specimen, and find equipment to contact Hamech."

"You make it sound as if you expect them to just let you."

"They're not expecting us to walk into their house. But once they figure out what's happened, you, Benji, or Dr. Zorba can't be anywhere near here."

"We're not leaving. You might need our help."

"Trust me when I say, we'll be fine."

"We're not going anywhere."

"You need to at least make sure the professor is safe."

"He is looking for a dear friend. He's not leaving either."

"Rory—"

Before he could speak, a loud rumble echoed from miles away, and after a few seconds, the ground shook. Two pillars of fire and smoke snaked up into the sky, looming over the tree line.

"*No*," Cy whispered, staring at the dark columns.

"What is that?" Benji asked, subdued panic in his voice.

Apolonia wore a proud smile. "That is Hamech."

Another explosion, and more smoke pillars and rumblings echoing across the sky made Tsavi touch Apolonia's arm. "We must go," Tsavi said. "He has found *Nayara*."

The warehouse transformed from being a glowing beacon of light to a red-and-blue strobe-covered hub of activity. An alarm sounded, and soldiers rushed out to fill every Jeep. They left the property spinning their wheels.

We crouched in the grass, trying not to be seen by the passing vehicles.

Tsavi smiled at Cy, excited. "We could not have planned this any better."

Cy's expression couldn't look more different. "Hamech is going to wipe out the city, Tsavi. Thousands of innocent humans will die if we don't find a way to contact him."

Tsavi nodded, and she, Apolonia, and Cy took off at full speed toward the warehouse. The armed guards who were walking the grounds had disappeared. They'd all probably left in the Jeeps.

It wasn't long before the aliens were out of sight, leaving us weak, helpless humans to wait in the grass.

Squatting in the field, I spent equal amounts of time watching in horror as the sky lit up and the ground shook and watching the warehouse, waiting for Cy or one of the women to signal us. A full minute went by and nothing.

Benji reached for my hand. I looked down at his open palm. I didn't want to be babied.

He sighed. "I just know you're scared, that's all."

"I'm not scared."

"You're not scared for Cy?" Benji gripped his rifle, keeping his mouth tight in an attempt to conceal how it made him feel to ask that question.

I glanced at him from the corner of my eye. "I think there are more important things…"

"No. Not really. Not to me. There's an alien parasite in front of us and an alien invasion behind us. Things are blowing up. People are dying. I'd kind of like to know."

"What? Is it you or him? You want me to choose out here in the field?"

"No."

"Then, what do you want me to say?"

"That you don't want him to stay."

"You just don't get it," I said, shaking my head. He didn't know what it was like to lose someone. He had no idea how it felt to say good-bye.

"I would if you told me."

"No."

"Does *he* know? What happened to you?"

I didn't respond. I couldn't. No matter how I explained it, Cy knowing something about me that I had refused to tell Benji more than once would be hurtful.

Benji's eyes fell away from mine, his jaw working under the skin.

"I didn't tell him. He just knew."

"I guess I could have known, too, if I didn't respect your privacy."

"He's leaving. You're not. I've already told you if it were the other way around—"

"I see the way he looks at you. I hear the way he talks to you, the things he says. He loves the woman I love. It bothers me," he said through his teeth.

"He doesn't love me! I'm different from what he's used to. I intrigue him. You see how Apolonia behaves. He got confused. But he *loves her!*"

"And you," he said, not missing a beat.

"Ugh!" I growled, crossing my arms. "Even if he did, which he doesn't, it wouldn't matter."

"What about that wouldn't matter? Because he could decide at any moment to put you on a ship and take you away from here? Away from me? Probably just out of spite because he hates me. He always has. Do you have any idea how that feels? For someone else to have that kind of power…to destroy you?"

"If I left, it would destroy you?" I asked, staring at him.

His eyebrows were pulled in, and his entire face was taut with anguish and worry. He did understand, after all, how completely a good-bye could change someone. How it could change everything.

"I kind of love you," I said.

His entire face morphed from desperation to a surprised smile. "You do?"

More explosions rattled the ground. They were getting closer.

Dr. Z touched his face with shaking hands. "They'll be at the college soon. We have no way to warn them. I...I should take Silver back."

I turned to him. "They can hear what's happening. Most everyone is gone for the holiday. The rest will be evacuated before you get there. And you'll never forgive yourself if you don't see with your own eyes that Brahmberger isn't in that building."

"I'll never forgive myself if students die because they didn't get out in time." The professor walked backward a few steps.

"Wait," I said, standing up. He turned his back on me and trekked back toward his moped. "You're going to get yourself killed. Dr. Z, I'm talking to you!" I yelled. No one from the warehouse could hear me over the alarm anyway.

"Take care of her, Benji." He hobbled in a half-jog and half-walk, and just as he disappeared beyond the tall grass, a huge explosion, double the size of the previous ones, lit up the sky so brightly that I had to take a step back and shield my eyes with my forearm.

"Dr. Z!" I screamed. "Get your ass back here!"

A gust of wind traveled toward us, bending down the grass and revealing Dr. Z pushing his moped to the road. My hair blew back, and so did Benji's.

"Whoa," he said. "Think that was Kempton?"

I shook my head. "I can't just sit here and wait. We have to do something. Try to stop Apolonia's father. Try to help Cy. Something."

"We can't just wave our arms in front of Hamech's ship, not without Cy or Apolonia."

"I'm not sure Cy will be enough."

"What makes you say that?"

"Because it wouldn't make my dad feel better to see you if he was looking for me."

Benji seemed to like hearing that. "So, the warehouse?"

I took a few steps closer to the two-story concrete building ahead of us. The ground shook in reaction to the boom miles away. "If they're being shot at, we wouldn't hear it over the alarm," I said.

Benji sighed. "I don't have much ammo left, but just say the word."

"Word."

We crouched while jogging to the side entrance of the warehouse. It was the same door I'd snuck into when I followed Cy there nearly two days before. I couldn't believe that only forty-eight hours had passed. It felt as if I'd been running for my life for months.

I reached up to the doorknob.

Benji stopped me. "This is too easy. Something isn't right."

"I bet they have a small group of soldiers guarding that damn rock, and the rest went to investigate the explosions. They probably thought it was us and have no idea they were walking into a fight with Hamech."

Benji turned to watch the fireworks over the tree line. "None of those men will be coming back."

The explosions were getting closer to the center of Helena and were happening more often, sounding more like an approaching thunderstorm than an interplanetary war.

"I feel like we should have gone with Dr. Zorba," Benji said.

"We can stop this from here." I turned the knob and pulled open the door, standing rigid when the barrel of a handgun touched my nose.

"Easy," Benji said. His rifle made a cracking noise as he dropped it to the ground.

The woman holding the gun to my face narrowed her eyes at me and then glared at Benji. "Oh. You are in so much trouble," she said.

"Shut up, Bryn."

My face screwed into disgust. "Who is she?"

Benji sighed. "My sister."

Bryn pushed out her bottom lip, and then she grabbed my jacket with her free hand and yanked me inside, shoving me up against the metal wall by my neck.

"I said, easy!" Benji yelled, following us inside.

Bryn retrained her gun onto my temple. "Dad has lost every bit of respect he's gained in Majestic the last twenty-plus years, Benji. You don't get to be mad about shit!"

Bryn wore green fatigues and a matching cap, her golden blonde hair shooting out in a short ponytail at the nape of her neck. Her high cheekbones and almond-shaped green eyes made her look more supermodel than soldier. Her perfect teeth reminded me of Benji's, and I started to wonder if his perfect looks were genetic or if, being second-generation Majestic, they had been engineered. Today, anything was possible.

"Really, I'm fine," I said to them both.

Bryn smiled. "You're nothing. After tonight, it'll be as if you never were. So, be a good ghost and shut the hell up. You've done enough to piss me off today."

I moved, slapping my hands together and simultaneously grabbing Bryn's gun and pointing the barrel at her forehead.

"Whoa!" Benji said, barely having time to react. "What was that?"

Bryn scrambled for the gun for a fraction of a second, but then her eyes widened with recognition that she had lost control of the gun, and her hands immediately went up.

"I don't think I'm done for the day," I said, cocking the gun when she shifted as if she were going to try to make a move on me.

"What else don't I know about you?" Benji asked, watching me hold the gun in awe.

"Clearly a lot!" Bryn growled.

"Stop whining," I said. "You didn't even tell me you had a sister."

"I did, too."

"No, you didn't."

Benji sighed. "At Theta Tau. The drinking game?"

I thought for a moment. "That doesn't count. I was drunk."

Benji and Bryn looked at each other, neither quite sure what to think.

"Where's Dad, Bryn?"

"He's here," she said, lifting her chin above the barrel of her gun. She was afraid, breathing hard. "They took him upstairs. They won't let me see him."

"Sorry to meet you like this, Bryn. I'm going to need you to take us to the rock."

She shook her head. "I don't know where it is. I don't have that kind of clearance."

"Dad does," Benji said.

Bryn's eyes widened. "Benji, you're going to get him killed by these people! Why are you doing this?"

"They aren't bad people, Bryn. They're trying to save us."

She frowned, shaking her head. "You've been brainwashed or something. You know that's not true."

"Walk," I said. "Take me to your dad."

Bryn's lips formed a hard line, and she closed her eyes. "You're going to have to kill me. I'm not taking you to my dad." She opened her eyes once to look at her brother. "I'll never forgive you for this, Benji."

He snarled back at her. "You *will* take us to Dad, so we can get that rock off this planet before it kills us all, or I'm going to kick your ass, you spoiled, close-minded, snotty little *bitch*!"

Bryn's eyes popped open, and we both stared at Benji, stunned. I'd never heard him swear *or* yell, and by Bryn's expression, she hadn't either.

I smiled at him. It was kind of sexy.

Just then, Benji blanched, and less than a second later, he dived for his sister and slammed her to the ground.

I didn't have time to react or ask what was going on before I had my answer. Apolonia's sword hit the wall, just on the other side of where Bryn's neck would have been.

Cy and Tsavi stood motionless, both just as shocked as the rest of us were.

"She's Benji's sister!" I yelled before Apolonia could take another swipe at Bryn.

Benji and Bryn stood—Bryn more slowly than her brother— and Apolonia pulled in her weapon.

"Rory," Cy scolded. "What are you doing here? I said to stay outside!"

"Do you have the rock?"

"No!"

"Have you contacted Hamech?"

"No!"

"Then, you're not getting much accomplished in here alone, are you?"

"Where's Dr. Zorba?" Cy asked, suddenly realizing he was gone.

"He went back to Kempton. He's making sure everyone got out before Hamech destroys the campus."

Apolonia looked to Cy. "Upstairs."

They bolted up a nearby set of metal stairs, and we followed. Benji held Bryn close. After navigating the hallway, Cy pointed at a door and then kicked it in. No one was inside, but it was full of radios and computers.

"Where is everyone? Did they all leave for *Nayara?*" Benji asked.

"No, some stayed behind, but we corralled them in the courtyard," Cy said.

Benji and Bryn traded glances. "Did you kill them?"

"Not all of them," Tsavi said. "But some didn't give us a choice."

Bryn fought her brother, slapping him in the face and beating the sides of her fists against his chest. "Let me go to him! I have to see if he's alive! Let. Me. Go!"

Benji kept hold of her until she collapsed against him and began to weep.

A boom, this time much closer, shook the building. Without a second thought, I bolted out the door and ran down the hallway, opening doors and trying to find an office with a window. Unable to find one, I ran to an exit door on the east side, which led to a metal railing that spanned the length of the building. Each end turned onto stairs that led into the courtyard. The remaining men, most of them in white lab coats, were standing among lifeless soldiers, facing in the direction of Helena, their faces lit by the glowing annihilation.

Hamech's ship had finally come into view. It was oval, beautiful, and a behemoth, floating over the north end of Helena toward the warehouse. Half of Helena was burning, but the huge ship persisted, dropping thick, gelatinous fire from its center and edges onto buildings, melting them like acid on Styrofoam. The viscous flames moved over the charred ground like liquid mercury, scorching everything in its path and joining other streams to form larger pools.

Two fighter jets flew over the warehouse, so low and loud that the walls rattled. I covered my ears and then watched in horror as they fired on Hamech. I wasn't sure which outcome would be worse—the fighter pilots not saving the city or Apolonia's wrath if her father's ship exploded. The ship belonging to Cy's Amun-Gereb shot the jets out of the sky, and they dropped helplessly to the town below. The jet fuel mixed with the flames on the ground, causing more explosions.

I put my hands on the rail and steadied myself as a powerful blast of air nearly drove me back against the warehouse. I gripped the rail, and my eyes squinted to shield them from the hot wind. It was overwhelming to see that much destruction and death. Where the earth wasn't orange with fire, it was red with glowing embers. Wind whipped through the blaze, making the inferno rise in pillars, as if it were reaching out from the pool of flames, trying to climb back to the ship. Fiery debris fell out of the sky like rain, and the early morning clouds were red, reflecting the devastation below. A quiet college town the day before, Helena now rivaled the bowels of hell.

"Rory!" Benji called, bursting through the door.

The view ahead made him stop in his tracks. He was in as much awe as I was. He slowly reached out for me with one hand, Bryn's 9mm in the other. I let his hand take mine. Neither of us was able to look away.

"My God," he whispered. "It's all gone."

TWENTY

THERE WERE ONLY TWO THINGS LEFT TO DO, and I had no idea how to accomplish either of them. Hamech's ship was moving slowly, but it was headed straight for the warehouse. We still weren't sure where the specimen was, if Tennison had reactivated the parasites, or if Brahmberger was being held captive somewhere inside the facility.

I shook my head. It seemed very hopeless.

Benji squeezed my hand. "It's not over yet." He pulled me down the gangway, and we descended the stairs.

"Frank Reynolds!" he screamed. "Dad!" He was pushing his way through the lab coats, looking at each face.

One man grabbed him. "Benji?"

"Sebastian!" Benji said, gripping the man's shoulders. "Where is my father?"

Sebastian shook his head, pushing his broken glasses up the bridge of his nose. "I haven't seen him since we were forced here. Rendlesham said you betrayed us, but Frank didn't believe it. None of us believed it. And we were right. You did it. You brought us the girl."

Benji glanced at me for a brief moment and then lowered his chin at Sebastian. "I need to know where you saw my father last. Is he alive? Have Tennison and Brahmberger recovered the organisms?"

"The rock still hasn't shown activity, but the girl," he said, glancing at me, "knowing her past resilience, we believe she could stimulate them. Before, they had reacted immediately to the aliens. In theory, they're more attracted to an extraordinarily strong host." He stood up tall, clearly proud of Benji. "We've just been waiting for you to complete the objective, sir."

All the breath left my lungs. Cy was right. Benji wasn't just a college kid who happened to be going to the right college at the right time. He wasn't just watching over me for his father. Benji was one of the twelve. He was Majestic.

All the things he proved capable of since the radio station weren't learned just from his father. He was a soldier, and Ellie was right. I was his target, and he had achieved his objective—to bring me to the warehouse.

Sebastian ducked when another explosion burst in the distance and then shook his head, looking afraid and desperate. "I don't know where your father is, Benji, but you've got to get us out of here."

Benji frowned and then walked over to the tall fence that surrounded the courtyard. He stood back, aimed, and shot at the large chain wrapped around the gate. While he was distracted by helping the lab coats escape, I bolted up the stairs, running as fast as I could across the gangway to the door.

As the door closed behind me, I heard heavy footsteps clanging against the iron stairs. Before I could make it back to the communication command center, Benji's fingers clenched my jacket, and I was yanked backward.

"Rory, stop!"

Before Benji could say another word, I maneuvered myself out of his grasp and elbowed him in the stomach. He folded in half, and then I grabbed the top of his sweatshirt and yanked him to the ground, stepping on the back of his neck with one foot and on the wrist that held Bryn's gun with the other.

"Please just listen!" Benji begged, his words garbled from his face being mashed against the iron catwalk. He pressed against the sole of my boot until he could look up at me. "I love you. That changed everything."

I pressed down harder, feeling my eyes burn. He'd lied to me before. He was probably lying now.

I pulled the 9mm from Benji's hand. He didn't fight me.

Stepping back, I aimed at the center of his forehead. "Don't be stupid, Benji. Stand up slowly. It would be a shame to kill you with your sister's gun."

He did as I demanded, standing up and keeping his hands in the air. "Rory—"

"Shut up." I felt my lip quiver. A week ago, I couldn't stand to hear him talk. Now, I was crying over him?

Benji reached out for me.

I lowered the handgun and fired a warning shot next to Benji's knee.

He hopped and yelped. "Dang it, Rory!" he growled, frustrated. "Don't listen to what you heard. Feel what you felt. Know what you knew."

"Walk," I demanded, gesturing toward the hallway.

Apolonia came out of the communication center, prepared with her weapon. Her eyebrows immediately pulled in, confused at the sight of Benji walking down the hallway with his hands up and me pointing a gun at him.

"Has he been compromised by the parasite?" she asked in her thick, awkward way.

"He is the parasite," I said, forcing him to walk into the room.

Cy stood up quickly when he noticed us walk in. "What—"

"I heard him," I said, my voice breaking. "He's Majestic. He lied to us. He was bringing me here to be a test subject, to infect me with the parasite."

Bryn laughed once without humor. Her eyes were red, blotchy, and moist. She was sitting on the floor, tethered to a desk with a phone cord. "You're not on anyone's side, are you?" she said to her brother.

Tsavi pulled another cord out of the wall and bound Benji's wrists.

"I'm on Rory's side," Benji said.

I shook my head at him and then left him with Tsavi and Bryn.

"What now?" I asked Cy.

"We're close."

I wiped sweat from my forehead. "So is Hamech. Helena is in ashes. The ship is headed here."

"Here?" Apolonia asked. She looked to Cy and then to Tsavi.

"The roof," Tsavi said.

"The specimen is being held between here and the only roof access. Soldiers will be there, guarding it," Benji said.

"We eliminated the soldiers in the courtyard," Tsavi said.

"They wouldn't have left the specimen," Benji said.

Bryn watched her brother, incredulous and then sad. She held her bound hands in front of her, resting her elbows on her knees. Placing her cheek against her wrists, she shook her head. "You're killing us all over a misfit girl who thinks you're a lying piece of shit."

Her words stung. I knew she believed them, but that just meant she wasn't in on Benji's plan.

"Rory, go with Apolonia and Tsavi. Show them the way to the roof. I'll keep working on communications," Cy said. "Try not to kill anyone," he said to Apolonia.

"I assume you're not going to hold the guards lying in the courtyard against me?" Apolonia said.

"They attacked first. But Benji's father is in the compound somewhere. I'd like to spare his life if possible."

"Hey," I said, offering a small smile to Apolonia. "You used a contraction. You actually sounded normal."

She blinked.

"I thought it sounded great," I said.

The corners of her mouth turned up just a tiny amount. A full-on smile broke out across her face, and for the first time, I didn't feel like she hated me. "Thank you."

We began to leave but turned around when Benji started making a commotion by pulling against his makeshift handcuffs.

"Don't send her up there, Cyrus," Benji warned.

Cy didn't look at Benji but back at the control panel. "Quiet."

"You're going to get her killed," Benji said, yanking on the cords. "Keep her here with you. Let the warrior princess and her BFF go upstairs to flag down the fire king. They don't need Rory's help."

Cy spun around in his chair and rushed Benji, stopping just an inch from his nose. "I. Said. Quiet," he hissed.

Benji looked at me, determined. "Don't go, Rory. There are soldiers up there. You'll be walking into a trap."

"I've seen what Apolonia does to soldiers," I said.

"There are worse things than soldiers, Rory. Please. Don't. Go." A deep line formed between his brows. His wrists were white, the skin straining against the cord. He was leaning toward me, desperate.

"I don't believe a damn word you say." I tucked Bryn's 9mm into the back of Cy's jeans. "Shoot him in the kneecap if he tries to escape."

"Gladly," Cy said, concentrating on the control panel.

As we left, Benji lost his temper, yanking and pulling against the cord and kicking at the desk.

"Maybe one of us should stay behind with Cyrus?" Tsavi said in the hall.

The walls shook from a shock wave, and I grabbed for Tsavi, so I wouldn't fall over. It felt as though we were on a ship in the middle of a stormy sea.

"We need to go. Cyrus can manage," Apolonia said.

Apolonia stayed in front of me, and Tsavi brought up the rear. Left and right directions proved difficult for Apolonia at first, but she caught on quickly.

Just a corridor away from the roof access, Apolonia pushed me against the wall and signaled for silence. After waiting a beat, she pulled out her pair of daggers and came around the corner. In the next moment, she was pulling an unconscious man around the corner and sat him on the floor between us.

"Is he dead?" I asked.

"I hope not. I hit him on the head with the handle of my *chechnahct*." She acted it out, making a quick downward motion with her dagger.

Tsavi checked his pulse. "He's alive."

I peered around the corner. *Jesus. Benji was right.* We had walked into a hive. There were twice as many soldiers guarding the rock as there were in the courtyard.

Apolonia nodded to an elevator shaft. "There is the roof access."

I shook my head. "I don't do elevators."

She leaned over as far as she could and pushed her back flat against the wall, nodding again. "There are stairs as well. We can sneak past the soldiers if we're careful. Cyrus would prefer that we bypass them rather than engage them and risk further bloodshed."

I peeked around the corner, in the direction of the soldiers. A room beyond the armed men was quarantined off by some type of clear plastic tarp, thin enough to see through. Some of the scientists were in full hazmat suits. Others were lying on tables.

I squinted to confirm what I'd seen. There were people definitely lying on the tables, but they weren't scientists. They were people of all ages, including young children. One table was empty. Mine.

A blast rocked the facility, which only made the scientists work faster. The soldiers seemed to be nervous and antsy, but they remained at their post.

"Apolonia, there are children in there. I think the scientists are baiting the parasites with them. We have to get in there."

A myriad of emotions scrolled across Apolonia's face. Most times, she seemed heartless, but the thought of children inside clearly affected her. She nodded. "I will get you in, but if I go against Cyrus's wishes by killing one or all of them, I will tell him you're to blame."

"Fair enough," I said, positioning myself behind the lethal, beautiful being I was actually beginning to like.

"Amun-Gereb will be on top of this place at any moment!" Tsavi hissed.

I was surprised she wasn't okay with the new plan. Tsavi was usually the more compassionate one, but she was clearly afraid. She had seen what those parasites were capable of and didn't want to be anywhere near them.

Apolonia rounded the corner, grunting and huffing with every jab and swish of her sword. Tsavi joined her, using only her hands. One by one, they cleared the soldiers, mostly debilitating them, but a few wouldn't stay down, so Apolonia had to make their incapacitation more permanent.

When they were all either unconscious or writhing in pain, Apolonia and Tsavi stood in the center, victorious. I stepped out.

"Well played," I said, smiling.

They both half-frowned, half-smiled.

"Well...played?" Tsavi said, laughing once and then looking to Apolonia.

"Well done," I said. "Good job. Way to kick ass."

"Kick...ass," Apolonia said. "I like this one."

In unison, we all responded to movement from the floor but too late. A rifle was already raised, and a spray of bullets pierced through Tsavi's torso. She cried out as Apolonia quickly removed the soldier's head.

We both rushed to Tsavi's side.

Tsavi groaned and then whimpered. Apolonia spoke to her in Ahnktesh. Tsavi was bleeding out, her dark blood pooling quickly beneath her.

"English," Tsavi said. "I like English."

"What do I do, Tsavi? Tell me what to do," Apolonia said. Her hands were shaking as they hovered over the dozens of bleeding holes in Tsavi's suit. Apolonia didn't seem to know where to start.

"The roof," Tsavi said. "Once Hamech arrives, take me to the...to the..."

"Infirmary?" I said.

Tsavi let out a breath. "Yes. Infirmary."

Apolonia looked around, her lips quivering. "I do not think we...I'm not sure we have time to wait to get Hamech's attention."

"I'll just rest here until you come get me."

Apolonia laughed once, a tear falling down her cheek. An explosion outside made the steel-and-concrete building shake like a scared child.

Apolonia lifted Tsavi from the floor and carried her through the plastic tarp, laying her on the empty silver table. The men in the hazmat suits watched, still and silent.

Apolonia turned to look through the medical supplies and instruments available, both scared and frustrated. A canister caught her eye, and she grabbed it.

A bubbling noise came from Tsavi's throat, and then she let out a gurgling long breath. Her body relaxed, and her head fell to the side.

"I must..." Apolonia looked around at everyone in the plastic-covered ten-by-twelve room, fidgeting. "I must signal my father. We can still save her." She ran from the room with the canister and up the stairs to the roof.

I stood, glaring back at the scientists in hazmat suits staring back at me, and then pushed through the plastic tarp. The machines inside beeped, buzzed, breathed, and pumped in rhythmic harmony.

Each of Tsavi's eyelids formed narrow slits, revealing her dark eyes and vacant stare. Just a few minutes before, she was walking, talking, alive. I wondered how long she could go without oxygen. *How long have I gone without it?*

"Tsavi," I leaned down, whispering into her ear. "Listen to me. Wake up. You can do it. It's easy." I felt my whole body trembling and tears burning my eyes. "Tsavi?"

"Don't waste your time, Rory. She's obviously gone," a scientist said. He removed his hood, and his ginger hair and blond eyebrows came into view.

"Help her," I begged, looking at the others on the table.

One African American girl and one Latino boy, both about eight or nine years old, lay on the other side of Tsavi in a deep sleep. On the other side were a middle-aged man and a silver-haired Asian woman who was nearing the last stages of her life. The monitors showed that their hearts were beating, but their brain waves were flatlined.

"Benji was told that you wanted the rock to protect us from Apolonia's people. Who is going to protect us from you?" I said, slapping an instrument tray off one of the small tables and taking a step toward the ginger.

Another still-hooded scientist backed away.

The little girl, her hair in gorgeous tight spirals, had stitches in her forearm. The boy had an open laceration in the same spot, and plastic tubing guided his blood to the rock.

The building shook again.

"You're baiting the parasites?" I said, so angry I was shaking. "With *children?*"

The ginger smiled with approval. "Rory, nice to finally meet you."

"Who are you?" I said, even angrier that he knew my name.

He chuckled. "I'm a little hurt you don't recognize me. Either you're not paying attention in class, or Byron Zorba is more jealous than I thought and doesn't teach his students about the most esteemed biomedical engineer of all time."

"Dr. Tennison?" I asked, surprised.

He didn't look at all like an evil mastermind. His face was pocked with old acne scars. He was greasy and potbellied. He didn't look like he was capable of tying his own shoes.

He smirked, disgustingly gratified. "I guess he does, after all."

I grabbed a scalpel and lunged at Tennison, but a strong, thick hand grabbed my wrist.

"Easy now!" the man laughed.

I pulled away. It was Rendlesham, still wearing his ridiculous crocodile boots.

"Don't be stupid, girl. You're outnumbered and alone. We don't want to hurt you," Rendlesham said, forcing me to drop the scalpel.

"No? And here I had you pegged as a sadist," I said, gesturing to the innocent people on the tables.

"No," Tennison said, motioning to me. "You're clearly an asset, smart and dangerous. We could use you on our team."

"I heard—as bait."

Tennison laughed at my response.

I pulled my hand away from Rendlesham. "What do you plan to do once that ship blows this place to hell? You're going to need more than a flash drive to preserve the data you've acquired in here."

"We know he's here for her," Tennison said, looking up. "She's already gone to stop him. We've already seen signs of life in the specimen. By the time they come to get it—"

"It'll already be too late?" I said.

"Precisely."

"For them or for us?"

"Them, of course."

"You can't control the organism that's in that rock, Doctor. It's a fast-growing parasite that has to be destroyed. It consumed every inhabitant of Cy's neighboring planet in less than forty-eight hours before Hamech incinerated everything but that one piece," I said, nodding to the rock.

The specimen looked different than it did in Dr. Zorba's lab. More porous, more worn down. Maybe they'd been scraping it, but the air in that room was definitely different—warmer, stuffier, thinner. They were tampering with the rock's environment, trying to reanimate the parasites, just as Cy said they would.

The timid scientist pulled off his hood. "Who told you this?"

My mouth fell open. "Dr. Brahmberger? You're...working for Majestic?"

He looked ashamed.

I shook my head. "Dr. Z's been looking for you for months," I said, glaring at him in disgust. "I'm glad he didn't stay here to be heartbroken over what you've become."

"Byron was here? Where is he? Did something happen to him?" Brahmberger asked.

"He went back to the campus to try to save whomever he could. You remember what that's like, don't you, Doctor? To be on the good side?"

Dr. Brahmberger only let that wound him for a moment. "Who told you about the organism?"

"It's a parasite."

"Says who?" Rendlesham asked.

"Cyrus. The signal you heard almost two years ago, Brahmberger? The parasites, via their hosts, directed that here. They were luring us."

"Where are these hosts now? What happened to them?" Tennison asked.

"They lost contact with them within ten minutes of touchdown."

"Scary story," Rendlesham said, insincerity dripping from his voice.

I looked to Brahmberger. "It's true."

He paused and then shook his head. "It will be contained here."

"Your curiosity is going to result in the same end," I said, looking to Brahmberger. "Do you want to be responsible for helping that thing eradicate our existence?"

"If it means I finally get the notoriety I deserve, I can live with that," Tennison said, situating the girl's arm closer to the rock.

Without missing a beat, I grabbed a pen out of his pocket and stabbed him in the eye. He cried out in pain and bent in half, clutching his face.

Brahmberger held out his hands but didn't try to stop me. Rendlesham started to grab for me, but a gun cocked, and all movement stopped.

Benji was on the other side of the barrel.

"Where is Cy?" I asked over Tennison's wails. I began to take a step toward Benji but hesitated.

Cy stepped out from behind Benji. "He convinced me."

"With a gun?" I asked, eyeing Benji.

His eyes were pleading, desperate for me to believe him.

"Quite the opposite actually," Cy said. "He freed himself and didn't attack me. Instead, he begged me to help him help you."

The building shook again, this time more violently, nearly throwing us all to the floor. Benji grabbed for me and kept me from falling headfirst into one of the tables.

I pulled away from his grip.

"Rory," he whispered, his eyebrows pulling together. Before he could speak again, Rendlesham moved toward us, and once more, Benji trained his gun on the doctor.

"Please try," Benji said, his eyes glossing over. His grip was so tight on his weapon that his hand was shaking, and the veins in his arm bulged. "I would love to shoot you in the face."

Cy recognized Tsavi and rushed over to her. "What? Tsavi? Tsavi!" He lifted her in his arms and then looked at me with wet eyes. "Hamech is three miles east of here. Where is Apolonia?"

"The roof."

Cy eyed the rock and laid Tsavi down gently. Then, he dashed out through a slit in the plastic walls and up the stairs.

Benji scanned the room, sickened by what he saw, until his eyes fell on the middle-aged man on the table. His eyes bulged. "Dad?" he cried. He immediately began disconnecting the man from the attached IVs and wires.

Bryn rounded the corner and rushed to her dad's table, her wrists still bound together. "Daddy?" she shrieked. "What did you do?" she screamed at Brahmberger.

He began to cry and backed away, sitting on a nearby stool. "What I thought…what I thought was right in the name of science."

"Dad?" Benji said, slapping the man's face lightly a few times. "Dad!"

Brahmberger went to a tray and picked up a syringe. "Here," he said, flicking the tube twice.

"Don't touch him!" Benji said, pointing Bryn's gun at him.

Brahmberger ignored him, pushing whatever liquid was inside the syringe into the hep-lock IV still taped to the man's hand.

We watched for a few seconds, waiting for whatever Brahmberger had done to him to be revealed.

The man blinked.

"Daddy?" Bryn said.

The building shook again, this time causing a bit of the ceiling to crumble to the floor. The steel frame creaked and moaned.

Benji helped his father from the table.

"C'mon! Bryn, help me!" Benji said.

I took a scalpel and cut the cords around Bryn's wrists.

Together, she and Benji lifted their father to his wobbly feet. Benji wrapped his father's arms around Bryn. "Get him out of here!"

"Benji?" he said, reaching for his son.

"I'm here, Dad, but you have to go." Benji hugged him once and then signaled for Bryn to go on without him. "Take him south, Bryn! Don't stop until you can't see the fires anymore!"

Bryn pulled her dad's arm tighter around her neck and bore most of his weight as she walked him out as quickly as she could.

Another explosion. This one rattled my teeth and sent me to my knees.

Benji helped me to my feet. "We've got to get out of here, too, Rory!" Benji said, tugging on my arm.

"The kids," I said, reaching back.

Brahmberger shook his head. "They can't be moved. They're both in a persistent vegetative state, as is the woman."

I took the 9mm from Benji and pointed it at Brahmberger. "You did that to them?"

"They came to us that way. I don't know why. I haven't asked many questions since joining Majestic. I've learned it is better not to know." He looked down at the girls. "I'll stay with them," he said, sitting back down on his stool in the corner. "It's the least I can do."

Rendlesham grabbed a few things as if he were about to leave, but Benji swiped the gun back from me and fired. I jumped, and Rendlesham was on the floor with a blown-out knee, next to a writhing Tennison.

"They should all stay with their patients," Benji said, his voice breaking.

He grabbed my hand and pulled me through the plastic tarp.

A loud clanging behind Benji and me didn't faze us, but the yells from Dr. Brahmberger did.

I turned, seeing Brahmberger backed against the clear plastic wall, his stool on the ground. He was staring at Tsavi, who was twitching and jerking in an unnatural way.

I took a step, but Benji stopped me.

"She's alive!" I said with a hopeful smile. "She woke up!"

Benji nodded to Tsavi's arm. When Cy had rested her back on the table, her arm had fallen onto the table the rock was perched on.

Thick dark red mucus was draining from the pores in the rock. At first, the substance appeared to be snaking up Tsavi's arm and entering her wounds, but when I looked closer, I could see it was not the mucus moving, but small creatures inside the red trail. They were slug-like in texture and appearance, each one about as big as a human thumb.

Tennison stood and pulled the pen from his eye with a yelp. Holding his wound, he approached Tsavi's twitching body with wonderment. "It's happening. It's the alien carcass! It has drawn them out!"

"We should go," Benji said quietly.

"What are you waiting for, Dr. Brahmberger? Get us a sample!" Tennison said.

Brahmberger fetched a petri dish and nervously scraped at the red matter.

"This is it," Tennison said, his hand hovering over Tsavi. "What we've been working toward for three years, Brahmberger."

Tsavi's back arched, and then her neck turned to the side. Her eyes were no longer slits. They were wide, bloodshot, and weeping the thick red mucus.

Brahmberger screamed, dropped the petri dish, and backed away as Tsavi rose from the table, her head, shoulders, and wrists twitching.

Then, the young boy began to twitch…and scream. Now that the parasites had found a familiar host, they were trying to embed themselves in the others. The humans.

My heart began to pound. Tsavi was now the host of the parasite. Tennison was right. It *was* happening. We were out of time.

"Babe," Benji said in a low voice, slowly tugging me back toward him.

I nodded, walking backward, trying not to attract their attention with any sudden movement.

Together, we walked calmly to the stairs despite the horrific shrieking coming from the plastic room.

"Shit," I said, staring at the huge piece of concrete blocking the stairwell and trying not to yell. "*Shit.*"

"Is there another way to the roof?"

I swallowed. "On the other side. There's an elevator."

"C'mon," Benji said, pulling me by the arm around and to the other side. He pushed the up button.

I shook my head. "I can't do this."

"What?" he said, turning to me.

The shrieking was growing louder.

"I don't do elevators. I can't…" I was breathing harder, my anxiety level climbing as the elevator neared.

"I'll be with you. We can't stay here."

The elevator opened. I looked around. "Maybe there's a window. I could climb up."

Benji stuck his foot in the doorway and cupped his hands over my shoulders. "It's just one floor."

"My parents were murdered, Benji. The men who killed them—they worked for Majestic. They got on the hotel elevator with us. They held a gun to my head and forced my parents to lead them to our room where they raped my best friend and tortured us before leaving us all to die. I haven't been in an elevator since." I sucked in air but still couldn't breathe. Just the thought of walking into that box terrified me.

"Rory, I need you to come with me—right now." He wasn't looking at me. He was looking past me.

I turned to see Tsavi standing behind me, twitching. The red mucus was pouring from her nose, eyes, and ears. I screamed and fell backward.

Benji pushed the button and then aimed his gun, shooting at Tsavi, keeping her back until the doors closed.

The elevator creaked upward, and Benji pulled me to his side with one hand, holding on to the rails of the ancient elevator with the other.

"Sorry," he said. "This probably isn't the best one to start off with."

"Just get me the hell out of here," I said, trying to stay calm.

The doors opened, and immediately, hot wind whipped across my face.

Benji pulled me along with him onto the roof. I fell to my knees, sobbing unlike I had since the moment I realized my parents and Sydney's deaths weren't a horrible nightmare.

Benji leaned down and lifted me into his arms, running across the rooftop to where Cy and Apolonia were kneeling over a canister, furiously trying to activate it.

An explosion set ablaze the field just one mile to the east. I could feel the heat against my face. My hair blew into my eyes from the firestorm raging just a mile away.

Cy stood, taking my cheeks in his hands. He looked to Benji with a frown. "Is she hurt?" he yelled over the roaring fire.

Benji set me on my feet. "Tsavi…" he said, breathing hard.

Apolonia stood, desperation in her face. "Is she dead?"

I shook my head. "Yes, but the rock…it…she's a host."

Apolonia's expression crumbled, and she walked away, screaming into the sky. Her body shook as she yelled, and then she leaned toward her father's ship, shouting something beautiful and full of rage in Ahnktesh.

"Will he see her?" Benji said.

"The canister is an energy source," Cy said, shaking his head in despair. "They must have harvested it from the *Nayara*. We could have signaled Hamech with it, but it's damaged. We can't get it to open."

Apolonia stood at the edge of the roof, tears streaming down her face, and then she took out her sword. Benji stood in front of me protectively.

"Hamech will not survive learning that he was responsible for my death," Apolonia cried.

Cy's hands went up to his head, and his fingers knotted in his hair. "We have to let him destroy the parasites."

Apolonia looked up at her father's ship and then back at Cy, nodding.

"I failed," Cy said, letting his hands fall to his thighs. "I failed you, Rory." He turned to his betrothed and took her into his arms.

"Will Hamech stop once he destroys the warehouse?" Benji asked. "Because if Hamech is going to destroy Earth anyway, instead of just waiting here to die, we should all get a fighting chance."

Cy nodded once. "He's been making his way here from the *Nayara*. He knew Majestic was headquartered here. Once he knows he eliminated those he thinks killed his daughter, he'll go back home."

"You're *sure*?" Benji said.

"I'm sure that the parasites must be destroyed."

Benji tensed and then held out his hand for mine. I took it, both of us staring up, waiting for our impending death.

Apolonia's long hair blew in the wind, dull and dirty, like her skin and clothes. We were all filthy, sweaty, and exhausted. Cy held her jaw, and she looked him in the eyes, tears glazing over her ice-blue irises, as her father's ship maneuvered, readying itself to fire on the warehouse.

She spoke in Ahnktesh. He replied in English.

"This isn't the end, my love," he said, broken and exhausted. "We'll see each other again soon."

TWENTY-ONE

APOLONIA'S FACE HARDENED, and her jaws worked as she clenched her teeth. "I can't give up."

She took her sword, swinging it toward me. Benji pushed me out of the way, and I fell to the ground.

The sword landed against the canister with a spark.

"We've already tried that," Cy said, holding his hands out.

Apolonia swung again. "I! Am going! Home!" she said, grunting as her sword hit the metal.

The canister finally opened, spraying an incandescent but luminous pink light into the sky. The warship was nearly on top of us.

A shriek sounded from down below. The parasites were infecting the dead soldiers in the courtyard. They were spreading.

"Hamech!" Apolonia screamed, waving at the massive vessel. She spoke in their language again, waving her arms in the air.

Benji helped me to my feet as Cy joined his betrothed in trying to get Hamech's attention.

"Look!" Benji said, pointing to the ship.

The entire ship lowered slowly, stopping just ten feet above us. A large square door opened, and a bridge lowered to connect the ship to the rooftop.

A man in blue robes, massive and as beautiful as his daughter, walked out. When he saw Apolonia, he ran for her, his arms wide open, followed closely by a small army of guards. She matched his pace, throwing herself into his arms. He hugged her tightly, his body shaking with relief and tears.

He didn't look at all like someone who had just murdered thousands of innocent people.

I smiled, seeing how safe Apolonia looked in her father's strong arms. I missed that feeling of security and surrender so much, and I was glad that she still had it.

The shrieking from the courtyard was getting louder, but another noise overwhelmed the awful sounds below. It popped and then sizzled.

"Incoming!" Benji yelled, using his body to shield mine.

The underbelly of Hamech's ship, fifty yards from the bridge, exploded, and then the AK-47s began to fire in a steady beat.

Benji crawled on his belly to the edge of the roof. "It's the other soldiers! They're back!"

Bullets sparked and ricocheted off Hamech's ship, and I covered my head with my hands and instinctively curled up into a ball.

And then, all at once, the shooting stopped and screaming began. Benji sat up on his knees, and I ran to stand next to him. The infected from the courtyard had overtaken the Humvees, and the soldiers were now on the ground, writhing and twitching, as the parasites overtook their bodies.

One of Hamech's men approached him and spoke quickly. The king's eyes flickered, and he spoke something I didn't understand.

Cy responded, his head slightly bowed, and then he looked back to me. "The ship's weapon is no longer functional. It has been damaged by the missile, Rory. We must leave. I can't leave you here to die. I won't."

Hamech spoke to Cy, and he appeared to argue but not for long, and then Cy gestured to Benji and me.

Hamech nodded to me and then spoke when he looked to Cy.

"He is asking about your character," Apolonia translated. "Cyrus had to reveal that Benji is Majestic."

Cy looked at me, sad. "Come with us, Rory. We're no longer able to save this place."

"What are you talking about? There are only six of them right now. We can destroy the warehouse."

He shook his head. "Not without the ship's weapon. By the time we return with a capable ship...Earth will be overrun."

"No," I said, looking at Cy, Apolonia, and her father. "No! We can still do this. Don't give up on us!"

Cy had sadness in his eyes. "You can come with us. Hamech has ordered that Benji be left behind."

"You know I won't leave him," I said.

"Rory," Cy began.

"We're worth saving! You know that! At least try!"

Cy looked to Benji. "Convince her."

Benji looked at me, his eyes full of conflict. "Go," he said, placing both his hands on my cheeks. "There's a reason you don't need anyone here. Because you're meant to go with them."

"No." I shook my head, pushing away from him. "No!" I looked to Cy, grabbing his arms. "Help me," I begged. "We can think of something! Maybe the Humvees have explosives. Maybe—"

"Now that the parasites have adapted to the environment, they're multiplying. You won't make it ten yards on the ground," Cy said.

I looked down at the canister. It was sparking, and the pink light alternated between bright and dim. I pointed to it. "You said it was a power source?" I asked, rushing over to it.

"Yes?" Cy said.

"Can we overheat it? Use it as an explosive?" I asked.

Cy frowned, "It's a powerful energy source, so yes. What are you getting at?"

"Ask him. Ask Hamech if I overheat the canister's core to destroy the warehouse, will he spare Earth?"

Cy shook his head. "No. You wouldn't be able to get out in time, Rory."

I offered a small smile. "I've told you...I can't die."

Apolonia's eyes lit up, and she spoke to her father.

Cy became desperate. "No! Get in the ship, Rory. You're coming with us."

Hamech responded to his daughter.

"What's he saying?" I yelled.

"No!" Cy screamed back. "Apolonia, no!"

Apolonia let go of her father and walked over to me, cupping my shoulders with her elegant long fingers. "Are you sure you want to do this?" she asked.

"Apolonia, no," Cy said, his voice low and stern.

"I'm sure," I said without hesitation.

Apolonia turned to her father, speaking the beautiful words I had fallen in love with, just as I had fallen in love with Cy and even Apolonia.

Hamech looked toward the edge of the roof just above the courtyard from where the shrieking could be heard, even louder than the roaring flames that were now a hundred or so yards away. Then, his eyes settled on me, a fatherly look of pride on his face.

He nodded.

"No!" Cy yelled. He reached for me, but Hamech's guards held him back.

Apolonia picked up the canister, manipulated its insides with little effort, and then handed it to me. "I see now why he feels so fond of you. It's been an honor, Rory." She leaned over and kissed my cheek.

"Rory, no!" Cy said, his voice breaking.

"Would you give him a lift?" I asked Apolonia, gesturing to Benji. "I know he didn't want to take him back to Yun. But just take him far enough away to keep him safe."

Apolonia nodded to her father's men. Just before they grabbed Benji, he pulled the canister from my hands and then shoved me into the arms of one of the soldiers.

"What are you doing?" I said, watching him pull his gun on the Amun-Gereb. The soldiers immediately pulled their weapons. "Benji!" I screamed, struggling in vain against the man holding me.

Benji smiled at me with so much love in his eyes that it made me choke back tears. "You were right, Rory," he said. "You can't die because I won't let you."

He turned on his heels and ran for the elevator that led downstairs.

"Benji!" I screamed so loud that my voice broke. "You promised you'd never leave me!"

Benji paused for just a moment, waiting for the elevator. He looked at me one last time and then stepped in. The doors closed in front of him.

Hamech gave an order, and the soldiers followed his daughter and her betrothed back to the ship, pulling me along with them.

"Benji!" I sobbed, fighting with every last bit of strength I had.

At the edge of the open door, the ship moved away from the warehouse and then sped off, quickly leaving it behind. The cold wind whipped around us, but I couldn't feel it. I wasn't sure I could feel anything. Within moments, the structure was engulfed in a huge ball of fire, dwarfing the inferno that was Helena.

The soldier finally let me pull away, and I fell to my knees. The ship slowed and then came to a stop, maybe ten miles from where the warehouse once stood.

Apolonia kneeled beside me, holding me, as we watched the warehouse burn.

"He died an honorable death," Apolonia said, touching her cheek to mine. "You were lucky to have him in your life."

I wiped my cheek. It felt gritty and cold. "He was the one I needed," I whispered. My lip quivered. "I should have known I would lose him."

TWENTY-TWO

HAMECH'S SHIP LOWERED just a few feet above a field, and I walked off the bridge to the grass below. A few days ago, my days consisted of being a bitchy, self-absorbed college student whose worst problem was an overenthusiastic admirer. Now, more alone than ever, I was left mourning that boy. The one who I had once foolishly wished would leave me alone...had.

Apolonia hugged me and returned to her father's ship.

Cy stayed behind. "I know it's not enough, but I'm so sorry, Rory. You've had to give up too much."

I stared at the fire and then looked to Cy. I offered a half smile. His gold eyes narrowed as he smiled back.

"Thank you for everything," I said, hugging him.

He hugged me back, kissing my hair. "You must know that they'll be checking back here for the parasite. If they detect it—"

"They'll blow us out of the sky? Now *that* I'm not sure I can survive."

Cy touched my cheek. "Don't worry. I'll come get you first."

"Good-bye, Cyrus."

"Actually, if you're going to embarrass me with my full name, it's Osiris."

I nodded. "Egyptian god. Dr. Z would have loved that."

Cy's face compressed. "You wouldn't give up two years ago, Rory. So, you can't now."

I lifted my chin, knowing why he was worried. He was leaving, and everyone else I cared about was dead. Everyone. "I couldn't even if I wanted to. I think someone up there enjoys watching me suffer."

"You can still come with us."

I shook my head. "I have to make sure people know what Benji and Dr. Z did here. How many people they saved."

Cy nodded. "Good-bye then. I will miss you terribly, Rory Riorden. You are my favorite human."

"You're my favorite Egyptian."

He hugged me once more and then returned to Hamech's ship.
He watched me as the vessel rose, and the door shut. Then, they
were gone.

By the time I reached the first pieces of smoking debris, the
morning sun was high in the sky.

The gel fire from Hamech's warship had burnt itself out the
moment they left, not scorching even a single blade of grass
outside its existing area. But the main pile of warehouse rubble was
still burning in some places.

I sat on a large piece of concrete about twenty feet from where
the warehouse once stood, touching my fingers to my hands. Dr. Z
was gone. Benji was gone. It was one thing to say I wouldn't give
up, but at the moment, I was likely the only living person left in
Helena. The sole survivor. Again.

I stepped over body parts and wreckage, half-hoping and half-
dreading that I'd come across Benji's body, wondering if I would
be able to recognize him if I did.

"Don't cry," I said to myself. "Don't you fucking cry," I said,
sniffing anyway.

I heard a groan and stopped.

The groan came again, and I followed it, walking carefully.

"If you're not going to cry…can I?"

My eyes widened when they zeroed in on where the voice was
coming from, and I saw Benji lying under a metal door, his hair
singed and parts of his clothes fried to a crisp. His arm, forehead,
and cheek were all blistered and charred, but he was alive.

"Benji!" I yelled, rushing over to him.

"Hi, babe." He grinned through the fatigue and pain.

"I don't believe it! How are you…how did you…" I wanted to
hug him, but I wasn't sure what was broken or burned.

"Think you could get this thing off me?"

I nodded. "I'll try." I began to lift and pull, and then I found a
pipe to wedge between the ground and the metal. It took me a few
tries, but I finally pried it open long enough for Benji to roll out.

He landed on his back again and let out a raspy breath.

I fell to my knees, trying desperately to find a place to touch him. "Where else hurts? Is anything broken? I can't believe you're alive!" I cried the last bit.

"I ducked behind this door. Luckily, when I was blown back, that huge piece of concrete and rebar broke my fall." He noticed my swollen red eyes and reached up to touch my face. "Have you been crying over me?"

"Shut up." I sniffed, laughing once. "Don't ever do that to me again."

"I promise," he said, his breath catching.

"Ribs?"

"Yeah."

"I'm not sure where the nearest hospital is. Or the nearest car."

Benji was trying not to move. He definitely had cracked a rib or two, but I began to worry he had internal bleeding.

I could hear sirens, but they were all closer to town.

"I'm going to, um…" I said, sniffing and worried all over again. "I need to find a car. We need to get you to a hospital."

Just then, a car engine caught my attention, and my head perked up. It was an orange Mustang with Bryn at the wheel.

"Benji?" she cried, slamming the car into park and jumping out.

"Help me get him into the backseat," I said. "We need to get him to a hospital."

Bryn nodded. "There's a hospital in Chester. Maybe twenty minutes away."

Benji growled with every movement, crying out loudest when we stood him up. He held his right arm against his chest. Benji's dad was in the front seat, still not quite conscious. Bryn helped him lean forward, letting me crawl into the back.

Benji cried out again as we maneuvered him into the back of the car. "I'm not sure all this pain trying to get to the hospital is worth medical attention." He rested his head on my lap and relaxed. "But *this* is definitely worth cracked ribs."

I touched each side of his face as Bryn pulled away from the burning wreckage of the warehouse. Benji grimaced with every bump.

"Sorry," I said, cringing every time he tensed.

"It's not so bad. Maybe I can even get a date out of this?"

I grinned. "No way."

"No way?" he said, his eyebrows shooting up. "Cheese and rice, woman, what's it going to take?"

I leaned down, just an inch from his face. "You can't get *a* date, but you can get a *first* date because I want more than just one."

Benji lifted his hand to the back of my neck and pulled me the short distance to his lips. As he kissed me softly, slowly, and passionately, I knew that I finally had the unconditional love, safety, and security I'd been missing.

I peered up through the back window at the smoky sky. Cy and Apolonia were somewhere up there, not knowing that I wasn't alone after all.

"I have a feeling we'll see them again," Benji said.

I looked down at his brown eyes and smiled. It was possible. *Anything* was possible.

I looked at the road ahead. For the first time in a long time, it felt like good things were coming, and for the first time since I died, I felt alive.

THE END

ACKNOWLEDGMENTS

As always, I wouldn't be able to put in the strange hours that I do if it weren't for my incredible husband, Jeff.

My children are so patient, and they understand that with great success comes great sacrifice. Thank you, my loves. Everything I do, I do it with you in mind.

This book was one of two that I've written outside of my comfort zone. Thank you to Abbi Glines and Colleen Hoover for cheering me on, and thank you to Kelli Smith for making me feel like I accomplished what I'd set out to do with this book.

Thank you to Miss Katy for letting me work all night and sleep all morning with nary a peep from the baby. You don't know how much that contributes to my finishing my books on time and sometimes early!

Thank you to Jovana Shirley for editing this book with so much efficiency and professionalism and for working it into your already busy schedule. I won't forget it.

Thank you to Danielle and the MP for being so excited for this book and for your tireless efforts to help spread the word.

Always last but never least, thank you to my readers who continue to support me so enthusiastically. Thank you for letting me live out my dream.

ABOUT THE AUTHOR

Jamie McGuire was born in Tulsa, Oklahoma. She attended Northern Oklahoma College, the University of Central Oklahoma, and Autry Technology Center where she graduated with a degree in Radiography.

Jamie paved the way for the New Adult genre with international bestseller, *Beautiful Disaster*. Her follow-up novel *Walking Disaster* debuted at #1 on the *New York Times*, *USA Today*, and *Wall Street Journal* bestseller lists. She has also written apocalyptic thriller *Red Hill*, a novella titled *A Beautiful Wedding*, and the Providence series, a young adult paranormal romance trilogy.

Jamie now lives on a ranch just outside Enid, Oklahoma, with her husband, Jeff, and their three children. They share their thirty acres with cattle, six horses, three dogs, and Rooster the cat.

Here's where you can find Jamie:

Website: www.jamiemcguire.com

Facebook: www.facebook.com/Jamie.McGuire.Author

Twitter: @JamieMcGuire

Instagram: JamieMcGuire_